Miss Love

EMMA MELBOURNE

Copyright © 2023 by Emma Melbourne.

Cover design by James at GoOnWrite.com

All rights reserved.

This book is a work of fiction. Any resemblance to persons living or dead is entirely coincidental.

No portion of this book may be reproduced in any form without written permission from the publisher or author, except as permitted by U.S. copyright law.

Prologue

Six Months Earlier

September, 1815

Dear Miss Fleming,

I am writing to give my condolences for the loss of your father and for your family's recent troubles. You have my deepest sympathy.

After a great deal of reflection, I have decided I must do the honourable thing and release you from our engagement. You were raised to expect a certain lifestyle, and without your dowry, I would be unable to support you in the manner you deserve.

Believe me, Miss Fleming, no one is more disappointed by this turn of events than I am. I trust we may remain friends.

Yours truly,
Percival Brooks

October, 1815

Dear Mr. Brooks,

You foolish man, I thought you knew our betrothal was in jest. As the daughter of a viscount and the granddaughter of a duke, I would never stoop to marry the son of a baronet.

But I fear I may be to blame, as I thought you understood how the game was played. Please accept my sincere apologies.

I am sure you will find another young lady who is worthy of your affection.

Miss Fleming
P.S. Go to the devil.
Amelia

One

Notes from the diary of the Earl of Langley

March, 1816
London

I never thought I would keep a diary, but boredom has driven me to it. Every Season is worse than the last. The balls are boring. My friends are boring. And all the young ladies in London are intolerably dull. After ten years on the town, I have yet to meet a woman who can string two intelligent sentences together.

Of course, my mother is after me to get married, as she thinks I need an heir. Perhaps having children would be interesting, but I doubt it. Certainly not if they were borne by one of the insipid young ladies I've met at balls. I'm only thirty-two, so there's plenty of time to worry about the succession.

But somehow Mother discovered that I'm known as the Stoneheart, and although I find the name amusing, she finds it worrisome. She's convinced that I'm lonely, and insists that if I simply offer marriage to an eligible young woman, love will follow. But I tried that once, and everyone knows how it ended.

Robert Stone, Earl of Langley

Matthews, the Earl of Langley's butler, looked down his nose at the young person standing on the doorstep of the earl's townhouse. It was an unfashionably early hour for a morning call, and the caller presented a decidedly unfashionable appearance, in a coat that hung on his slight frame and trousers that dragged on the ground.

"The earl is not at home this morning," Matthews said haughtily.

Miss Amelia Fleming took a deep breath, squared her shoulders, and presented her brother's visiting card. "I believe he will want to see me," she said, in her best impression of her brother's voice. Amelia felt a moment's guilt at paying a visit disguised as her brother, but it vanished almost as quickly as it came. Someone had to confront the earl, and her brother William had shown no desire to do it.

Matthews' eyebrows rose to his hairline as he read the name on the card, and he stepped back as though he had seen a ghost.

"Viscount Cliveden," he said, sounding stunned.

"Yes," Amelia nodded.

It took Matthews a moment to gather his wits. "You must be the son," he said finally.

Amelia gave him a strange look. "Yes."

"If you'll wait a minute, my lord, I will ask if the earl will see you," Matthews said.

Amelia was left standing on the doorstep while he went to find Lord Langley. When Matthews scratched on the door of his lordship's dressing room, his haughty expression gave way to a look of apprehension. He was relatively new to the household, and he couldn't predict how the earl would react to the news of his early caller.

There was no answer to his scratch on the door, so Matthews knocked timidly.

"If you mean to knock, do it properly," came a voice from inside the room. "I have no patience for people who scratch at my door."

Matthews hesitated, unsure whether to knock properly or simply go in, as Langley clearly knew he was there.

"You might as well come in," Langley called. "No need to heighten the suspense."

Matthews found Lord Langley in the process of tying his cravat, while his valet, Timms, hovered solicitously by his shoulder.

"Viscount Cliveden has called, my lord," Matthews said nervously, holding out the tray bearing the visiting card.

Langley raised an eyebrow. "What a surprise."

There was a moment of silence while Matthews waited for further instructions. None came.

"I told him you were not at home, my lord," Matthews finally continued.

"Matthews, you can be remarkably foolish sometimes," Langley said. "I am certainly at home to Viscount

Cliveden. I have been waiting for him to call for almost a year. Show him to my study and tell him I will be with him directly."

Amelia was shown to a handsomely furnished study. "May I take your hat, sir?" Matthews asked.

Amelia raised a protective hand to the top hat that covered the long red hair she had carefully pinned in a knot. "No thank you, I'll keep it."

After she had waited for a quarter of an hour, she noticed an elegant chess set on a small table in front of a fireplace. She moved to examine the pieces, which were beautifully carved in mahogany and ivory. To pass the time, she began a match against herself, walking around to the other side of the board after playing a piece. After several moves, the furrow of anxiety left her brow.

By the time Lord Langley strolled into the room a half hour later, White was several moves away from checkmate. Amelia was so engrossed in the game she didn't hear the door open, and she jumped when the earl spoke.

"I am honoured, Cliveden," Langley said. "And at such an early hour, too."

"I was afraid that if I waited, I would lose my nerve," Amelia admitted. Now that she had seen Lord Langley, she regretted having come. He was an intimidating figure; tall, dark, and fashionably dressed in a burgundy waistcoat and buckskin breeches that showcased his athletic physique. His eyes were the colour of coffee but held none of the warmth.

Langley strode further into the room and surveyed his visitor through a quizzing glass. He saw a slender youth with blue eyes, fair skin, and a smattering of freckles across a straight nose. The caller wore shabby clothes and a determined expression. For an instant, Langley's face betrayed surprise, but it came and went so quickly that Amelia thought she had imagined it.

"Really, Cliveden, you don't need to go to such lengths to convince me you're short of funds," Langley drawled. "I am not such an ogre that I would begrudge you the cost of decent clothing. Whoever designed that coat should be shot."

Amelia flushed. "While you may find the situation amusing, sir, I can assure you I do not. I am fully aware of the debt that I owe you, and I have come to explain that I can't pay you yet."

"One might ask why you continue to play the tables when you have a debt of honour you can't pay."

"My lord, I was overcome by grief and not thinking rationally. I gambled with the hope of winning enough money to pay the debt. I believed that if I played long enough, the odds would turn in my favour."

Langley raised an eyebrow. "Not a mathematics scholar, are you, Cliveden?"

Amelia's eyes flamed with anger before she swallowed her pride. "I realize it was foolish, and I have come to ask if we could reach an agreement to pay the debt in instalments. My estate, Cliveden Manor, is entailed and heavily mortgaged. But the land is good, even if it hasn't been optimally managed. I have been working to improve the crop yields, and I think there is a realistic hope of making it profitable very soon. I could pay you a little every year."

The earl was quiet for a minute. "And if I agree to take payment in instalments, do I have your word that the gambling will stop?"

Amelia shifted uncomfortably in her chair. "I will try my utmost to stop it, my lord."

"You beg me for patience, but you can't give me your word?"

Amelia looked more uncomfortable still.

"It's a family weakness, my lord." She hesitated. "There may be a way to hasten repayment."

"Oh?" asked Langley.

"My sister's marriage," Amelia said in a rush.

The corner of Langley's mouth quirked up. "You'll forgive me, Cliveden, for having some reservations. I don't think it will answer. You have just confessed a family weakness for gambling, and although my pockets are deep, I'm not sure they're deep enough to support a lady with gambling in her blood." He paused. "And there is something distasteful about taking a woman in payment of a debt."

Amelia laughed. "Oh, not you, sir. I realize Amelia has no hope of marrying into the nobility. But our birth may still be worth something, and a wealthy merchant or merchant's son may be within our reach. Two years ago, Mr. George Garland approached our father about a match with Amelia, which Papa declined, as Amelia's affections were otherwise engaged. But now her engagement has ended, and we hope that Mr. Garland will renew his suit."

"Your sister must be beautiful."

"Oh no, sir," Amelia said earnestly. "Isabelle is the beauty of our family. But Amelia's looks are tolerable, and I believe she has a chance of a good marriage."

"Wouldn't the beauty of your family have a better chance of making a good marriage?"

"Oh, I could never sacrifice Isabelle. She's very young, and still dreams of finding the sort of love she reads about in novels." Amelia smiled. "But Amelia's a practical girl. She won't mind."

"How fortunate for your family."

"Yes. The thing is, sir, Mr. Garland places a great deal of importance on social position."

"He is a social climbing mushroom," agreed the earl.

"Yes," said Amelia, biting back a laugh. "And our family's reputation is unfortunately somewhat tarnished. Since the–" she paused and searched for the word. "Since the incident with our father, many of the doors of the *ton* have been closed to us. You and your family are very influential, and I believe that if you wanted, you could smooth our path back to society."

Langley played with the ribbon of his quizzing glass. "Wouldn't people think it was odd, after the incident?"

"Oh, I'm sure we could come up with a story that would satisfy people. We could let people believe that the debt had been paid, and–"

"But the debt hasn't been paid," Langley pointed out gently.

"We don't have to lie, if that's distasteful to you," Amelia agreed. "You could just say something vague that hinted that it had, and the news would spread through the *ton*."

"What exactly would I say?" asked Langley, looking amused.

"I would have to think of exactly how to phrase it," said Amelia. "But I'm confident I could come up with something." She hesitated. "But I had another idea."

The earl sighed. "You had better tell me."

"You could pretend to be courting Isabelle."

Langley curled his lip and said nothing.

"Everyone would believe it, she really is very beautiful," said Amelia earnestly. "If I explain the situation to her, I'm sure she'll go along. You could take her driving and dance with her at balls."

"How old is Isabelle?"

"Seventeen," Amelia answered.

"Do you know how old I am?"

"No, sir."

Langley noted that his visitor's voice had risen in pitch, and he smiled. "I'm thirty-two. Almost twice Isabelle's age."

"Hardly that, sir," said Amelia.

"Oh no?"

"You're two years short of double."

"You're right," he said with a small smile. "I see that you have a head for arithmetic, even if you don't understand gambling odds."

"I've always been good with numbers," said Amelia defensively.

"If you say so," said Langley skeptically. "But we've strayed from the point. You were suggesting I court a young lady half my age–"

"Over half," Amelia cut in.

"A young lady slightly more than half my age, who I assume has not yet been out in society, and whose family stands in my debt."

"Pretend to court, sir," Amelia corrected. "I never imagined that you would actually offer for Isabelle."

"What would be the conclusion of this little drama?" the earl asked curiously.

"Oh. Well, once Amelia has secured an offer of marriage from Mr. Garland, or someone like him, you could stop paying attention to Isabelle."

"What would the *ton* think of that?"

"I expect people would think you decided you did not suit."

"And what would that do to Isabelle's chances of marriage?" he asked. "People would assume I had found her wanting."

Amelia considered the problem. "Maybe you could pretend to be engaged and she could cry off."

"Are you suggesting I set myself up to be jilted a second time?" he asked dryly.

Amelia flushed. "I wasn't aware that you had been engaged before," she said quickly. "I see how that would be a problem."

The earl walked over to study the chessboard.

"White is four moves from checkmate," he remarked. "Do you often play chess against yourself, Cliveden?"

"I used to play against my father, sir. Since his death, I have had trouble finding an opponent, so I occasionally play against myself. It is not as enjoyable as playing against an opponent, but it serves." Amelia smiled. "You have a magnificent chess set."

"I'll play you for the debt, Cliveden," Langley said abruptly. "If you beat me at chess, we'll call things even."

Amelia smiled. "Is this a trap, my lord? I have just promised to stop gambling."

"Not exactly, Cliveden. You promised to do your very best to stop. You explained that it's an—er—family weakness."

"I have nothing to wager, my lord, and I won't make a bet I can't pay."

"Then it seems you don't share the family weakness, Miss Fleming," Langley said smoothly. "And I don't make bets with ladies."

Two

Amelia jumped in surprise. In her confusion she knocked off her hat, revealing a messy knot of red hair.

"How did you know?" she asked.

"Miss Fleming, only a fool would be taken in by that outfit."

She bristled. "Your butler didn't think anything was amiss."

Langley nodded. "I am ashamed, Miss Fleming. As you have discovered, I am employing a fool."

Amelia laughed in spite of herself. "How long have you known?"

He sighed apologetically. "That Matthews is a fool? I suspected it within several days of hiring him. But it is very hard to find competent staff."

Amelia stared at him in confusion and then in frustration. "That wasn't what I meant. I don't care about your butler!"

"I'm sure he would be disappointed to hear it."

"How long have you known that I'm not William?" she persisted.

"Since I walked into the room. You have a different shape than your brother."

"I didn't think you'd met William," said Amelia. "Had I known, I wouldn't have tried to pass myself off as him. But we've always looked so much alike, and I'm quite tall and skinny, so–"

"I've never met your brother," Langley interrupted. "But even in those ridiculous clothes, you don't look like a man."

"And you let me continue under false pretences?" she asked indignantly.

"You were the one who began the deception."

"Yes, but once you realized I was not my brother you ought to have said."

"Forgive me, Miss Fleming," said Langley. "You have my word that the next time a young lady pays me a morning call disguised as a man, I will inform her as soon as I realize it."

Amelia laughed again. "It sounds absurd when you put it that way." She had prepared for this interview so carefully, but she felt like the conversation was getting away from her.

Langley nodded. "I'm glad you agree." He paused and looked her in the eye. "I wish to be clear on one point. The next young lady to pay me a call in disguise will not be you. When you next do me the honour of paying a call, you will come as yourself, with a chaperone."

Amelia nodded meekly, suddenly struck by the impropriety of what she had done.

"I beg your pardon, sir. I just thought that someone needed to see you, to discuss the matter openly, and I thought you might not want to see me if I came as myself. I apologize for wasting your time."

Langley smiled. "On the contrary, Miss Fleming, I can't recall when I last spent a more interesting half hour. Does your mother know you're here?"

"Mama has gone to her family in France. She left the day after Papa's incident."

"That was shortly after Boney's return," Langley mused. "It would have been a dangerous time for a lady to be travelling in France."

"Oh yes, but Mama wouldn't have cared about that," explained Amelia. "She's always been fearless, even reckless. Papa used to joke that there was a streak of madness in her family, and she didn't disagree. Sometimes I thought she was disappointed that her children were so conventional."

Langley privately thought that Amelia's decision to visit him disguised as her brother suggested she shared more of her mother's character than she thought.

"Why did she flee?" he asked abruptly. "Surely such a fearless lady wasn't afraid of the scandal?"

"Oh, Mama didn't care a fig for the scandal," said Amelia dismissively. "But she is terrified of poverty. And although her brother has had his own difficulties over the past few years, with the war and all, he is still in a better position than we are."

"Fortunate for her," Langley remarked. "So she left her conventional children to fend for themselves?"

"Well, William had just come of age," Amelia

explained. "And Aunt Lizzie, Papa's sister, has lived with us for several years. So Isabelle and I have a chaperone, and everything is proper."

"I am relieved to hear that the proprieties are observed," said Langley dryly. "Does Cliveden know you're here?"

She coloured. "Not precisely."

"I didn't think so."

"I was trying to convince him to come himself. I told him that if he didn't come, I would, but I don't think he believed me."

"He is a fool, Miss Fleming."

"He is very young," she said defensively.

"He's older than you, is he not?" asked Langley.

"Yes. He is almost twenty-two," she admitted. "I'm twenty."

"Yet you haven't had a Season?"

"No. Mama planned to bring me out two years ago, but I became betrothed to an old friend. But the betrothal has ended."

"Who was it?" he asked quietly.

She shook her head. "It's not important."

"I think it is."

Amelia sighed. "Percy Brooks. He's the second son of a baronet whose estate borders ours. We played together as children, and two years ago we reached an understanding. We didn't marry immediately, as he was working as a secretary at the embassy in Vienna. And then, after the incident–" She paused.

"The incident in which your father threw himself in the river after I ruined him at cards?" asked Langley bluntly.

"Yes. Although to be fair, Mama doesn't believe he threw himself in the river. She insists it was an accident. I understand he was quite drunk."

"Best to let her think that if it gives her comfort."

"I'm not sure if it gives her comfort, but she says he wouldn't have had the guts to do it deliberately," said Amelia matter-of-factly.

Langley nodded. "And your Mr. Brooks? Did he cry off because of the scandal?"

"He cried off because of the loss of my dowry," Amelia said brusquely. "His family has also had financial difficulties, and Percy has almost no money of his own. Without my dowry, we would have had nothing. I don't think I would have minded, but Percy said it wouldn't be fair to me."

"I'm sorry."

Amelia shrugged. "An affair of the heart is always a gamble," she said philosophically, although her expression belied the lightness of her tone. "And the good news is, I'm free to seek a match that will be more helpful to my family."

"George Garland," said the earl thoughtfully. "Are you acquainted with him?"

"No, but Papa thought he was harmless."

"High praise indeed," said Langley wryly. "So you're committed to this idea?"

"Yes. Garland or someone like him," said Amelia. "I've often wondered if things would have turned out differently if I'd married him two years ago. Papa would have had the settlement, and he might not have felt compelled to play so much, and maybe–"

"The result would have been the same," said Langley

ruthlessly. "Your marriage would only have delayed the inevitable. Your father would have run through the settlement money, and then he might have tried to marry your beautiful sister off to another wealthy cit. He would have run through that money too and had to face the crisis then. Of course, that's assuming that you don't have an endless supply of beautiful sisters available for sale."

"That's a cruel way to look at it."

The earl raised an eyebrow. "Yet you don't argue it's inaccurate."

"No," Amelia admitted. "But most people would not put it quite so bluntly."

"You may have heard, Miss Fleming, that I'm known as the Stoneheart."

"I'm not foolish enough to take that seriously," Amelia scoffed. "It sounds like the villain in a fairy tale."

"Quite so," agreed Langley, the ghost of a smile on his lips. "But coming back to the point, it is nonsensical for you to think that you failed your father. If anything, you failed me."

"You, my lord?" asked Amelia in surprise. "Because I haven't been able to pay the debt?"

"Don't you see, Miss Fleming, that if you had married Mr. Garland your father's ruin would have been delayed by several months, and it would likely have been at someone else's hands? My name wouldn't have been associated with the scandal."

"But that's ridiculous!" she said incredulously.

The earl shrugged. "No more ridiculous than you blaming yourself for your father's inability to stay away from the gambling tables."

"Well," she said, disconcerted. "I wish you'd reconsider my suggestion to pretend to court Isabelle. I'm sure we could find a way to end things without embarrassing either of you, and I think it would increase my chance of a good marriage."

The earl was silent for a moment and appeared to be considering it.

"But if you don't think you could do that, there may be other ways," Amelia continued. "I could offer you other services, perhaps on your estate–"

"Certainly not," Langley interrupted angrily. "I won't consider it."

"William said you'd say that," said Amelia, looking disappointed.

She had finally succeeded in shocking Langley. "You've discussed this with your *brother?*" he asked. His opinion of William had never been high, but he could hardly believe that he would offer his sister's virtue in payment of a debt.

Amelia nodded. "He said that no man wants a woman to give him advice on managing his estate."

"Managing his *estate?*" Langley sputtered in disbelief.

Amelia nodded again. "I've spent a lot of time over the past several years researching agricultural methods to maximize the productivity of our estate." She smiled modestly. "We've increased our crop yields by sixty percent over the past four years."

"*Crop yields?*" asked Langley.

"Yes, crop yields," said Amelia. "I know it sounds dull, but it can significantly increase an estate's income. I've worked with many of our tenant farmers to introduce some new methods, because when the tenants do well, they're more likely to pay their rent reliably. Our estate was poorly managed to begin with, so I doubt your lands would see the same degree of improvement as we have. But there may still be ways–"

"Miss Fleming, I have a land agent," Langley cut in.

"Yes, and I'm sure he's very capable," she agreed. "But the thing is, sir, I've been very motivated. My family needs money quite desperately, so I've devoted a great deal of time to reading and experimenting. I think I could help your land agent."

"Out of the question," he said firmly.

"Oh," said Amelia dejectedly. "Well, if you don't think I could help your land agent, and you don't wish to pretend to court Isabelle–"

"I don't."

"Then the only option I can see is for us to pay you in instalments. A little every year."

"There is another option," he said, staring at her intently.

Amelia met his eyes, hardly daring to hope. "There is?"

Langley nodded. "I could forgive the debt."

Amelia flushed to the roots of her hair. "And what would you want in return?"

"Nothing."

"Nothing?" she asked in disbelief.

"Nothing," Langley confirmed. "Miss Fleming, I owe your family an apology for the part I played in your father's difficulties. I knew he was on the rocks, and I should have stopped playing long before things reached that point."

MISS FLEMING FALLS IN LOVE

Reason warred with emotion in Amelia's mind. She had long thought that only a monster would continue to play a man on the brink of ruin, but hearing Langley admit it forced her to see the other side. "If he hadn't lost to you, he would have lost to someone else," she said practically. "He had a weakness for gambling."

"And it would eventually have ruined him," Langley agreed. "But there was no need for me to be the instrument of it, and for that, I bear some responsibility. Miss Fleming, I have always thought it was unfair for your family to suffer for your father's folly, and I understand he left you in a hole from which very few men could climb out. I'm fortunate to be in a position where I don't need the money. Had Cliveden had the courage to come and discuss the matter, I would have told him so long ago."

Amelia hardly knew what to think. The offer seemed too good to be true, and it left her unsettled. She worried Langley thought she had been hoping for this offer from the start, and her pride wouldn't let her accept it.

"My lord, you have mistaken my intention," she said. "I didn't come to ask you to forgive the debt. It is a debt of honour, and we are an honourable family. It will take several years, but we will pay it in full."

Langley looked at her with growing respect. "Your sentiments do you credit, Miss Fleming."

Amelia nodded. "I hope to get some money to you by the end of the month." She stood. "I've stayed too long already. Good day, my lord."

Langley stood as well. "I suggest you put on your hat. Poor Matthews is easily shocked."

Amelia put on her hat, and Langley frowned.

"A curl has escaped from under the hat," he told her.

Amelia took off her hat and found the errant curl. She looked around the room for a mirror but found none, so she tried to pin it up by feel. Unfortunately, her blind efforts caused a larger section of hair to come loose from the pins.

Langley sighed. "Will you allow me?"

Amelia nodded. Langley walked over and gently rearranged the pins. His fingers, cool and sure, brushed her neck as he pulled up a fallen lock of hair. The line of her throat was delicate and feminine, and Langley smiled. It was ridiculous to think that anyone could mistake her for her brother.

"There. I think that will hold until you get home. Is your coach outside?" he asked casually.

"I'll walk. It's not far."

"Miss Fleming, you will not walk across town in those clothes," he said firmly.

"Why not? I walked here in them."

Langley changed tack. "I have a pair of horses in need of exercise," he began.

"Oh, I would love to," Amelia said impulsively, thinking that Langley was offering to let her ride one of his horses. She had always loved to ride and hadn't had the opportunity in months, and she knew the earl's horses would be splendid.

She remembered she was wearing her brother's clothes. "I'm afraid I'm not dressed for it," she said, the disappointment plain on her face. "I would look odd riding sidesaddle in these clothes. But I've ridden astride before, and I really don't think anyone would recognize me, so perhaps–"

"My coachman will get up to mischief if I don't keep him occupied," Langley interrupted. "I was going to suggest you go home in my coach." His words were polite, but the look in his eyes invited no argument.

"Thank you, my lord," said Amelia.

Three

Letter from Miss Amelia Fleming to her mother, Viscountess Cliveden

Chère Maman,

I miss you very much. Things have been difficult here. William has taken to gambling to try to recover our fortunes, but so far he has only added to the debt. I've begged him to stop, as he's never had a head for cards, but he won't listen to me.

We're trying to economize, but I fear we're falling further behind. Prices just seem to go up, I don't understand how the shopkeepers can justify it. I'm convinced the fishmonger is cheating us.

I hope Isabelle will fall in love with someone who is both rich and kind, but we haven't been invited anywhere, and it's very hard to meet eligible men without going to parties or balls. Aunt Lizzie is trying to get us vouchers for Almack's, but so far she hasn't been successful. I don't think the ton would dare close its doors to you, and I wish you would come home.

I went to see the Earl of Langley today to discuss Papa's debt. He was insufferably rude, and he seems to have a very high opinion of himself. I understand why people call him the Stoneheart, as he's arrogant, overbearing, and generally miserable. The best thing I can say about him is that he appears to be in fine physical shape. However, this does not atone for his rudeness.

Your loving daughter,
Amelia

~

Amelia had a lot to think about on the drive home. The Flemings' townhouse was also in Mayfair, only a few blocks from the earl's, but the residences had little else in common. While Langley's house was immaculately kept, the Flemings' was the shabbiest on the street. Amelia lived with her elder brother William, Viscount Cliveden, her younger sister Isabelle, and Mrs. Elizabeth Crenshaw, their father's widowed sister. Their finances only stretched to three servants: a cook, a manservant, and a maid, and the ladies of the household frequently helped with the domestic work. Everything of value had been sold, and there were dark rectangles of unfaded wallpaper where the paintings used to be.

Amelia knew they would soon have to give up the house itself, and part of her wished William would sell it quickly, as a clean break would be preferable to limping along like a wounded creature. She wondered if Langley had the right to claim the townhouse as payment for the debt. He hadn't looked like the sort of man who would send a bailiff to kick them out of their home, and he certainly hadn't looked like he needed the money. But then, he was known as the Stoneheart. One never knew.

Amelia had hoped to get inside without being seen, but the coach drew up outside the townhouse just as Isabelle and Aunt Lizzie were leaving to go shopping. Isabelle's eyes widened at the sight of Amelia descending from the coach, and Amelia wished she had asked the coachman to let her off at the corner of the street. She consoled herself with the thought that the coachman was unlikely to have listened to her, as Langley had given him clear instructions to deliver her to the doorstep.

Isabelle feigned a fall on the step to draw her aunt's attention, and then discovered a minuscule tear in her skirt. She insisted on returning inside to inspect the damage, and Amelia was able to slip around the side of the house and enter through the servants' door. She stayed in her room until dinner, stewing over her highly unsatisfactory interview with the Earl of Langley.

Isabelle wasn't able to corner Amelia until after their aunt retired to bed, but as soon as Aunt Lizzie went upstairs, she confronted her sister.

"Amelia, was that *Langley's* coach that brought you home this afternoon?"

Unfortunately, William chose that moment to enter the room in search of a misplaced snuffbox. He stared at Amelia incredulously.

Amelia saw no point in denying it. "Yes," she said, hoping they wouldn't press her to explain further.

She had hoped in vain. "Why were you in Langley's coach?" William asked, in some alarm.

"I paid him a visit to discuss the debt."

"Oh, Amelia," William said reproachfully. "Why would you do that? You know we can't pay him."

"Well, ignoring the situation is hardly going to make it go away," Amelia said practically. "If you recall, I wanted you to go yourself."

"And I intend to call upon him," William said resolutely. "Just as soon as I've won enough money to pay the debt."

Amelia sighed, and Isabelle looked anxious. "William, you know it's highly unlikely that you'll win enough to pay him," Amelia said gently. "So far, your losses have greatly outweighed your winnings, and–"

"I've been trying very hard, Amelia, but luck has been against me," William said defensively. "But the luck is bound to turn. A fellow can't have miserable hands every time. It's simple statistics."

Amelia sighed again. "But William, don't you see, the odds are reset with each hand? The cards, or the dice, have no memory of past outcomes." She had explained this to William countless times, but so far it didn't seem to have stuck. She had always thought her brother was a reasonably intelligent man, but he was in the grip of a delusion that if he played long enough, he would emerge a winner. Amelia was familiar with this type of madness, as she had seen it in her father.

"I just know it's highly improbable that I'll keep losing. I can't give up, Amelia," William said firmly.

"William, I'm only suggesting that you give up gambling. Not that we give up trying to pay the debt," she explained. "I suggested to the earl that we could pay him in instalments, a little each year."

William laughed bitterly. "I can only imagine what he thought of that suggestion. A gentleman doesn't pay a debt of honour in instalments, Amelia. He probably laughed you out of his house."

"Actually, he offered to forgive the debt," Amelia said slowly.

William gaped at her. "Forgive the debt?" he asked in disbelief. "In exchange for what?"

"Nothing," Amelia explained. "Langley said he understands Papa left us in a hole from which very few men could climb out. And he has enough money. So he offered to forgive the debt."

Hope slowly dawned on William's face. "But Amelia, this is wonderful! Such a weight off my shoulders. Why didn't you tell me at once? I'll have to pay him a visit to thank him, and–"

"I turned him down, of course," Amelia said matter-of-factly.

"You what?" William asked, nonplussed.

"I turned him down. It is a debt of honour, William, and it must be paid. As must all our other debts."

"I think you're both crazy," said William, shaking his head. "Langley for offering to forgive the debt, and you for turning him down."

"Well, if you had gone to see him yourself, as I urged you to do, you could have swallowed your pride and accepted his offer," said Amelia tartly.

William mulled that over. "Maybe there's still a chance. I'll call upon him tomorrow, explain that you were out of your senses, and beg him to renew the offer."

"Oh William, no," said Amelia. "He's a haughty, superior, and disagreeable man. But if our name is to be respected in the *ton*, and for the sake of our pride, we must pay him."

William flushed. "He may be a better man than you think if he offered to forgive the debt. It's not your business, Amelia. Leave me to settle things with him myself."

"I'm not sure that's a good idea, William," Amelia said carefully. "It might be awkward." A few days ago she had wanted nothing more than for her brother to call upon Langley to discuss the debt, but she feared that with William's current attitude, nothing good could come of such a meeting.

"Oh, Amelia, did you pretend to be William?" Isabelle asked with a laugh. "Is that why you were wearing his clothes?"

"Wearing my clothes! Really, Amelia!" exclaimed William in frustration. "It's bad enough when you do that in the country, but in town! If anyone found out you would be ruined."

Amelia had formed the habit of occasionally wearing William's clothes to ride through the fields at Cliveden Manor, their family's estate. His breeches were more comfortable than her skirts, and from a distance, she was often mistaken for her brother. She had quickly realized it was good for the tenants to think the viscount was taking an interest in his land.

"Relax, William," said Amelia impatiently. "Nobody will find out. And Lord Langley knew perfectly well who I was."

"Well, if Langley knew who you were, it seems he

found out," William grumbled. "You must have given him quite an opinion of our family."

Amelia privately thought that of all the things her family had done, her attempt to impersonate her brother was one of the least objectionable, but she held her tongue.

The next morning, Matthews opened the door to another man who claimed to be Viscount Cliveden and requested an audience with the earl. As this caller appeared different from the one he had admitted the day before, Matthews was at a loss for what to do. He approached the earl's bedchamber and knocked loudly on the door.

"Must you knock so loudly so early in the morning?" the earl complained. "I'm barely awake." His valet smothered a laugh, and Langley turned to look at him.

"Do you find that amusing, Timms?" Langley asked.

The smirk vanished from Timms' face. "No, my lord," he blurted.

Langley nodded. "Well, Matthews?"

"A man has called, asking to see you," Matthews began. "He claims to be Viscount Cliveden, but if I may say so, he looks different from the Viscount Cliveden who called yesterday. A little taller, I think, and with slightly coarser features. The differences are subtle, my lord, but I don't think it's the same man."

"Your powers of observation are as acute as ever, Matthews," said Langley with a sigh. "I suppose I had better see Cliveden. Show him to the study and tell him I'll be with him directly."

"But my lord," said Timms anxiously. "Have you considered that this man may be an impostor, here for some nefarious purpose? He may try to overpower you once he gets you alone."

Langley raised an eyebrow. "Perhaps you had better wait outside the door, Timms, so that if he tries to overpower me I can call for help."

Matthews chuckled inwardly, as Timms was a good foot shorter than Langley and running to fat.

When Langley entered his study half an hour later, he found his visitor pacing in front of the fireplace. The chessboard was untouched.

"My lord," William said with a deep bow. "It's an honour to meet you."

Langley took a seat behind his desk. "Cliveden," he acknowledged.

"I expect you know why I am here," William began timidly.

"You'll have to enlighten me," Langley said politely.

William's next words came out in a rush. "My lord, I know my sister came to visit you yesterday, and I want to explain. Amelia gets funny ideas sometimes, she's been that way since we were little. She doesn't really understand how the world works. I don't know what exactly she said to you, but I want to apologize–"

"Why do you want to apologize if you don't know what she said?"

"What?" asked William, taken aback. "Oh. Yes. Well, I know it was improper for her to come, and it's really none of her business, and–"

"Do you know, Cliveden," said Langley thoughtfully.

"I don't think she would have felt the need to come if you had come yourself."

William flushed. "I was planning to come, my lord. I just hadn't found the time."

Langley nodded. "No doubt you are busy. Managing an estate can take a great deal of time."

"Yes, my lord," said William slowly, aware that Amelia had taken over many of the responsibilities of the estate.

"Well," said Langley. "You're here at last. I imagine you would like to discuss a schedule for the payment of your father's debt."

"Actually, my lord," William began nervously.

"Yes?" The earl's dark eyes were hard, and William was finding it hard to think.

"Amelia said you offered to forgive the debt," William said quickly.

"I did make that offer," Langley confirmed. "But she explained it was a debt of honour, and she insisted you would pay it. I'm afraid I insulted her. I won't make that mistake again."

"Ye-es," said William uncomfortably. "The thing is, my lord, Amelia wasn't really speaking for the whole family. She's very proud, you know, and not always practical. That's actually the reason I came today, I hoped you might . . ." He trailed off, unable to give voice to his thoughts.

"Insult you by offering to forgive the debt?" suggested the earl.

"Yes," said William miserably.

"My dear Cliveden, I wouldn't dream of it. Your sister showed me the error in my thinking."

"My lord, I will speak plainly," said William desperately. "I wish I could pay the debt, truly I do, but I can't. I don't have the money. I'm not sure I will ever have it. So if you could see your way to forgiving the debt, or even reducing the amount, I would be forever grateful."

"What is your gratitude worth, Cliveden?"

William flushed again. "I had hoped you would be a gentleman," he said angrily, standing to leave.

"Do you know, Cliveden, I hoped the same of you," Langley said coolly. "Matthews will see you out."

Four

The following day, the Earl of Langley paid a call at a fashionable townhouse a short walk from his own. The butler greeted him deferentially and showed him into a comfortable sitting room, where an attractive young lady was playing the pianoforte. She had Langley's features cast in a feminine mould, with raven hair, dark brown eyes, and an aquiline nose.

Lady Diana Templeton rose from the piano to greet her brother. "Robert!" she said, with an expression of genuine pleasure.

Despite the seven years between them, Langley and Diana had been close since childhood. As a young girl, Diana had worshipped her elder brother, and lived for the day he came home from Eton for the summer. He had been kind to her, and had spent many afternoons taking her riding or swimming on their estate. Diana had found him much more interesting than her sister Mary, who preferred indoor pursuits like reading and needlework.

"This is unexpected," Diana said with a smile.

"You can be honest, Diana, if it's an inconvenient time, I'll go away again."

"Don't be silly, Robert, you know I'm always pleased to see you," she said. "I'm just not used to entertaining gentlemen in the morning."

"I'm sure Templeton would be glad to hear that."

Diana's laugh held a bitter note. "Sometimes I wonder if he cares. I think he's bored with me."

"Then he's a fool, Diana," her brother said seriously.

"He's hardly a fool, Robert."

"I've long suspected it, you know."

"I think the reason the two of you don't get along is that you're so much alike."

The earl raised an eyebrow. "I wouldn't have said that Templeton and I don't get along, but if he's making you unhappy, that's likely to change. Why do you think we're alike?"

"You're both tall, dark, and intimidating."

Langley sighed. "It's the curse of my life, Diana. Always judged on my looks."

Diana laughed. "You know what I mean. You're both so–" she paused and searched for the right word. "*Intelligent,* it's off-putting."

"Thank you."

"It wasn't exactly a compliment, Robert," said Diana with a sad smile.

Langley looked at her with concern. "What's going on, Diana?"

"I don't know. It's just that Templeton's never here. I knew he had a frightfully important job with the diplomatic service, but I never dreamed he would spend so much time abroad. I thought things would be better now that the war is over, but if anything, it's worse. And when he's in town, I never see him, because he's always working. On the rare occasions we do talk, he's impossibly *polite*." She looked down at her lap. "I think he's disappointed that I still haven't given him a son. It's been over a year."

Diana hadn't married until the advanced age of twenty-four, and there had been a time when her family had doubted she would ever marry at all. Blessed with birth, beauty, and fortune, she had enjoyed tremendous success during her first London Season, and turned down five offers of marriage from eligible gentlemen. During her second Season she had been pursued by a wealthy duke, who was confident he would succeed where lesser men had failed, but she turned him down as she had the others. By her fifth season, she still hadn't met a man whom she liked well enough to marry, and she had developed a reputation for being proud and a little eccentric. She spent her time riding, playing the pianoforte, and enjoying harmless flirtations with men who understood that they wouldn't lead anywhere.

The *ton* had raised its eyebrows when she danced three times at a ball with The Honourable Giles Templeton, a serious young man with political aspirations. Lord Langley had raised his eyebrows when, two days after the ball, Mr. Templeton called to request his permission to ask for Diana's hand. As the second son of a viscount, and in possession of a comfortable fortune inherited from a maternal uncle, Templeton wasn't a brilliant match, but he was certainly an eligible one. Langley had given his consent, fully expecting Diana to turn him down as she had the others. But Diana had surprised the *ton*, her brother, and Mr. Templeton by saying yes, and the wedding took place a month later. The jealous gossips said Diana had stared down a lifetime of spinsterhood and settled for the only man still interested, but the more charitable observers said she had fallen in love.

"At least you've silenced the old ladies who thought you and Templeton married so quickly because you were with child," Langley remarked. He had never been sure what to think of his sister's relatively hasty marriage.

Diana looked startled. "Were people really saying that, Robert?"

"No one was foolish enough to say it in my hearing, but I'm sure there was speculation," he said honestly. "I know I wondered."

She burst out laughing. "You could have asked me."

"It was easier not to know the answer. In any case, I'm sure the lack of a child is more Templeton's fault than yours. Have you explained to him that he'll have to spend some time in town for that to happen?"

"*Robert*," she said reproachfully.

"Come now, Diana, don't pretend you don't know how it works," he said dryly. "It seems the Stone siblings aren't destined to find love."

Diana snorted. "You could have any lady you wanted, and you know it," she said unsympathetically. "If you knew how often I am accosted by mothers of eligible young ladies, curious about whether you plan to attend such-and-such ball, or if you prefer blue or yellow gowns, or even your favourite hair colour–"

"Red," he said abruptly.

"I beg your pardon?" Despite a close relationship with

her brother, Diana was often left wondering if he was being serious or satirical.

"Red hair. Pink gowns," he elaborated. "Say something ridiculous and they'll stop asking."

She smiled indulgently. "Don't you realize you're in an enviable position? Many men have to work very hard to secure a lady's affections."

"They would be better served by working to increase their wealth," Langley said cynically. "I think they would find the result was the same."

"One failed engagement hardly gives you the right to say you're not destined to find love," Diana protested. "And don't pretend you were in love with Selina, because I won't believe it."

Five years ago, Langley had been betrothed to Lady Selina Thorpe, the only daughter of a duke. Their fathers had been childhood friends, and had long talked of a match between their children. Although he had initially chafed at the idea of marrying a girl his father had chosen, Langley, then Viscount Granton, had come to accept the match. At eighteen, Selina was pretty enough, and although she had a certain degree of reserve, she seemed as intelligent a woman as a man could expect. As Selina could never be found without her mother, and her mother was an ignorant busybody, Langley hadn't made a great deal of effort to get to know his intended bride before his wedding day. He hadn't been raised to expect love in his marriage, and he thought Selina would fill the role of his countess as well as anyone.

But Selina Thorpe had other ideas. On the day of their wedding, she had arrived at the church looking as pale as a ghost, and after taking several steps up the aisle, had cried out 'I can't do it,' and run out of the church.

The *ton* thought Langley had handled his bride's defection like a man with ice in his veins. After Selina ran out, her mother had assured the guests that her daughter's flight represented nothing more than 'maidenly nerves,' and bustled out with the apparent intention of bringing her back. The minister had been too flustered to say anything, but Langley had coolly announced that whether or not the bride returned, no wedding would take place unless another groom could be found. He had told the guests that although the day's programme hadn't been as advertised, he trusted it had been entertaining, and walked calmly out of the church without a hint of emotion. That evening, he had played cards at his club as though it had been an ordinary day. This performance earned him the name of the Stoneheart, a name that still stuck and which caused his mother a great deal of concern.

Selina's father had later explained she had run off with her sweetheart, a penniless soldier she had met at a ball the previous year. Nonetheless, there had been some spiteful gossip to the effect that there was no sweetheart, and she had simply been terrified at the prospect of marriage to a man she found cold and intimidating. One story held that she remained unmarried, and was now living with an aunt in Scotland. Langley didn't know what to believe, and frankly, he didn't care. Selina had made it clear that she wasn't the bride for him, and he was thankful she had done so before they had taken the irrevocable step of marriage.

"I wasn't in love with Selina," he admitted to his sister.

"But that's the problem, a man can't force himself to fall in love with any woman who happens to be convenient. I have standards, Diana, and I believe that you're the only sensible woman of my acquaintance."

She laughed. "Perhaps you need to expand your acquaintance. How many balls have you been to this season?"

"One," he admitted unrepentantly.

"And did you dance with anyone?"

Langley smiled sardonically. "You must understand, Diana, that I can't only dance with one girl, as it might raise expectations. So in order to ask one young lady to dance, I must be prepared to dance with several. I find I lack the courage."

"It's a wonder that you bothered to go to one ball."

Langley nodded. "The truth, Diana, is that I questioned the decision as soon as I arrived. But I had heard a rumour that Thornton was thinking of selling his chestnuts, and I wanted the chance to discuss it with him before it was generally known. 'Twas his godmother's ball, you know."

"You went to a ball to buy a horse?" she asked incredulously.

"A pair of horses, Diana," he corrected. "And the finest pair I've seen in years. Beautiful steppers, and a delight to drive."

"I take it you bought them?"

"Oh yes," he said. "And for an excellent price, too. Really, a far greater bargain than any of the other ladies on display that evening."

"You'll have to let me drive them sometime."

He nodded. "We'll go out one day."

MISS FLEMING FALLS IN LOVE

"Really, Robert?" she asked hopefully, for Langley was notoriously possessive of his horses.

"Yes. On the condition that you don't tell Adrian, as he would demand to drive them too. You're the only one of my siblings I would trust to handle them."

"You have my word not to tell Adrian, or Mary," Diana promised. "I had a letter from Mary yesterday and she seems very happy." Their sister Mary had wed a wealthy Scottish landowner and was currently expecting their third child.

"Somehow, I always forget about Mary."

"She has beautiful children," Diana commented with a wistful expression.

"Mary's children are terrors," said Langley. "She brought them to visit me the last time she was in town, and I had to hide in my study."

Diana laughed. "And the funny thing is, they love you. Whenever I see them, you're all they talk about. It's Uncle Robert this and Uncle Robert that."

He sighed. "I don't encourage them, I assure you. I don't know how such a dull couple managed to produce such spirited offspring." He paused. "Do you think Mary was unfaithful to John?"

"*Robert*," Diana chided.

"You're right, we shouldn't speculate," he said shamelessly. "On a more pleasant subject, I've come to beg a favour. I heard you were planning to throw a ball."

"Oh? Where did you hear that?" asked Diana, who had been planning no such thing.

"*Ton* gossip," Langley said mendaciously.

"I see. Would you like me to throw a ball, Robert?"

"Well, it would be convenient," he admitted. "Especially since you were already thinking of it. And I'm convinced you would be a brilliant hostess, Diana."

She rolled her eyes. "Yes, Robert. I will throw a ball. But I still don't understand why I'm doing it."

"There is a young lady," he began.

Diana's eyes widened as she leapt to the obvious conclusion. "Finally! Robert, I'm so pleased! And mother will be overjoyed!" To say that Diana was surprised by the request was an understatement. Since Selina had left him at the altar five years ago, Langley had largely withdrawn from society. He managed his three estates shrewdly, spent occasional evenings at his club, and was rumoured to keep a former opera dancer in a snug house in Marylebone. But he rarely attended balls or parties, and the mothers of eligible daughters who had secretly rejoiced at the end of his engagement had long despaired of him ever asking another woman to marry him.

"Much as I hate to disappoint you and Mama, I'm not looking to marry her," Langley said bluntly. "She seems to be quite an eccentric. But I need you to help bring her family into favour in the *ton*."

Diana's brow wrinkled in confusion. "Who is she? Do I know her?"

Langley sighed. "Miss Amelia Fleming."

Diana's mouth fell open, and it was a moment before she spoke. "That's a surprise," she finally said.

"Yes," he agreed. "It seems their lives have been difficult since the incident last year."

Diana looked at him curiously. "Is your conscience troubling you, Robert?"

"I don't have a conscience, Diana. But it may be in my

interest to assist them. Miss Fleming is pursuing a match with George Garland."

"That parvenu?" Diana scoffed.

"Yes," Langley confirmed. "And the Flemings are unlikely to pay their debt unless one of them marries well."

"Well, that rules out marriage to Mr. Garland."

Langley smiled. "I should have said unless one of the Flemings marries rich."

Another thought struck Diana. "Are you short of funds, Robert?" she asked with concern. She thought it highly unlikely, as her brother was rumoured to be very rich, but she couldn't think of another explanation for his interest in the Flemings' affairs.

"What? No. Why would you think so?"

"I wondered why you're suddenly concerned with the Flemings' debt."

"It had slipped my mind until recently. But Miss Fleming feels honour-bound to pay it, so I feel honour-bound to assist her in acquiring the funds."

"I see. While you were listening to gossip, did you hear of a proposed date for this ball?"

"If I recall, it was planned for next week?" he suggested hopefully.

"Robert," Diana said reproachfully. "There's no way I can plan a ball in a week."

"I thought you were already planning one?" he asked innocently.

"Two weeks. That's the soonest I can get everything organized. You wouldn't want me to host a shabby affair."

"Thank you, Diana," he said. "Send me the bills, and let me know if you need any help with the staff. I'd be happy to send you Matthews. If you like, you may keep him. The man's afraid of his own shadow."

"He's probably just afraid of you," she said with a laugh. "So I'm to invite Miss Fleming and, I presume, her mother?"

Langley shook his head. "Lady Cliveden is in France with her family. Miss Fleming is living with an aunt. You may as well invite Cliveden, although I suspect he's too lily-livered to come to a ball where I'm likely to be in attendance. And you'll have to invite Garland, of course." He paused. "Miss Fleming has a sister, Isabelle. You may as well invite her, too."

"Is Isabelle beautiful?" Diana asked casually, wondering if this was the true reason for his interest in the Flemings.

"I'm told she's incomparably beautiful," he said, but he spoke with such disinterest that Diana dismissed the thought.

"The Hunts are in town, they came to call this morning," she said. "I guess I'll have to invite them to this ball."

"Why would you have to do that?"

"They're your nearest neighbours in Kent, Robert, it would be an insult not to invite them."

"Do you think they would cut our acquaintance if we didn't?" he asked hopefully.

"You are the most provoking man," Diana said. "It is no wonder that you are still unmarried."

"Although I suspect I would have a chance with Miss Hunt," he mused, throwing his sister into a fit of giggles.

"No one would accuse you of giving the girl encouragement."

"I have done her a service," he said. "I prepared her

for the rejection that she has undoubtedly faced in her first Season."

"Well," said Diana. "If I throw this ball, I will have to invite the Hunts."

"You couldn't argue it was a small, select affair? Close friends, that sort of thing?"

"If I did, how would I explain the inclusion of the Flemings? Or Mr. Garland? Unless the two of you have become close friends," she teased.

"I might surprise you, you know."

~

When Mr. Templeton walked into his drawing room half an hour later, he found his wife staring thoughtfully out the window.

"Hello, Diana," he said.

She jumped. "Giles, you startled me," she said with a laugh.

"I'm sorry," he said stiffly, taking a chair across from her. He was a fine-looking man, dressed impeccably, if somewhat severely, in a navy waistcoat and black pantaloons.

"Don't be sorry," she said with a smile. "I was distracted. Robert called today, and he wants me to throw a ball." She looked at her husband uncertainly. "Of course, provided you have no objection."

"Do you wish to throw a ball, Diana?"

"Yes, I think I do," she said. She needed something to occupy her mind.

"Then I have no objection."

"Robert offered to pay for it."

"I do object to that," Templeton said. "If my wife wishes to throw a ball, it is only right that I stand the expense."

"All right," she said. "I was going to plan for a date in two weeks. It will be a rush, but I think I can manage it. Will you be in town?"

"Are you hoping to dance with me, Diana?" he asked lightly.

"Of course. You are my husband."

"I'll be in town."

Five

Notes from the diary of the Earl of Langley

I can't believe I ever complained of boredom. I now look back fondly on the time when I didn't find a Fleming in my study every day, wanting to discuss some outrageous idea about their debt. I must say that I much prefer Miss Fleming to her brother. It will take some effort to untangle their affairs, but I think it will be worth it.

When Langley returned home from visiting his sister, he found his younger brother Adrian in his study with a bottle of scotch open in front of him. At twenty, Adrian was tall and slender, with fair hair, blue eyes, and a cherubic face.

"Robert!" he said, looking startled. "I wasn't expecting you."

"I'm sorry to have surprised you in my study," Langley said dryly.

"I meant I wasn't expecting you so soon," Adrian amended. "I thought you'd spend the afternoon at your club."

"And yet, here I am," said Langley. "Help yourself to a drink, it may help with the shock."

Adrian flushed. "Well, I was hoping it would help," he began. "You see, I need to talk to you about something."

"Rusticated again?" Langley asked. Adrian was in his third year at Oxford, and although he had not distinguished himself academically, he was nonetheless well-known to the Chancellor. The previous year, he had been rusticated for setting a sheep loose in his college.

"Yes," admitted Adrian. "How did you know?"

"Fraternal intuition."

"Well, this makes it easier," said Adrian. "I must say, I was dreading having to tell you. So I thought, you know–"

"You thought that if I found you in my study, drinking my good scotch, I would take a more favourable view of the situation?"

"Yes! No! That is, I'm not sure. You have such a confusing way of speaking sometimes."

Langley sighed. "It seems I have many things to apologize for today." He took a seat and faced his brother. "What happened, Adrian?" His eyes were kinder than his tone.

"Well, Robert, it started with a monkey." Adrian paused and appeared to consider his next words carefully.

Langley sighed again. "Was anyone injured?"

"No!"

"Were any crimes committed?"

"No!" said Adrian defensively.

"Were any young women compromised? Should I expect an irate father to descend upon us and demand an offer of marriage?"

"No," Adrian said, looking insulted. "You know me better than that, Robert."

"All right, then. We'll leave it there." Langley surveyed his brother. "You look worn out, Adrian. A spell of rest might be a good thing."

"Oh, I'm all right," said Adrian. "To be honest, I was a bit nervous about telling you I was sent down, and now that it's done, I'm feeling much better. You weren't nearly as upset as I feared you would be."

Langley smiled ironically. "I'll try to do better next time."

"Oh, there won't be a next time," Adrian reassured him. "Robert, I never expected that one monkey could be such a nuisance. I regretted buying him almost immediately, and I almost gave him back, but I'd already told the fellows about the prank, and I would have looked pretty foolish not to go through with it. But I've learned my lesson, and there will be no more monkeys."

"I'm pleased to hear it," said his brother, who had very little hope that this would be the last of his younger brother's scrapes. "Will you try to continue your studies in town?"

Adrian looked surprised. "What? No, I don't think I could study in town, and it really wouldn't be a good use of my time, now that the Season's begun. I've sent a note round to Corky, and–"

He was interrupted by a knock on the door.

Matthews entered timorously. "I'm sorry to interrupt, my lord, but a young lady has arrived. She says her name is Miss Fleming, and she insists you will want to see her." Matthews had not known what to make of the slightly shabby young lady who had addressed him by name and confidently requested to see the earl, but her accent proclaimed her a lady of quality, so he had decided to inform Langley.

"Well, Robert, that's rich!" Adrian exclaimed, "Lecturing me about young women when you're expecting a visit from your own inamorata."

At that instant, Amelia Fleming appeared at the door to the study, looking nervous but resolute. She wore a faded blue day gown, and her hair was styled in a simple twist.

"I say, Robert, she doesn't look like your usual style of young lady," Adrian said loudly. Langley glared at him and rose quickly to meet Amelia.

"Miss Fleming, this is an unexpected pleasure," he said smoothly. "Allow me to introduce my brother, Mr. Adrian Stone."

Adrian winked at his brother and looked at Amelia with interest. "Fleming? Isn't that the name of the viscount who–"

"Is Miss Fleming's brother," Langley interrupted quickly.

Adrian appeared to be thinking hard. "Yes, but wasn't it her father who–"

"Was the viscount before her brother," Langley cut in again. "Miss Fleming, I know you'll accept Adrian's apologies. He has an engagement this evening and was just leaving."

"As it happens, I do have an engagement. I'm dining with Corky and then we're going to see a play. The one about the dog."

Amelia and Langley both looked confused.

"Which one is that?" asked Langley.

"You know, the one about the man who tames a dog. *The Taming of the Something*, I forget the breed."

Understanding dawned on Langley's face. "He means *The Taming of the Shrew*," he explained to Amelia.

"That's the one!" exclaimed Adrian. "I wonder if they have a real dog on the stage, or if an actor plays the dog? The dog would have to be particularly well trained, I think."

"But it's not–" Amelia began.

"Quite," cut in Langley. "I'm sure it will be most enjoyable, and I look forward to hearing all about it tomorrow. You'll want to get going, you don't want to be late."

"You're right," Adrian agreed. He bowed to Amelia. "Pleasure to make your acquaintance, Miss Fleming. Evening, Robert."

"Enjoy yourself," said Langley.

"Oh, I shall," said Adrian blithely. "It's wonderful to be back in London. Sometimes I wonder if there's any point in me going to Oxford at all."

"I've wondered the same thing myself," said Langley, with the ghost of a smile on his lips.

Amelia burst into laughter as soon as the door closed behind Adrian. "Why would you let him think it was about a dog?" she asked when she had collected herself. "Now he'll be disappointed."

"Adrian likes dogs," said Langley shamelessly. "I'm

not sure what he thinks of shrews. If we had enlightened him, he might never have left."

"Oh. Well, it's quite convenient, because I wanted to speak to you," Amelia confessed.

"I thought you might," said Langley. "But before we get into that, where is your chaperone?"

"Aunt Lizzie refused to come," Amelia explained. "She said nothing would induce her to visit the Stoneheart."

He didn't appear insulted at her use of his nickname. "Your maid?"

"She said it was more than her job was worth," said Amelia. "I tried to explain that you're just a man, but she wasn't convinced."

"You need a firmer hand with your servants, Miss Fleming."

"If I had the funds to pay my servants, I might take your advice," she said tartly. "But as it stands, I haven't been able to pay our maid in a month. She has received nothing but room and board, so if she doesn't wish to pay calls on bad-tempered men I'm sure I can't blame her."

"I apologize, Miss Fleming," Langley said quietly. "What did you wish to speak to me about?"

"Well," she began uncomfortably. "When I first visited, you offered to forgive the debt."

"And you explained it was a debt of honour, and you felt bound to pay it," he reminded her gently.

"Yes." Amelia took a deep breath. "But, after consulting with my brother, I–we–have decided that we would like to accept your kind offer to forgive our family's debt." She looked at Langley anxiously.

Langley raised an eyebrow.

MISS FLEMING FALLS IN LOVE

"What changed, Miss Fleming?" he asked.

"I've had a chance to discuss it with my brother, and we decided that if you're generous enough to forgive our family's debt, we should not be ashamed to accept."

"Miss Fleming, I think you owe me the courtesy of an honest answer."

She looked down at her shoes before raising her eyes to meet the earl's. "William lost heavily at cards two days ago," she said bluntly. "I understand he called upon you in the afternoon and left feeling like he had something to prove. He bet the townhouse and lost, and the new owner is giving us six weeks to move out."

"I'm sorry to hear that," said Langley, looking at her with genuine sympathy.

"Thank you. So, you see, we have no assets left. Everything of value has already been sold." She laughed bitterly. "We even tried to sell some hideous candlesticks that we thought were gold, but we were told they're brass. Papa must have sold the originals and had copies made." She laughed again. "They're so incredibly ugly, I don't know why he bothered having them copied. If he was determined to buy brass candlesticks he could have chosen a more pleasing design. But it ensures that although we have lost everything else, we retain possession of the ugliest brass candlesticks in England."

"I'm sorry," Langley said again.

"Yes," said Amelia. "You see, I always knew we'd have to sell the townhouse eventually, and I know we should have sold it to pay our debt to you." She flushed. "We could have paid off part of our debt and used some of the money for improvements to the estate. Recovery would have been hard, but it still seemed possible. But now, because of one night of play, the townhouse is gone too." She closed her eyes for a moment, then opened them and faced him bravely.

"My lord, when I first came to see you, you were kind enough to offer to forgive the debt," she began. "At the time, I didn't appreciate the offer as I should have." She paused, hoping for some encouragement, but she received none. Langley's dark eyes were uncompromising.

"So I came to say that if your generous offer still stands, we would be very grateful to accept," Amelia said, trying to keep the desperation from her voice.

"I'm sorry, Miss Fleming, but the answer is no."

"No!" she exclaimed. "Is this a game to you? I don't understand why you would offer to forgive the debt and then change your mind three days later. Do you take pleasure in playing with my emotions?"

"Believe me, Miss Fleming, it's not a game to me."

"What then? Have you experienced a sudden loss of fortune?" she asked. "Is it not only the Fleming men who are foolish enough to throw away their money at play?"

"No," he said, and paused, as though considering whether to say more.

"And despite your resolve not to renew your offer, you still let me humble myself? Did you enjoy hearing me beg?"

"No," Langley said again. "Trust me, Miss Fleming, I don't find this situation enjoyable. I know it must be hard to understand, but I think in time you will appreciate the reason."

"I don't see how I can trust anything you say, but I understand why you're known as the Stoneheart," she said. "I appreciate that I've been wasting my breath, and I won't take up any more of your time."

She rose and walked towards the door.

"How will you get home?" Langley asked, planning to call for his coach.

"Without your help, my lord," she said firmly.

Six

Isabelle was the first to see the purple phaeton pull up outside the Flemings' townhouse. "Amelia, you have to see this," she called to her sister. Amelia joined her at the window, pleased to have an excuse to abandon the entirely unsatisfactory set of accounts that had been sent from Cliveden Manor.

"What a strange vehicle. I've never seen anything like it," Amelia remarked. The phaeton had been painted a deep shade of aubergine, and boasted a yellow stylized G on the panel.

As the sisters stood staring, the driver handed the reins to his groom and descended. He looked to be in his mid-thirties, with a large frame, fair hair, and a florid countenance. The points of his collar were excessively high and excessively starched, suggesting he aspired to join the dandy set. Although she had never met him before, Amelia guessed his identity immediately. "It must be Mr. Garland," she told Isabelle.

Mr. Garland was the owner of four highly profitable

textile mills in Manchester. His grandfather had founded the first mill, and his father had grown the business into a small empire. The family's growing wealth had allowed the current Mr. Garland to be educated at Harrow and Cambridge, and he had been raised to think of himself as more than the son of a tradesman. Unfortunately, the aristocracy hadn't shared this opinion, and Garland had spent the past decade on the fringes of high society. When he inherited the mills three years previously he had chosen to remain in London, and he compelled his managers to travel to meet him four times a year to review their quarterly reports. His father had left the business in such good order that it hadn't suffered from his neglect, and indeed, his managers thought his neglect far less harmful than his interest would have been.

At the beginning of the Season, Mr. Garland had made it known that he was in the market for a wife of noble birth, and after considerable nagging from Amelia, William had paid him a morning call. After fifteen minutes of awkward conversation, William had made it plain to Mr. Garland that he was quite welcome to court Amelia. Almost two weeks had passed with no sign of him, and Amelia had begun to fear he wasn't interested. But now he was here, ascending her front steps.

Mr. Garland looked surprised when Amelia answered the door herself.

"Miss Fleming," he said, bowing deeply. "Your brother told me you were beautiful, but he didn't do you justice." He had practised that phrase several times on the drive over and was quite pleased with how it came out.

Amelia dropped into a curtsy. "Pleased to meet you, Mr. Garland," she said politely.

"My dear, it's truly an honour to meet you. Always an honour to meet an honourable lady," he said with a chuckle. Amelia forced a smile at the attempted witticism.

"Your brother mentioned you liked to drive, and I came to ask if you cared to come for a ride in my phaeton?" he asked

"Thank you, I would," she said demurely. "Give me a minute to get my hat and pelisse." Aunt Lizzie joined them at the door and gave her approval to the outing. Amelia was glad that Isabelle did not make an appearance, as she hoped to keep Mr. Garland away from her lovely sister for as long as possible. She would hate for him to transfer his affections to Isabelle, for she knew Isabelle would feel obligated to marry him, and she was determined not to sacrifice her sister.

Amelia got ready quickly, and Mr. Garland was soon assisting her into his vehicle. "It's a brand new phaeton, just delivered last week," he explained proudly. "I chose the colour myself, and the monogram is based upon my own design. I thought of doing a double G, but I decided that a single G makes more of a statement. After all, Miss Fleming, very few men are fortunate enough to have the same initial for their first and last names."

"Indeed."

"Aren't the horses splendid, Miss Fleming?" he said proudly. "I bought them last week at Tattersall's. Had to pay a pretty penny for them, of course, but I think they're worth it."

Amelia privately thought the horses were too short in the neck and would tire quickly, but she nodded politely.

"When I was at Cambridge, Miss Fleming, I was acquainted with a duke's son, who had the most perfectly matched team of bay horses you've ever seen."

"How interesting," Amelia murmured, at a loss for what else to say. She suspected that when Mr. Garland said he was acquainted with a duke's son, he meant he had seen him at a distance at least once.

Mr. Garland had very little use for Latin or Greek, and had left Cambridge after two years without completing a degree. This didn't prevent him from boasting of his time at Cambridge to almost everyone he met, and by the time they reached the park, Amelia was heartily sick of hearing about it.

She was relieved when he returned to the subject of his horses. "I intend to try to match this pair," he told her. "I have bought a coach in a similar style to this phaeton, and I believe that if one can afford it, a coach should always be drawn by a team."

"I agree, Mr. Garland," she said, giving him a bright smile. Although there was plenty of space in the phaeton, Amelia felt as if Mr. Garland was sitting uncomfortably close to her, and she surreptitiously tried to inch away.

Mr. Garland's driving was more exciting than his conversation. On the way back from the park, he narrowly missed colliding with a barouche, a lamppost, and a boy selling oranges, and Amelia was relieved to make it back to her street without any major incidents. As they neared her house, they came upon the Earl of Langley, riding towards them beside a fashionable young lady.

Several paces behind them, a man in a groom's livery led a beautiful white Arabian horse.

Garland did not recognize the earl or his sister, but he recognized the fine cut of their clothes, and he was pleased to have spectators. He attempted to maintain his speed until they were directly in front of the Flemings' townhouse, when he abruptly reined in his horses. Unfortunately, one of the horses objected to this command and decided to bolt. The phaeton veered wildly into the middle of the street, and narrowly missed colliding with Lord Langley, who deftly turned his horse out of the way.

Garland pulled on the reins with all his strength but seemed powerless to stop his horses, which were galloping down the street at a dangerous pace. The phaeton bounced and swayed, and Amelia kept a white-knuckled grip on her seat. They were approaching a busy intersection, and she closed her eyes and resigned herself to a crash.

All of a sudden, she heard another set of hoofbeats, and she opened her eyes to see Langley galloping beside them at a breakneck pace, looking perfectly at ease. Amelia watched in disbelief as he caught up with their horses, then reached over and caught the bridle of the horse closest to him. Langley spoke gently to the horses, and when he slowed his own horse, Garland's pair slowed with him. They came to a stop mere feet from the intersection, where a grocer's cart was lumbering by. Without Langley's intervention, they would have crashed into it.

Langley rode around to Amelia's side of the carriage, dismounted, then reached up to help her down. She was relieved to feel the ground under her feet and annoyed to find herself trembling.

"Thank you, my lord," she said, trying to keep her voice calm. "I'm all right, I'm not going to swoon. I just need some space." Langley was still standing unusually close, and his proximity was making her lightheaded.

"Certainly," he agreed, but he made no move to step away. She looked at him in confusion.

"I'm afraid you'll have to release my arms," he said apologetically, and Amelia realized she was still holding on to his forearms as though her life depended on it. She abruptly let go of him and took a step backwards.

"Thank you, sir," said Garland, who was still seated in the phaeton. "It seems I have bought quite a spirited pair of horses. I had the situation under control, of course, but I still appreciated your intervention."

Langley gave him a dismissive nod.

"I'm afraid we haven't been introduced," Garland said.

"I see nothing to fear in that," said Langley dryly.

"What?" asked Garland. "Oh. Well, you're right, it's easily remedied. George Garland, at your service."

Langley sketched a bow. "I am Langley," he said, with an air of resignation.

Garland's eyebrows rose. "Lord Langley," he simpered. He stood in the phaeton and attempted to bow, and in doing so, almost lost control of his horses again. "It is an honour to meet you." He looked from Langley to Amelia. "Are you acquainted with Miss Fleming?"

Langley looked at Amelia, and a smile tugged at his lips. "You might say that, yes."

"I see," said Garland. "I wonder if I ever met you at Cambridge?"

"I don't recall," said Langley. "I have a lamentably poor memory, you see."

"Oh, me too, me too," agreed Garland, as though a poor memory was an impressive achievement. "But I think I would have remembered you."

"I'm flattered, Mr. Garland," said Langley, who was rapidly growing bored with the conversation.

Garland flushed, then turned back to Amelia. "Miss Fleming, if you would care to climb back into the phaeton, I will drive you back to your door."

Langley gave him a look designed to depress pretension. "Do not trouble yourself, Mr. Garland. I will escort Miss Fleming to her door."

"Oh, it would not be any trouble," Garland assured him. "And you have your horse, my lord."

"I assure you, I am able to control him," said Langley. "Good day, Mr. Garland."

It was a dismissal that even Garland could not mistake.

After Garland drove off, Amelia hardly knew how to behave with Langley. The last time they met she had told him she understood why he was known as the Stoneheart. Now he had saved her from a road accident that, if not fatal, would almost certainly have resulted in catastrophic injuries. She had never learned the etiquette for such a situation.

"Thank you, my lord," she said simply.

"See that it doesn't happen again, Miss Fleming," Langley said curtly.

"It was hardly my fault," she said, stung.

"I'm sure that fellow employs a coachman. If you

must drive with him, insist that someone else holds the reins."

Amelia was spared the need to reply by the arrival of Diana, mounted on a pretty bay horse, followed closely by the groom leading the white Arabian.

"I must say, that was exciting," said Diana mischievously. "How brave you were to drive with him!"

Langley rolled his eyes. "Some might have said foolish. Miss Fleming, allow me to introduce you to my sister, Lady Diana Templeton."

"It's a pleasure to meet you, Miss Fleming," said Diana with a smile. "My brother has told me a great deal about you. You must call me Diana."

"Thank you," said Amelia, surprised that Langley had spoken of her to his sister. "Please call me Amelia."

"We came to see if you wanted to ride with us," continued Diana. "Although after that experience, perhaps you would rather have a break from horses for a time."

Amelia realized that they had been in her street for the express purpose of calling upon her, and they had brought the beautiful white Arabian for her to ride.

"You came to ride with me?" she asked, dazed.

"Yes, unless Cliveden wishes to ride Cirrus sidesaddle," said Langley dryly.

Amelia looked at the horse, who stood patiently staring at her through intelligent brown eyes, and then up at the earl, who was looking at her in much the same way. The memory of their recent quarrel was still fresh in her mind, and the last thing she had expected was for him to show up with his sister to take her riding.

"Thank you, I'd love to," she said. "I'll have to change, if you don't mind waiting."

"Not at all," Langley said politely. The corner of his mouth lifted. "It will give us an opportunity to recover from the excitement."

Amelia flew up to her bedchamber and into a dove-grey riding habit, which, despite being three years old and well-used, was not far behind the current fashions. When she rejoined Langley and Diana, who had been walking their horses up and down the street, Diana commented on how well she looked in it.

"Yes, I believe the fashions for riding habits don't change as quickly as those for morning dresses," Amelia commented ruefully. "They're far more durable, too. What I really need is for one of the leaders of the *ton* to make it fashionable to wear a riding habit for all occasions."

Diana burst out laughing, and Langley smiled. The groom led Cirrus over and prepared to assist Amelia into the saddle, but Langley gave him a nod of dismissal and threw her up himself.

They set off toward the park, with Langley riding a distance behind them to give the ladies the opportunity for private conversation.

"This is lovely," Amelia remarked, relishing the feeling of the early spring wind on her face. "It's been months since I had a chance to ride. We had to sell almost all our horses, you see, and besides that, I've rarely had the time."

"I know my brother regrets the part he played in your family's misfortune," Diana said awkwardly. "I cannot imagine what you've suffered."

MISS FLEMING FALLS IN LOVE

"It's been a hard year," Amelia acknowledged. "But I am trying to be optimistic and to see the good in it. I was engaged, you know," she confided. Diana was a good listener, and Amelia found herself sharing secrets that she had previously only shared with Isabelle. "When Percy learned I lost my dowry, he ended the engagement. I've since realized it was a fortunate escape. I would hate to be married to a man who cared more for my dowry than he did for me."

"Were you very much in love with him?" Diana asked sympathetically.

"I don't think so," said Amelia cautiously. "I certainly thought I was at the time. And I was very upset when he wrote to end the engagement. But the feeling passed so quickly; there was so much to do that I didn't have time to dwell on it." She paused. "I think I was more in love with the idea of being married to Percy than I was with Percy himself."

"I can understand that."

Amelia turned to look at Diana. "How did you know you loved Mr. Templeton?"

Diana gave a funny little smile. "I met him at a ball," she began. "He was the most serious man there, and I learned after that he rarely went to balls. He brought me a glass of punch. Then he called on me, and we went riding, and he told me stories about the funny customs practiced by diplomats he had met on the Continent. He had ambition, and he was so vastly different from any other man I had ever met."

"He sounds wonderful," said Amelia honestly.

"Yes, he does," agreed Diana. "Unfortunately, I have since learned that his wish to marry me had far more to do with ambition than with love. He wants to be Prime Minister, and my family has a great deal of influence."

"But that doesn't mean he doesn't care for you."

"In the first few weeks we could hardly go a day without an argument," Diana admitted. "Everything I did seemed to irritate him."

"He sounds like a most unreasonable man," said Amelia sympathetically.

Diana nodded. "He once flew into a rage because I rode in the park in the morning without a groom. I suppose rage is the wrong term, as he's rather cold-blooded. But he tried to forbid me to ride alone." She smiled impishly. "The next day I went out half an hour earlier, while it was still dark, to prove he couldn't control my behaviour."

"What did he say to that?" Amelia asked curiously.

Diana looked down. "Well. He apologized, actually. Told me that if I wished to make reckless decisions and endanger my safety, that was my right. Then he left for Vienna."

"I see," said Amelia. "So you still ride in the mornings?"

"No," said Diana slowly. "I find it's no longer enjoyable." She sighed. "Some would say it is my fault for daring to choose my own husband." She gave Amelia an overly bright smile. "But no good will come from dwelling on that. I'm giving a ball in two weeks, and I'd be honoured if you and your family would come. The invitation cards will go out tomorrow." Diana's smile was now conspiratorial. "I intend to invite Mr. Garland too."

Amelia realized Langley had wished to introduce her

to his sister so that Diana could help promote a match between her and Mr. Garland. After an initial, inexplicable sense of disappointment, Amelia reminded herself of all the reasons marriage to Garland was a good idea. It had been her own scheme, after all.

Seven

"Let me lead, Amelia," William said in frustration.

"I'm trying, William, but I can't predict where you're going to go next," she said testily. "I don't think you're doing it properly." Diana's ball was three days away, and Amelia had asked William to help her practice the waltz, but an hour of stumbling around the sitting room hadn't improved her confidence.

"I never have trouble when I partner Isabelle," he retorted.

"You're right," she admitted. "I'm sorry, William." Although dancing came easily to William and Isabelle, it had always been difficult for Amelia, and her childhood dancing lessons had been extremely frustrating for both her and the dancing master. She had an easier time with country dances, which had a set pattern of steps she could memorize, but the waltz required her to follow an unknown pattern in response to imperceptible cues from her partner. Amelia thought it was highly unfair that such a useless skill could influence her marriage prospects.

"Maybe you should rest," suggested Isabelle, who had been playing the pianoforte for them.

"That's an excellent idea," said William, whose toes were sore from being stepped on. "It might be best if you just don't waltz, Amelia. Mr. Garland doesn't look like the waltzing type, and it's highly unlikely that anyone else will ask you."

"What an optimistic view of my situation," Amelia said sarcastically.

"What?" asked William. "Oh, I just meant you're not acquainted with any other gentlemen. Except for Lord Langley, of course, but he hardly ever goes to balls. And even if he did, it's not like he'd ask you to dance. Can you imagine?" He laughed at the thought of his sister dancing with the earl.

"No, I can't imagine," Amelia lied, forcing herself to smile at William. She hadn't told her brother that Langley's sister was hosting the ball.

"Who's hosting this again?" William asked. "Friend of Aunt Lizzie?"

"Lady Diana Templeton."

William's forehead wrinkled as he tried to place the name. "Are you sure she's good *ton*? I mean, it seems strange that she invited Garland."

"She's Langley's sister," Amelia admitted.

William's mouth fell open. "Langley's sister? Why would Langley's sister invite us to a ball?" He paced in agitation. "Do you think he's trying to lure us into his sister's home to press us for payment?"

"Don't be silly," said Amelia impatiently. "I think he's

trying to do us a kindness. I told him that since the scandal, we've been largely shut out of society."

"You told him that?" asked William in disbelief. "But Amelia, it makes us look weak."

"No weaker than we did already." Amelia was glad she hadn't told William the other details of her conversation with the earl, as she could only imagine what he would think of her suggestion that Langley pretend to court Isabelle. Now that she knew Langley better, Amelia had to admit it was ridiculous to think of him as a match for her sister.

"Well, I won't be going to that ball," said William. "I'm going up to change, I've plans with Freddie Micklebury tonight."

"Where will you go?" Amelia asked tartly. "We barely have enough money for food, you can't afford to go out on the town. How will you pay for the hackney and the drink?"

"I'm just going to Micklebury's rooms, and I'm going to walk," said William stubbornly. "Really, Amelia, things aren't that desperate yet."

Amelia stared at him in disbelief. "William, we've lost the townhouse, and you said yourself that the bank won't give you any more credit. We are far beyond desperate."

He flushed. "I'm the viscount, Amelia. That's for me to worry about," he told her defensively. The guilty look in his eyes made Amelia suspect he planned to spend the evening gambling.

William's expression the next morning told Amelia he had played and lost, and she decided it was time for more drastic action. That afternoon, she changed into a kitchenmaid's dress and apron, and walked the now-familiar route to Langley's townhouse. She had chosen her moment carefully, and slipped in through the servants' entrance when dinner preparations were at their peak. The chaos in the kitchen allowed her to pass through it unnoticed, and luck led her down the hallway to a storage closet that was just big enough to serve as a hiding place.

Amelia could hear the clock in the entrance hall as it chimed the hours, and she thought time had never passed more slowly. She closed her eyes, but despite her exhaustion, she couldn't sleep. Every so often, a prickling sensation convinced her there were bugs on her legs, but when she tried to brush them away, nothing was there.

When she finally emerged from the closet at two in the morning, Amelia's joints were stiff and her head ached. The house was dark, and she crept along with one hand on the wall until she found a candle that had been left burning in the entrance hall. She took the candle and made her way to Langley's study, where she was pleased to find his desk unlocked.

Amelia didn't see her father's IOUs, but she found a large stack of banknotes, a gold-enamelled snuffbox, and a stack of letters. The first three letters were from Adrian, and he followed a pattern; after telling his brother about some prank he had pulled, such as stealing a mate's cravats and knotting them all together, he closed with an appeal for more money. The fourth letter was in French, in a delicate hand, and signed by someone named Celestine. Celestine was apparently grateful for a gift of jewellery, but although Amelia read French fluently, she couldn't make sense of the rest of the letter.

"You won't find it, Miss Fleming," came a voice from the doorway.

Amelia shoved the desk drawer closed and looked up to see a man striding toward her, holding a candle. The candlelight cast him in shadow, but Amelia knew instinctively that it was Lord Langley. She turned to run, hoping to escape through a window, but she had left her candle on the desk, and she found herself staring into darkness. Amelia realized she was trapped, and she turned to face the earl.

Langley surveyed her calmly, apparently unsurprised to have found Amelia in his study in the small hours of the morning, and raised an eyebrow at her maid's apron.

"Would you believe I was cleaning your desk?" Amelia asked.

"No."

"I didn't take anything," she said defensively.

"I didn't think you had." His tone was cool, but she thought his dark brown eyes looked more amused than angry.

"You can check. It's all still there, the money, the snuffbox–"

"But not the IOU from your father."

"I didn't take that either," she protested. "It wasn't there. All I found were some letters." She looked down guiltily, then met his eyes again. "I admit I read some of those, but it was hard not to. I had to make sure the IOU wasn't there."

"Of course," said Langley conversationally, as though

it was the most natural thing in the world. "Did you learn anything interesting?"

"Your brother has atrocious spelling," she said. "And Celestine—is she your sister? I wondered if she was practising her French, I could barely make heads or tails of her letter."

His eyes widened at the mention of Celestine, and he was debating how to reply when Amelia spoke again.

"You know, my mother is French, so I grew up speaking the language. I would be happy to tutor Celestine if she would like."

Langley coughed. "Celestine is not my sister," he said awkwardly. "And I believe French is her first language." Langley wasn't surprised that Amelia hadn't understood the letter, as it was peppered with slang she was unlikely to have learned from her mother.

"Oh," Amelia said curiously. Although she was naïve, she knew it was improper for a woman to write to a man who wasn't her brother. "Who is she?"

"Celestine is no one of importance." As he said it, Langley realized it was true. He would buy her more jewellery as a parting gift.

"That's a cruel thing to say."

"You're right," he acknowledged. "I should have said that Celestine is a lovely woman, but she is no longer of importance to me."

Amelia nodded. "I should get home."

"How did you get in?" he asked curiously.

"Through the servants' entrance during the dinner hour. I hoped no one would notice me in a servant's dress, and if anyone did, they would assume I was new. As it happened, I didn't see anyone. I hid in a closet for hours. I think I must have been directly under your longcase clock, and when I heard it chime two o'clock, I thought it was safe. I thought I was being so quiet, I'm surprised I woke you."

"I have just returned home."

"Ah, you were out carousing," Amelia said with disapproval.

"At least I wasn't housebreaking," he retorted. "I'm surprised you didn't apply for a post in service here, so you could search the house at your leisure."

Amelia smiled enigmatically. "How do you know I didn't?" she asked, wishing she had thought to do so. "I certainly wouldn't have done so myself, as my red hair is quite recognizable, but I could have installed a friend. Perhaps one of my maids is sleeping in your servants' quarters as we speak."

The corner of his mouth lifted in amusement. "Just so you're not tempted to come back and search through other private things, I can tell you, on my honour, that you won't find your father's IOU in this house."

"I won't come back," she said firmly. "I regretted coming almost as soon as I arrived, and not only because the closet was uncomfortable. I know there's no difference between taking the IOU and taking the banknotes, however hard I tried to convince myself otherwise." She paused. "It was a moment of weakness borne of desperation, but I have recovered."

"I'm pleased to hear it. Have you recovered enough for a game of chess?" Langley wasn't sure what madness had come over him. It was almost three in the morning, and he had come home from his club weary and tired. But suddenly he was awake, energized, and wanted nothing more than a battle of wits with the redhead who had broken into his study.

Amelia chewed her lip. "I won't play for money."

"Of course not. We'll play for pride."

Langley led her over to the chessboard and set his candle beside it.

"Interesting dress," he commented. "A new fashion?"

"It's a maid's dress, as you well know, and you won't convince me you've never seen a maid before," said Amelia pertly.

He smiled appreciatively. "You're right, but I've never seen a maid who looks quite like you. Have you chosen a dress for Diana's ball?"

Amelia flushed. "I'm considering various possibilities," she lied, for didn't own anything remotely suitable for a society ball and didn't have the money for a new gown. Isabelle planned to wear one of their mother's old ballgowns, but as Amelia was considerably taller than her mother, that wouldn't be an option for her.

Langley nodded and turned his attention to the chessboard.

"Ladies first," he said chivalrously, turning the board so she would play white.

"Oh no," said Amelia. "I don't want an unfair advantage."

Langley picked up two pawns, one black and one white, then held both hands behind his back.

"Right or left?" he asked her.

"Left," she said confidently. He brought his left hand forward and opened it to reveal the black pawn. Amelia carefully turned the board back around, leaving the white pieces in front of Langley.

"White goes first, my lord," she said.

Langley moved a knight. He did not expect a difficult match, and he paid more attention to his opponent than to the game. The candlelight cast flickering shadows across her face, and Langley was mesmerized.

Amelia knew he was staring at her and didn't know what to think. She wondered if he was still angry at her for breaking into his house, but although his gaze was intense, at times she thought she caught him smiling.

Langley drew his eyes away from Amelia's face and back to the board, and was surprised to see she was ahead. He had been moving his pieces like an automaton, and he was at risk of losing the game. Although he had initially considered letting her win, he had quickly abandoned that idea as unsporting, and the prospect of a true loss irked him. He forced himself to focus, and it took his best effort to force a stalemate.

"You play very well, Miss Fleming," he said, looking at her with new respect.

"So do you, my lord." She didn't know the time, except that it was very late, and she feared the servants would be up soon. "I should get home."

"Allow me to escort you."

"I don't suppose there's any point in arguing." The truth was that Amelia had no wish to argue, as the thought of walking home by herself in the wee hours of the morning was not appealing.

"None at all," Langley agreed, and offered her his arm.

∼

Langley remembered Amelia's remark about placing a spy in his servants' quarters while Timms was assisting him to dress the next morning.

"Timms," he asked pensively. "Do you know if the household has taken on anyone new recently?"

"My lord?" asked Timms.

"Servants, Timms. Specifically, female servants. Any new housemaids?"

"None that I can think of, my lord," said Timms.

"I see. Have you heard any strange talk in the servants' hall recently? Anyone behaving strangely?"

"Nothing comes to mind, my lord," said poor Timms, who privately thought that the only person behaving strangely was Langley himself. "Do you have a concern about the service, my lord?"

"Oh no, I have no complaints," said Langley. Timms almost laughed at that. Although Langley rarely complained, his staff were well aware that a seemingly insignificant error could serve as a grindstone for his cutting wit.

"I'm pleased to hear it, my lord."

"Thank you, Timms. Keep your eyes and ears open downstairs."

"Certainly, my lord."

～

Two days later, Amelia was going through a sheaf of unpaid bills, trying to decide whether to pay those that were the longest overdue or to pay a small fraction of each, when she heard a determined knock at the door. When she opened it, she was confronted by a middle-aged man wearing tradesman's clothes and an unpleasant expression. He stuck his foot in the doorway and shouldered his way into the entrance hall. Not for the first time, Amelia wished for their old butler, whose glare alone would have sent this obnoxious individual scurrying back down the steps.

He nodded disrespectfully at Amelia. "I'm here to see Viscount Cliveden. Don't try to tell me he's not at home."

Amelia took a deep breath. "He's not at home," she said truthfully. "If you would like to leave a card, I'll make sure he receives it."

"I wouldn't like to leave him anything," he said insolently. "I've already supplied him with a new coat, along with three bills for it, and I've received no payment. So I've come to have a talk."

Amelia's heart sank, as she couldn't remember a tailor's bill among the lot she had just reviewed. She did, however, recall that William had purchased a new coat several months ago.

"I'm sorry," she said. "But as I said, Viscount Cliveden is out. If your bill appears to be in order, I'll settle part of it." She flushed, ashamed. "I'm afraid you'll have to wait for payment of the whole."

His face took on a calculating expression. "I see he has the funds to pay a housemaid, but not to pay his debts," he said. Amelia realized she was still wearing the apron she now used around the house to preserve her dresses. She fought a mad urge to laugh. The tailor had mistaken her for a servant.

"I might be convinced to take a different form of payment," he said, leering at Amelia. When he reached for her shoulder, Amelia reacted without thinking and slapped him hard across the face. He gaped at her in surprise.

"Now I've soiled my hand," she said disdainfully. She took advantage of his shock to shove him out the door, which she locked and bolted before she collapsed, trembling, against the wall.

When a determined knock came again moments later, she yelled through the door without stopping to think.

"I can only assume you want your other cheek slapped," she shouted, trying to speak loudly enough to be heard through the door but coolly enough to maintain her dignity. "But I'm not fool enough to open the door to you again."

"I'm disappointed to hear it," said the Earl of Langley, his voice full of amusement. "And I thought we had parted on good terms."

Amelia recognized his voice and her heart sank, but she realized that there was nothing to do but face him. She undid the lock and opened the door.

"My lord," she said sheepishly.

He cast his eyes down her faded dress and stained apron. Unlike the tailor's, his gaze didn't make her feel cheap.

"Hard at work, I see."

"Yes," Amelia replied simply. "I wasn't expecting callers. We have very few."

"Maybe that's because you threaten to slap them," he teased her gently.

"Only the ones who deserve it." She said it lightly, but her expression troubled Langley.

"Where is your butler?" he asked abruptly.

"He left several months ago," said Amelia. "He preferred to work in a household that could pay him. We have a manservant, but it's his day off." She hated to invite Langley in, as the house was more of a mess than usual, but she couldn't keep him standing on the doorstep. She threw the door open fully and stepped back. "Please come in, my lord."

"Thank you, but I can't stay. I've come because Diana asked me to give you this," he said, holding out a dressmaker's box. "She thought the colour was flattering in the modiste's shop, but it didn't suit her when she tried it on at home. She thought it would likely fit you, and it would complement your hair."

The box bore the name of one of the most expensive modistes in London, and Amelia couldn't resist. She lifted the lid and stared at an exquisite ballgown of powder blue silk. She ran her fingers over it reverently. It was finer than anything she had ever owned.

She glanced down at the silk dress and then back at the earl. "I can't accept this," she said sorrowfully. "It's too much."

"Well, Diana can hardly send it back," he said practically. "Borrow it for the ball. You can give it back to her after."

"All right," Amelia agreed dubiously. "Thank you. And please thank Lady Diana. It is really very generous."

"I believe she will enjoy seeing you wear it. Miss Fleming, whom were you expecting to find on your doorstep this afternoon?"

The abrupt change of subject caught Amelia off-guard. She couldn't think of a lie, and she flushed.

"Just an impertinent tailor, looking for payment," she

said, trying to make light of it. "I dealt with him, and I was prepared to do so again."

Langley looked annoyed. "Where's your brother?"

"He's out," she said shortly.

"Your chaperone, then?" he asked. "Surely she would be better able to deal with such people. Or perhaps you shouldn't answer the door when your brother and your manservant are away. You don't know who could be on the other side of it."

"But I might miss calls from earls bearing gowns," she said, trying to make a joke of it.

"There is nothing funny about it, Miss Fleming," Langley said curtly. "You should arrange for Cliveden to stay home when your manservant is away."

"Thank you for your concern, my lord, but I really don't think it's any of your business," she retorted.

Langley realized she was right, but it felt like it should be his business, and he searched for a justification.

"You forget, Miss Fleming, that your family is in debt to me."

"And you think this gives you the right to tell us who should answer the door?" she asked incredulously.

He sighed. "Let's just say, Miss Fleming, that of all the members of your family, I think you're the most likely to raise the money."

"Because I'm willing to marry for it." Amelia's cheeks were flushed, and her blue eyes were blazing. Langley thought she looked spectacular when she was angry.

"Because you're intelligent and resourceful," he countered. "Don't think I've forgotten that you increased the crop yields at your brother's estate by sixty percent. So it's in my interests to ensure you're safe."

She sighed, surprised and disarmed by the fact he remembered what she had told him during their first meeting. "If you must know, I answer the door to the bill collectors because my aunt and sister are distressed by hearing them pound on it," she explained. "I'm well able to deal with them, and I don't think I'm likely to come to harm in Mayfair, in broad daylight."

"Perhaps not," Langley admitted. He didn't doubt her ability to deal with bill collectors, but he was troubled by the fact that she had to do so. "But I still think Cliveden should stay home when your manservant is away."

She nodded. "If William asks for your opinion on the subject, I'll share it with him."

Langley realized he had received the best answer he could hope for.

"Thank you, Miss Fleming."

She nodded again. "Good day, my lord."

Eight

As the household's only maid was assisting Aunt Lizzie, Amelia and Isabelle helped each other dress for Diana's ball. Isabelle had found a pink ballgown of her mother's that fit her to perfection, and accessorized it with a strand of pearls her father had given her for her fifteenth birthday. Amelia had sold all of her jewellery, so she pulled a few curls down from her chignon to distract from the fact that her shoulders were bare.

She inspected the effect in the mirror and sighed. "All the curls falling down will make everyone think I don't have a lady's maid," she said to Isabelle, feeling discouraged. "And although that's true, I would prefer that not everyone knew it. I suppose I should take it down and start over."

"Oh no," said Isabelle seriously. "You look lovely, and that dress fits you beautifully. How fortunate that Lady Diana was getting rid of it."

Although Diana's invitation had included William, his sisters could not convince him to come. He made a vague excuse about having plans with friends, but Amelia suspected he wished to avoid Lord Langley. She thought William was looking particularly haggard, and hoped he had the sense not to try anything desperate.

As they no longer kept a coach, Amelia, Isabelle, and Aunt Lizzie took a hackney to the ball. Despite the short notice, Diana's ball was turning into one of the social events of the season, and carriages jammed the street in front of the Templetons' house. Of the two hundred invitations Diana had sent, over one hundred and fifty had been accepted.

To Amelia and Isabelle, who were attending their first ball, everything seemed impossibly grand. The torches lining the walkway illuminated exquisitely dressed couples, and Amelia was very glad that she had accepted Diana's castoff gown.

Diana and her husband received them in the entrance hall. Diana's warm smile gave Amelia confidence, but when she reached the ballroom, where a dozen couples danced the cotillion, her nerves made themselves known again. She had struggled to waltz with William in the privacy of their sitting room, and she knew it would be far more difficult to dance under the critical eyes of the *ton*.

Aunt Lizzie started toward some chairs along the wall, and Amelia and Isabelle followed. They stepped to the side to avoid a pair of ladies moving in the opposite direction, and Amelia found herself face-to-face with her former fiancé, Percival Brooks.

"Percy!" she said impulsively, holding out her hands to him. For a moment, his betrayal was forgotten, and his familiar face seemed like a port in a storm.

But the expression on his familiar face was like granite. After the briefest of nods, he turned and walked away, leaving Amelia with her hands outstretched and a look of hurt confusion on her face. Isabelle put her arm around her sister and dragged her after their aunt, who had continued toward a cluster of empty chairs and had missed seeing her niece receive the cut direct from her former fiancé.

"Stupid!" Amelia berated herself. "I should have cut him! I certainly have no wish to talk to the man, it was a case of reflex asserting itself before reason could overrule it."

"No one noticed, Amelia," Isabelle consoled her.

"Oh, but they did," said Amelia, who had seen the curious expressions on the faces of several interested bystanders, and was convinced that rumours of her humiliation were now rippling through the ballroom. "And as very few people knew we were engaged, there will now be speculation on why Percival Brooks felt unable to acknowledge me. Besides the usual reasons, of course."

"I'm sure they'll just assume he's a stickler for propriety, and did not want to converse with a young lady with whom he was not acquainted. Remember how Binnie used to lecture us about things like that?" Isabelle asked, referring to their former governess.

"Vaguely," said Amelia. "I think you paid more attention than I did."

"I remember you told her that if ladies in polite society were constrained by so many silly rules, you would seek to take your place in an impolite set," Isabelle said with a smile. "She was quite scandalized."

"Binnie was easily scandalized," remarked Amelia ruefully.

The sisters set the topic aside when they reached their aunt, who had found several empty chairs along the wall.

"This is turning into quite a crush," said Aunt Lizzie happily. "Why, I believe that's Lady Jersey over there! What a piece of luck to have secured an invitation. The Stones are very well connected, and you're very fortunate to have come to Lady Diana's notice. But I always trusted that young ladies of good breeding and proper behaviour would find their places in society."

Although Amelia knew their invitation to the ball had resulted from a series of highly improper meetings with Lord Langley, she didn't contradict her aunt.

Diana interrupted them to introduce a shy young man who wished to dance with Isabelle. Amelia watched her sister take her place in the set, reflecting that Isabelle looked as though she hadn't a care in the world. She felt a pang of envy, wishing that she could forget their troubles as easily as Isabelle seemed to do, or that she possessed the beauty that would motivate an eligible young man to request an introduction.

Mr. Garland arrived while Amelia was indulging in this rare moment of self-pity, and she forced herself to smile at him when he came to claim a dance.

"Miss Fleming, you are looking remarkably beautiful tonight," he said as he led her out to the floor. Amelia imagined that all the eyes in the room were upon them. Mr. Garland had evidently wished to make a splash at his first *ton* ball, for he wore a loud blue and white striped waistcoat and yellow silk knee breeches. His shoulders were uncommonly bulky and his waist unnaturally narrow, an effect that his valet had achieved with padding, tight lacing, and a great deal of effort. Amelia didn't know how it had been done, only that it looked ridiculous. She took a deep breath and reminded herself that he was unimaginably rich.

∽

"I don't see why we didn't take the curricle," complained Adrian, as he and Langley descended from Langley's coach outside of Diana's house. "I could have driven the greys."

"And there you have your answer," said his brother ruthlessly. "I was not in the mood for a road accident."

"I'm a very capable whip," protested Adrian. "Just because of the one incident with the chicken–"

"I wasn't aware that you tried to drive a chicken," interrupted Langley. "I was thinking of the time you capably drove my horses into a ditch."

"Because they were spooked by a *chicken*!" exclaimed Adrian hotly. "It's not as though I deliberately drove them into the ditch."

"It might have been better if you had," reflected Langley. "Then you could have argued you were indeed a capable driver, struck by a mad wish to drive into the ditch and destroy my carriage. As it stands–" he broke off when he realized his brother was no longer listening to him, but had turned to ogle a curvaceous blonde who was being handed down from a coach. Shaking his head, he ascended the steps to his sister's house.

Marsden, the Templetons' butler, bowed to Langley.

"Good evening, my lord," he said deferentially. As Langley handed his hat and greatcoat to a footman, he heard Marsden speaking to Adrian.

"Good evening, sir," Marsden said, supercilious now. "Do you have an invitation card?"

"An invitation card?" Adrian sputtered. "I am Adrian Stone, her ladyship's brother."

"I understood her brother was at Oxford," said Marsden implacably. "So I must insist on an invitation card."

Langley turned and smiled at the butler. "You are a credit to your position, Marsden."

"Come on, Robert," said Adrian angrily. "You can't let him turn me away! Just because I'm the youngest, you try to leave me out of everything, and it's not fair! I won't stand for it!" Several other latecomers stood behind him, unabashedly watching the scene.

Langley sighed and turned back to Marsden. "He is indeed her ladyship's brother," he said apologetically. "Whether he is welcome at her ball is a separate question entirely, but it's awkward to have him throwing a tantrum on her doorstep. There's no way around it, Marsden, you'll have to let him in."

Marsden gave a respectful nod to Langley. "As you wish, my lord."

Adrian thrust his hat and greatcoat at a footman and followed Langley to the ballroom, a sulky expression on his face.

"What, are you making faces to scare the young ladies?" Langley teased him.

"I learned it from you," said Adrian, although he realized his brother was looking unusually cheerful.

MISS FLEMING FALLS IN LOVE

Langley laughed. "Touché, Adrian. I guess I have developed something of a reputation. I have no wish to waste my time on young ladies who are too easily scared."

~

Langley's gaze raked across the room until he found Miss Fleming dancing with Mr. Garland. Beside her, Isabelle danced with a young baronet.

"What a beauty," commented Adrian, mistakenly thinking his brother was staring at Isabelle. "Planning to try your luck?"

"What?" asked Langley, more sharply than he had intended. "No."

"Well if you're not, you won't mind if I seek an introduction," said Adrian blithely. "That hair! It's like spun gold."

"What?" asked Langley again, momentarily confused. He had spent some time considering how to best describe Amelia's hair, and had decided it varied with the light. By daylight it was fiery, in candlelight titian, but never spun gold. He followed the line of his brother's gaze and realized that Adrian had been speaking of Amelia's sister. "Oh. You're referring to Miss Isabelle Fleming."

"If you say so," Adrian agreed. "The blonde beauty." He paused. "Wait a minute. Is she also related to the viscount?"

"Yes," Langley said curtly. "So leave her alone."

"I think not," said Adrian. "Just because you and her father had a little awkwardness at cards doesn't mean I should stay away from her."

"It was more than a little awkwardness, and it means we should do everything possible to avoid causing further harm to her and her family," said Langley with an expression that would have petrified most men.

But Adrian was not like most men. He set his mouth in a stubborn line, and Langley realized that his efforts to steer his brother away from Isabelle were having the opposite effect. He changed tack.

"I'll introduce you if you insist," Langley said with a sigh. "But I've heard she's a bluestocking." He felt a qualm of conscience, which he assuaged with the logic that it would be easier for the Flemings to deal with such a rumour than with Adrian's infatuation with Isabelle.

Adrian's mouth fell open. "No," he said in disbelief. "Not with such a face. Dash it all, Robert, a girl can't have the face of a Venus and the mind of a bluestocking! It isn't right."

"And yet it's true," said Langley, affecting a sad tone. "She is a very keen reader." That, at least, he knew to be true, for he remembered Amelia mentioning that her sister read novels. "I've also heard she attends literary salons." This was entirely false.

Adrian swallowed. "Maybe she could be reformed," he said hopefully.

Langley laughed. "Come now, Adrian, you don't reform a bluestocking. She seeks to reform you."

"But Robert, I've got a pretty strong character," said Adrian bravely. "I think I could resist her attempts to educate me."

"Oh, I've no doubt," agreed his brother. "But imagine the effort. Why, you'd hear politics at the breakfast table, poetry at dinner, and who knows what in the bedroom."

MISS FLEMING FALLS IN LOVE

"Yes," said Adrian, looking downcast. "You're right, Robert. I don't think it would do." He brightened. "I suppose I could ask her for one dance, but no more, as I certainly wouldn't want to raise her expectations."

"You're wise, Adrian."

Distraction arrived in the form of Mrs. Hunt, the wife of a landed gentleman whose estate bordered Langley's primary seat in Kent. This good lady was resplendent in a violet gown and a matching turban accented with ostrich feathers. She lost her footing as she passed Langley, forcing him to reach out to steady her.

Mrs. Hunt regained her balance and feigned a look of surprise. "My lord, I didn't see you there," she said with a curtsy and a laugh. "Mr. Stone," she nodded to Adrian before turning back to Langley. "And now I am in your debt, for I'm sure I would have fallen flat on my face if you hadn't been there to catch me. I will have to find a way to thank you."

"I assure you, ma'am, no thanks are necessary," Langley said quickly.

"Nonsense. I always pay my debts," she said with a fulsome smile. She looked over her shoulder and beckoned to a timid young lady standing behind her.

"Letitia, my dear, here is Lord Langley," she said brightly, pulling her daughter to stand beside her. "This is Letitia's first Season, you know, and I am ashamed to say that her childhood was quite sheltered," she continued, in the tone of a parent who was not ashamed of it at all. "I keep telling her it is quite proper for her to talk to our friends and acquaintances, especially such close neighbours as yourself and Mr. Stone."

A few slight alterations to her features could have

turned Miss Letitia Hunt into a very pretty girl. She had beautiful blonde hair and a good figure, which was currently displayed to advantage in a modish gown of cream muslin. But her pale blue eyes were set a smidgen too close together and her nose was a trifle too blunt, as though some mischievous fairy had flattened it during her infancy. As she was painfully shy, there was no personality to distract from her physical deficits, and the sum of her features seemed less than its parts.

Langley bowed politely to Letitia. "Miss Hunt," he said kindly.

Letitia blushed. "My lord," she whispered in a voice so soft it was barely audible.

"But why aren't you dancing, my lord?" Mrs. Hunt asked archly. "I am sure you would have no trouble finding a partner." Langley resented being manipulated, but he had always pitied Letitia, who was clearly browbeaten by her overbearing mother.

"If Miss Hunt would do me the honour, I would be pleased to join this set," he said smoothly, reflecting that the dance had to be at least half-done.

Mrs. Hunt smiled in satisfaction, while her daughter looked terrified as she placed her hand in his. Langley could feel her hand trembling as he led her out to the dance floor.

"Come, Miss Hunt, I'm not an ogre," he joked, trying to put her at ease.

"No, my lord," she said seriously.

Langley reflected that dancing with Letitia was like dancing with a doll. She was a tolerable dancer and knew the steps, but she brought no emotion to it, and answered his questions with a 'yes, my lord' or 'no, my lord', depending on what reply she thought he expected. Langley found his eyes straying to Amelia, who was dealing patiently with Garland's many missteps. Langley found himself at risk of mistaking his own steps and forced himself to focus on his partner.

Amelia had seen Langley join the set, and from across the room he and his partner appeared beautifully matched. The distance hid the imperfections of Letitia's features and her lack of conversation, and Amelia saw only a lovely blonde in a fashionable gown dancing with the best-dressed man in the room. For there was no doubt in her mind that Langley was the best-dressed man at the ball. Certainly, his collar points weren't as high, or his cravat so elaborate as those worn by the men in the dandy set, but his clothes were quietly elegant and fit him to perfection. Amelia wondered if he would ask her to dance, then chided herself for thinking of it. He had done her a great favour by procuring her an invitation to the ball, and she had no reason to expect him to dance with her at it.

When the set ended, a footman gave Mr. Garland a message that his carriage had suffered a scratch in a collision with a curricle. Garland rushed out of the room to inspect the damage, and Amelia was left to find a seat against the wall. She watched Percival Brooks dance with a petite young lady dressed in peach.

"Her name is Miss Rushton, and her fifty thousand pounds is the most attractive thing about her," came a voice over Amelia's shoulder. She turned and saw Langley standing next to her, looking maddeningly handsome. He handed her a glass of champagne.

She took the champagne and lifted her chin. "I don't know who you're talking about," she said mendaciously.

Langley smiled. "You're a terrible liar, Miss Fleming," he said gently.

"And I thought I lied rather well. I think with proper training I could be quite good. But my governess preferred to focus on useless accomplishments, like the piano, and watercolours, for which I have no aptitude whatsoever." She sighed. "Does Miss Rushton really have fifty thousand pounds?"

Langley nodded. "So they say. It's fortunate for her, because she would have a hard time finding a husband without it. Can you imagine looking at that nose across the breakfast table for fifty years?"

Amelia tilted her head to the side in contemplation. "For fifty thousand pounds, I think I could tolerate it. If I couldn't, I would arrange for her to be served breakfast elsewhere."

The earl burst out laughing, drawing stares. He was not known as a man who laughed easily or often.

Amelia sipped her drink. It was only her second glass of the evening, but she wasn't accustomed to champagne, and she felt as though it was fizzing through her entire body. "If I couldn't banish Miss Rushton from the breakfast room I would drink champagne every morning," she mused. "She is already looking more attractive than she did twenty minutes ago."

Langley feigned a look of alarm. "I wouldn't have given you champagne if I'd known it would addle your brain."

"I am not addled," she said defensively. "And I'm not

sure I can trust your judgment on the matter of Miss Rushton. You probably don't find anyone attractive."

"You have no idea whom I find attractive, Miss Fleming," he said lightly.

"This conversation is highly improper," Amelia said nervously.

"It is," Langley agreed. "Dance with me instead." A quadrille had ended, and the musicians were beginning a waltz. Langley took the empty champagne glass from her hand and set it on a table.

"This is a mistake, my lord," Amelia said, as he led her out to the dance floor. "I'm a horrible dancer."

"I rarely make mistakes, Miss Fleming," Langley said with a smile.

"You would have done better to ask Isabelle to dance. She dances like a dream, while I'll likely step on your toes."

"Perhaps I like to live dangerously."

Nine

Diana floated across the dance floor in her husband's arms. "I'd forgotten how well you dance," she said, smiling up at him.

"Not nearly as well as you do," Templeton said lightly.

"I imagine the ladies in Vienna are very accomplished at the waltz?"

"I imagine they are," he agreed. "You would know as well as I do, however, as we have no leisure for dancing while we're there."

"It sounds awfully boring," Diana remarked. "When do you have to go back?"

"I leave next Monday."

"And how long will you be gone?"

"A month, if everything goes as planned."

"Do many of the men take their wives with them?"

"Some. But I think it's hard going for the ladies. Most don't speak the language, and it's lonely."

"I see," she said. "I suppose I could learn German. I'm not entirely brainless."

"Don't worry, Diana, I won't ask you to come. I know how much you would dislike it," he reassured her.

"You are very kind, Giles," she said listlessly.

∽

To Langley's amusement, Amelia spent their first trip around the dance floor staring at his shoes.

"Do you approve of them, Miss Fleming?" he asked.

She looked up in surprise. "Approve of what?"

"My shoes. You have been giving them your full attention."

"They are very nice shoes," she said seriously. "I have been working very hard not to step on them."

Langley laughed at her frank answer, and she smiled up at him. Her face was flushed, and the dress brought out the blue of her eyes. She wasn't a classic beauty, but her charm was undeniable, and in the muted light of the ballroom she was bewitching. Langley thought she would be wasted on a man like Garland, who would undoubtedly prefer a classic beauty, and wouldn't appreciate the qualities that made Amelia interesting.

Amelia found waltzing with Langley much easier than dancing with William. Although she was acutely aware of his hand on her waist, she didn't feel like she was being pushed around; rather, it was as though she instinctively knew where to step.

"I haven't had much practice with the waltz," she confided. "I think our dancing master thought I was a lost cause. I tried to practice with William, but I never knew where I was supposed to move, and he got frustrated. But dancing with you is quite different from dancing with William."

"I would hope so," Langley said dryly.

"I wanted to thank you for inviting me to the ball, my lord," she said hesitantly.

"It's my sister you should thank."

"And I intend to," she said seriously. "Not only for the ball, but for this lovely dress. I can't believe it wouldn't suit her colouring, as I think she would look good in whatever she wore. In any case, it fits perfectly. It's almost as though it was made for me."

"How fortunate," commented Langley.

"And as I doubt your sister even knew of my existence a month ago, I am grateful to you for both the dress and the invitation."

"Are you reconsidering your plans for revenge?" he teased.

Amelia blushed. "I never thought of revenge, my lord." The room suddenly felt very warm.

"Oh come now, Miss Fleming, I could tell you were disappointed that I thwarted your efforts at housebreaking. The hostilities have been paused for the ball, but I know the detente will be temporary."

Amelia looked up at him cautiously, thinking that the arm on her waist didn't feel hostile at all.

"So if you've been plotting revenge, I won't hold it against you," Langley said lightly.

"In truth, my lord, I've had many ideas, but since the evening I — er — visited your study, I knew I wouldn't put them into action. I believe in fair play, and my actions that night were out of character."

"In that case, you can tell me your ideas," he said.

"After all the work I've done to bring about this ball, I think I deserve the entertainment."

"All right. I thought of trying to fleece you at cards," she confessed. "There would be a sort of justice in that. But I expect you play cards as well as you play chess, so I couldn't think of how to do it."

He inclined his head. "You flatter me, Miss Fleming."

She snorted. "I assure you it's unintentional."

"Did you have any other ideas?"

"Well, I thought of abducting Adrian and holding him for ransom," she admitted. "I thought I could manage it if he was intoxicated."

"Undoubtedly," Langley agreed.

"But I couldn't work out what I would do with him when the liquor wore off."

"You were afraid I wouldn't want to ransom him back?"

"Something like that," she said with a laugh.

"You didn't think of abducting me?"

"I wasn't sure I wanted you," Amelia said frankly.

Langley missed a step in the dance. "I beg your pardon?" he asked once he had recovered his equilibrium.

"Well, if I held you captive, who would pay the ransom?" she asked reasonably. "I thought of your mother, but I wasn't sure if she had independent means."

"She does," said Langley.

"Oh," said Amelia. "Regardless, a ransom demand might distress her, and my quarrel is not with her."

"On the contrary, Miss Fleming, my mother would be delighted to hear I had been abducted by an eligible young lady."

"Oh," said Amelia in some confusion. If she hadn't known better, she would have thought he was encouraging the idea. She gave her head a small shake. "In that case, it seems the only remaining obstacle is your physique."

"My physique?" Langley asked, looking amused.

"Yes. You look like you are in the habit of boxing, or fencing, or whatever gentlemen of leisure do to stay fit. I don't think you would be an easy man to subdue."

"Miss Fleming, did you know that this is the most interesting conversation I have ever had at a ball?"

But Miss Fleming didn't reply. She had had two glasses of champagne without any dinner, and it was taking all of her concentration to stay upright. Her vision blurred, and she stumbled forward against Langley's chest. He caught her easily and was about to set her back on her feet, thinking she had just taken a wrong step, when he realized her eyes were closed. He lifted her easily into his arms and carried her toward the door.

Along the way they attracted a great deal of attention, and couples stopped dancing to watch. Diana followed them to the hallway and directed Langley to a private sitting room, where he laid Amelia down gently on a rose-coloured sofa.

"I'll ring for my maid, I'm sure she has smelling salts somewhere," said Diana, reaching for the bell. "What did you say to frighten her so badly, Robert?"

Langley didn't appreciate her joke. "She must be ill," he said curtly. "Miss Fleming is not the type of girl who faints." He turned to a footman who was standing by the door. "Fetch Mrs. Templeton's doctor immediately."

The footman nodded and was turning to go when

MISS FLEMING FALLS IN LOVE

Diana stopped him. "Wait a minute, James," she instructed. "Robert, I'm sure she just fainted." She knelt beside the couch and chafed Amelia's wrists. "She'll come around, and I'm sure she wouldn't want us to make a fuss. This was her first ball, so it's no wonder she was overwhelmed. Was she drinking champagne?"

"Yes," Langley muttered, hating himself for having given it to her. "I don't care if there's a fuss, send for the doctor."

Diana was surprised to see that her brother's face was tense and his dark eyes anxious. "She won't thank you for it, you know," she said mildly, but she instructed her footman to go for the doctor. He passed Isabelle in the doorway, with Mrs. Crenshaw right behind her. "Don't worry, Mrs. Crenshaw, Isabelle," Diana said reassuringly. "Miss Fleming has fainted, but she's already coming around."

~

Amelia woke up in an unfamiliar room, with Aunt Lizzie, Isabelle, and Lady Diana Templeton bending over her with concerned looks on their faces. Behind them, Langley was pacing the room. Amelia had never seen him look so agitated.

"Thank goodness you're awake," said Diana. "How are you feeling?"

"Dizzy," Amelia admitted. "What happened?"

Langley walked over to join them. "You fainted, Miss Fleming," he explained.

"How did I get here?" asked Amelia in confusion, as she had no memory of leaving the ballroom.

"I carried you," Langley said abruptly.

"Oh," she said in confusion. "I'm sorry to have caused so much trouble. I've never fainted in my life before. She turned to Diana. "I feel so silly, and I've ruined your ball."

Diana smiled. "The ball is not ruined," she assured her kindly. If anything, the guests would think Amelia's fainting spell was a fine addition to the evening's entertainment, but Diana knew better than to tell Amelia that. "It was a momentary distraction, and I'm sure it's forgotten already." Indeed, Amelia could hear music and chatter from the next room.

"Don't try to get up," Langley admonished, for Amelia was trying to push herself into a sitting position. "The doctor will be here soon."

"Oh no," Amelia protested. "I don't need a doctor. It's just that I didn't sleep well last night because I was so nervous about the ball, and then I didn't eat any lunch. And then there was the champagne, I'm not used to it."

"That may be, but we've sent a man to fetch Diana's doctor. You can discuss it all with him." Langley turned to another footman who was hovering anxiously by the door. "Miss Fleming needs something to eat. Bread and butter, biscuits, something bland."

"I think I should go home," began Amelia, who dreaded the thought of discussing the incident with Diana's doctor. She had no doubt that the physician was frequently called to see aristocratic ladies who swooned, but she had always thought herself above such feminine weaknesses. There was also the matter of the doctor's fee, which would further strain her finances, but which she was determined Langley wouldn't pay. "I don't want to waste the doctor's time, when–"

She was cut off by the appearance of Percy Brooks, who rushed in looking upset. He knelt beside her on the sofa and took her hand in his.

"Amelia, I'm sorry," he said earnestly. "I knew that our first meeting would be painful for you, but I didn't think you would take it so hard. I thought it would be best to act as though we'd never been acquainted, but I see that was a mistake. "

"What?" she asked in confusion, trying to pull her hand away from his.

"I never meant to hurt you, you must believe that," Percy continued. "I cared for you—I still care for you— very deeply, and had circumstances been different, nothing could have altered my affection. We were both victims of fate. And I had no notion that the sight of me would provoke a swoon."

Langley snorted. Since Amelia had woken up, much of the tension had left his face, and he was looking much more like his usual self. "If I wanted a melodrama, Mr. Brooks, I would go to the theatre," he said cuttingly. "This is hardly the time or the place for such drivel."

Amelia still felt as though her brain was functioning at half-speed, and it took her a minute to process that Percy thought she had fainted from the stress of seeing him. The truth was that she hadn't spared a thought for Percy since Langley had asked her to dance.

"I hate to disappoint you, Percy, but this had nothing to do with you," she said. "If anyone is to blame, it is Lord Langley."

The others in the room turned to stare at the earl, who stood silently, with his arms folded across his chest.

Percy's face was stormy. "If he insulted you, Amelia, I'll–"

"There was no insult," she said quickly, realizing how her words could be misinterpreted. "He was a perfect gentleman. He convinced me to dance a waltz, and the effort of following both the steps and the conversation overwhelmed me."

"You will improve with practice, Miss Fleming," said Langley kindly.

"You should go back to Miss Rushton, Percy," Amelia said matter-of-factly. "I'm sure she will suit you very well. Especially if you choose to build a second breakfast parlour."

Langley burst into laughter, and the others stared at Amelia in concern.

"She's right, Brooks," Langley said. "Although the sight of you may not distress Miss Fleming, the sight of your cravat distresses me. You should return to the ballroom. Or better yet, go home."

Percy flushed at the insult, but turned back to Amelia.

"Do you truly want me to go?"

Amelia nodded. "Yes," she said simply.

"I'm sorry, Amelia," said Diana, after the door had closed behind Percy. "My husband wished to invite him, I think they met through their work at the embassy. I didn't know."

"It's all right," said Amelia philosophically. "I can't expect to go through life without meeting Mr. Brooks."

A maid hurried in and set a tray of bread and butter on the table next to Amelia.

"Oh, I can't," Amelia protested, turning to Diana. "I'm

still not quite myself, and would hate to spill something on your beautiful dress."

Diana looked confused. "I beg your pardon?" she began, but a look from Langley silenced her

"My sister would thank you for an excuse to get rid of it, because it's clearly not her colour," Langley said quickly. "Eat."

Amelia obediently spread butter on a slice of bread.

The next interruption came in the form of Mr. Garland, who bustled into the room and bowed deeply to Langley and Diana.

"This is a cursed night indeed!" he exclaimed when he saw Amelia lying on the sofa. "Miss Fleming, I can't recall when I have been more distressed. First my carriage, and now this!"

Langley's lips twitched, and Diana shot him a reproachful look.

"It's a lot of fuss about nothing, I feel fine now," Amelia said, taking a sip of tea. "But I would like to go home."

"Of course," said Garland, trying to hide his disappointment at being forced to leave the ball early. His first *ton* ball, and he had spent the better part of it arguing with an imbecile of a coachman about a scratch on his carriage. "I would be pleased to escort you home."

Amelia felt irrationally disappointed. Although her lightheadedness had passed, she still didn't feel like herself, and there was something reassuring about having Langley standing next to her with his arms folded, as though he were standing guard.

"Thank you, Mr. Garland, you are very good," she forced herself to say.

"Someone will find you a bucket," promised Langley.

"A bucket, my lord?" asked Garland, looking perplexed.

"In case Miss Fleming is unwell in the carriage," Langley explained smoothly. "It's very difficult to clean the interior of a coach."

Garland had a vision of his upholstery covered in vomit, and his face fell. "Oh. Oh, yes, of course," he said bravely.

"Or if you prefer, I could escort Miss Fleming and her party home," Langley suggested.

Garland brightened. "I wouldn't want to put you to any trouble," he said, but the hopeful look in his eyes said otherwise.

Aunt Lizzie looked uncomfortable. "Lord Langley, you are very good," she began carefully, "but–"

"Oh, I assure you I'm far from good," Langley said easily. "I've been looking for an excuse to leave, and Miss Fleming has kindly supplied one. It's no secret that I don't enjoy this sort of event, but I thought since my sister was hosting a ball, I should make the effort to attend."

Diana made a noise that sounded like a cross between a giggle and a snort.

"In any case, Miss Fleming, I would be delighted to drive you home," Langley said.

"Thank you," she said, for there was nothing else to say. Langley asked a footman to send for his coach.

"I will escort you to Lord Langley's coach," said Garland, bending over and holding out an arm. "Dear Miss Fleming, please lean on my arm."

"There's no rush," said Langley, looking at Garland with contempt. "My coachman is quick, but he can't work miracles, and it will be ten minutes before he has my coach at the door. Sit back down, Miss Fleming, eat a little more bread and butter."

She wanted to rebel against his autocratic tone, but she had no desire to stand outside waiting for the coach, or even worse, to wait in the entrance hall where she would be exposed to the scrutiny of curious eyes. Although she hated to admit it, Langley was right. She took another slice of bread.

Langley turned to Garland. "Mr. Garland, you strike me as a man who enjoys dancing," he said politely. "I would hate for you to feel obliged to wait here with us when you have already missed so much of the ball due to the misfortune with your coach."

Mr. Garland looked conflicted, but he resisted temptation. "I will wait with you, Miss Fleming," he said nobly. "I don't believe I could enjoy dancing with the knowledge that you are unwell."

"Thank you, sir," said Amelia, who secretly wished he would leave, as she found his conversation exhausting.

"Miss Fleming, did I ever tell you about my plans for Garland Castle?" he asked. "I bought an estate in the north, and although the current house is nothing to speak of, I intend to tear it down and build the most magnificent mansion in the country. I've already hired an architect, and we're currently planning the fireplaces. There will be one in every room, of course, and those in the great rooms will be done in Italian marble. I am looking for an artist to help with the designs, as it must be both noble and timeless, and–"

Amelia's eyelids felt heavy, and she leaned back against the arm of the sofa.

"The Elgin Marbles," suggested Langley.

"What?" asked Garland, taken aback.

"Lord Elgin has brought back a collection of sculptures from the Parthenon in Greece. They're over two thousand years old," Langley explained. "Your artist could copy the style. In fact, I heard Elgin was looking to sell them, and quickly, too. He might be willing to negotiate."

"Well, I'm not sure," said Garland. "I don't think I want anything secondhand. That kind of thing may be acceptable to some people, but I have artistic sensibilities."

"It sounds like you're something of a connoisseur," Langley remarked. "What's your opinion of the painting on the far wall? I've been told it's a Turner, but I have my doubts."

Garland walked over to the painting and stood chewing his lip, apparently deep in thought.

Langley rose to his feet. "I expect my coach will be ready." Before Garland knew what had happened, Langley was walking out the door with Miss Fleming on one arm and Aunt Lizzie on the other, with Isabelle following close behind them.

Garland bustled after them but was intercepted in the hallway by Diana.

"Mr. Garland," she said smoothly. "The supper buffet is ready, and I think you'll quite enjoy the salmon tarts." Before he knew what was happening, Garland was led down a hallway to a large room in which several tables were covered with a great variety of dishes.

Langley handed Amelia into his coach, which was richly upholstered in dark blue. "Oh," said Amelia. "We forgot the basin. I don't feel sick anymore, but just in case."

"I'm not concerned about the coach, Miss Fleming," Langley said kindly. "It can be easily cleaned."

"Oh," Amelia said again. This seemed at odds with his earlier comments, but her brain was too foggy to analyze it.

Somehow Aunt Lizzie and Isabelle ended up seated across from Amelia, so that when Langley joined them, he sat beside her. The bench seat was narrow, and she could feel the warmth of his leg inches from her own. Amelia rested her head against the side of the carriage, closed her eyes, and listened as Langley entertained her aunt and her sister with small talk for the duration of the drive home.

Ten

"I don't believe it," said William, staring at Amelia across the breakfast table the next morning. They were alone at the table, as Isabelle and Aunt Lizzie were still asleep. "You swooned?" He looked gratified to hear that his practical sister had done something so silly.

"I felt unwell and then I fainted," Amelia corrected. "I'm perfectly fine now."

"Did you lace your corsets too tight?"

"No," said Amelia. "But it was warm, and I had a glass of champagne, and–"

"Ah, you were drunk as a wheelbarrow," said William, who was enjoying the story immensely. "I don't think that sort of thing is good *ton*, my dear."

"I wasn't drunk, William," Amelia protested.

"I find that hard to believe," he said. "If you drank champagne and fell into a swoon, it sounds an awful lot like you were drunk. Did you make a scene?"

"I'm afraid so," she admitted. This question had been troubling her since she awoke that morning. "Lord

Langley was very good, he carried me out of the ballroom, and–"

"*Langley* carried you?" William asked in amazement.

"Yes. I was dancing with him when it happened, and I guess I fell into him." She had a vague memory of falling against his chest before passing out.

"Well, that explains the fainting," said William. "Dancing with the Stoneheart could do that to any girl. He gets a certain look in his eyes, you know, that turns a man queasy. What I don't understand is how you came to be dancing with him in the first place."

"He was quite pleasant, actually," said Amelia, and realized that he had been. "I was watching Percy dance with a perfectly awful girl, and Lord Langley came and asked me to dance. I think he dances better than you do," she reflected. "It was easy to follow his lead."

William snorted. "You didn't even try to follow my lead, you wanted to lead yourself."

"In any case," Amelia said with dignity, "he asked me to dance, and when I fainted, he carried me out of the ballroom. He even sent for Diana's doctor, but I didn't want to wait for him. So Lord Langley drove us all home."

"It sounds like he was actually quite decent," said William grudgingly. "Surprising, really. I thought he just invited you to this ball to further your interest with Mr. Garland. But maybe he was trying to make Garland jealous."

"I don't know," said Amelia, who had devoted considerable energy to the question of Langley's motivation. "I don't think he really needs the money. He has so much, I can't imagine it will make a difference to him."

"You can never have too much money," said William,

with the confidence of one who could only dream of such a problem. "Speaking of which, how did it go with Garland? Do you think he's likely to make you an offer?"

"I don't know," Amelia said again. "It's early days yet."

"I'm surprised Garland didn't bring you home."

"Oh, he offered, but Langley said he wanted to leave anyway," explained Amelia, deciding not to mention Garland's fear of having his upholstery soiled.

"It's very strange, Amelia," said William, shaking his head. "I don't understand Langley at all. Do you think he's mad?"

"Of course not!" Amelia exclaimed defensively. "Why would you say that?"

"His behaviour doesn't make sense," said William bluntly. "He makes you an offer to forgive the debt, which you, incomprehensibly, throw back in his face. Then I go to see him and he behaves, well, like the Stoneheart. But the next thing you know, he's arranging for his sister to invite us to a ball. It's deranged."

Amelia remembered that William didn't even know about her other visits to the Earl of Langley, which made for an even stranger series of events.

"I think you're reading too much into it," she said dismissively. "I imagine he barely thinks of us at all."

At that moment, Barlow entered with a letter for William. "This was brought round for you, sir," he said.

William slid his butter knife under the seal, leaving a smear of butter on the paper. His face went white as he read the note.

"It's from Langley," he explained grimly.

Amelia could barely hide her curiosity. "What does he say?"

William tossed it across the table toward her.

"You might as well read it. I'm going up to dress." He rose from the table, and Amelia realized he was still wearing his nightshirt.

After William left, Amelia spread open the sheet and read the note, which was written in a bold, upright hand.

Dear Cliveden,

I will do myself the honour of calling upon you this afternoon to discuss a matter of some importance. I hope to find you at home.

Sincerely,
Langley

Amelia's heart sped up. She couldn't decide if the prospect of seeing Langley again filled her with more excitement or dread. She reminded herself that he planned to call upon William, not her, and she might not even see him. Amelia assumed William would see him in the study, and she realized she would have to clean it.

The sound of hurried footsteps interrupted her reflections, and she found William in the entrance hall, shrugging into his greatcoat. He had clearly dressed in a rush, as his red hair was dishevelled, and he had not even troubled to put a waistcoat on over his shirt.

"Where are you headed, looking like that?" she asked him.

"Not sure yet. Probably Micklebury's again. I'll spend the day," he explained, reaching for his hat.

"But Langley wrote he intends to call this afternoon."

"And this way, you can honestly tell him I'm not at home. If I leave now, we can claim I never got his letter." He paused, struck by another thought, and gave Amelia a searching look. "Promise me you won't try to meet with him without me."

"I certainly won't promise that," she said indignantly. "He sent you a perfectly polite note, advising you of his intention to call. It's beneath your dignity to run away."

"I can't afford dignity," said William practically. "Maybe you and Isabelle should leave too. Go walk in the park with Aunt Lizzie."

"We can't walk in the park all afternoon," Amelia retorted. "Aunt Lizzie would tire after half an hour."

William shrugged. "Suit yourself. If, by some happy chance Langley renews his offer to forgive the debt, try to get it in writing. I've never met such an unpredictable man." With that, he put on his hat and dashed out the door.

Amelia returned to the breakfast table to find Isabelle spreading butter on a slice of toast, wearing a pale pink muslin gown and a dreamy expression. She had left her hair in the two braids she wore to sleep, and looked more like a schoolgirl than a young lady who had attended her first *ton* ball the previous night.

"Did you sleep well, Isabelle?" Amelia asked.

"I hardly know," Isabelle admitted. "I was so excited after the ball that I thought I would never sleep, as I kept reliving it in my head. Oh Amelia, it was just like something out of a novel! The dresses, the music—I've never seen anything like it. And this was apparently a relatively small event!"

"It was spectacular," Amelia agreed.

Isabelle's expression changed to one of concern as she remembered how the evening had ended. "Are you feeling better, Amelia?" she asked. When they had returned from the ball Amelia had gone straight to bed, so there had been no opportunity to discuss the evening's events.

"Yes, I'm well," Amelia reassured her. "Only embarrassed to have made such a scene. I hadn't eaten very much, and I had a glass or two of champagne."

"I see," said Isabelle slowly. "Did Langley say something to distress you? I know you said he didn't, but I wondered if you were just ashamed to say so."

"No," Amelia said firmly. "It had nothing to do with Langley at all." Her conscience told her that was a lie, that the sensation of twirling around the dance floor in his arms had been just as intoxicating as the champagne, but she would never admit it to Isabelle. "Langley's behaviour was above reproach."

"He certainly behaved like a gentleman after it happened," Isabelle agreed. "He carried you out of the ballroom like a true romantic hero. And the way he kicked Percy out of the room, and drove us home in his coach; really, it was incredibly chivalrous."

"Careful, Isabelle," Amelia teased. "If you keep talking like that, people may think you've fallen in love with him."

"I doubt that," Isabelle said with a laugh. "He's so intimidating, I can barely put two coherent words together when he speaks to me."

"He's just a man, Isabelle," said Amelia, a trifle impatiently.

"Yes. But a very formidable one."

"So if not Langley, did anyone else at the ball catch your interest?" Amelia asked.

Isabelle appeared to consider the matter. "I danced with several very pleasant gentlemen. One of them, Mr. Bailey, is also an admirer of Byron's poetry, so we had an interesting discussion about that. I also danced a set with Lord Langley's brother, Mr. Stone." She smiled at the memory. "He seemed to be trying to explain the plot of some play. I couldn't make heads or tails of it, except that he was convinced it would be improved by the addition of a dog."

"I believe many plays would."

"I suppose," said Isabelle doubtfully. "But it's hard to have a meaningful conversation while dancing. You're always being separated from your partner by the movement of the dance, so you can't say more than a couple of phrases at a time."

"Except for the waltz."

"Yes," agreed Isabelle. "But even with a waltz, it's hard to get to know a gentleman over the course of one dance. And as Aunt Lizzie told us that dancing two sets with the same gentleman could lead to gossip, and three would be considered positively *fast*, I think it will take several balls to learn a man's character."

"Yes," Amelia said thoughtfully, wondering if they would ever get another invitation to a society ball. She feared her fainting episode wouldn't add to her credit with the *beau monde*.

A knock at the door interrupted her reflections. It seemed too early for morning callers, and she feared it was another tradesman trying to collect a debt. She could hear Barlow talking to someone, and she hoped he would be able to turn him off without too much trouble.

Her heart sank when Barlow came to find her in the breakfast room.

"A Mrs. Hunt has come to call," he said apologetically. "I explained that Mrs. Crenshaw has not yet come down, but Mrs. Hunt said she would wait. I have put her in the sitting room."

As the name meant nothing to Amelia, she assumed that Mrs. Hunt must be an acquaintance of her aunt's. It was a nuisance that she had called while her aunt was still asleep, but it couldn't be helped. If they were lucky, she would be an acquaintance with some social influence. "I will see her, Barlow," she said. "Please send in tea."

"I'll join you," said Isabelle, and the sisters made their way to the sitting room.

Amelia had little experience with society fashion, but she suspected Mrs. Hunt was overdressed for a morning call. She wore a gown of deep blue velvet, embellished with many flounces and furbelows, and a matching hat.

"Mrs. Hunt," Amelia said with gentle dignity. "I am Miss Amelia Fleming. This is my sister, Miss Isabelle Fleming. I'm afraid my aunt is not down yet, but I'm sure she'll join us soon. I have sent for tea."

"In fact, Miss Fleming, it's you I've come to see. It's not a pleasant errand, but I believe it's my duty."

Amelia's lips twitched. She had always appreciated the ridiculous, and it was clear that contrary to her claim, her visitor was enjoying herself immensely.

"One should never shirk a duty," she agreed.

Mrs. Hunt nodded. "I feel the same, Miss Fleming."

She paused as Barlow entered with the tea tray, and a heavy silence reigned until he withdrew.

"Much as it pains me, I felt I had to come and tell you what people are saying," Mrs. Hunt continued in a condescending tone.

"Dear me," said Amelia lightly. "You make it sound quite frightening." She picked up the teapot. "Will you take tea, Mrs. Hunt?"

"No, thank you," said Mrs. Hunt, irritated by her hostess's apparent unconcern. "The talk certainly is frightening, Miss Fleming."

Amelia set down the teapot. "Don't tell me that Napoleon has escaped again?" she asked with feigned anxiety.

"What?" asked Mrs. Hunt, looking taken aback. "No."

Amelia let out a sigh of relief. "Parliament no longer intends to repeal the income tax? That would be a heavy blow indeed, although in our case, the government would have to fight our other creditors for payment."

Mrs. Hunt had not expected to like Amelia, but her dislike of her pert hostess was growing by the minute.

"It has nothing to do with tax," she ground out. "People are talking about you."

"About me?" Amelia asked. "Dear ma'am, I fear you are mistaken. I hoped to make a splash at my first ball, but I had little expectation of doing so. I can't imagine I have done anything to excite such interest."

Mrs. Hunt gave a satisfied smile. "Being new to town, you may not be familiar with our customs," she said smugly. "I am sorry to be the bearer of this news, Miss Fleming, but your actions at the Templetons' ball last night are being talked about throughout the *ton*."

Amelia feigned confusion. "My actions?" she asked, perplexed. "I know I am not the most accomplished dancer, but I don't think I was as bad as that."

Mrs. Hunt stared at her in disbelief. "Miss Fleming, you fainted in Lord Langley's arms! I don't know if you were simply overwhelmed by your first taste of high society, or if it was a deliberate attempt to get yourself alone with him. But it didn't go unnoticed."

Amelia remembered where she had heard Mrs. Hunt's name before, and realized she was the mother of the blonde beauty who had danced with Langley.

"Why Mrs. Hunt," Amelia said with a laugh. "Surely no one would be silly enough to make a scandal over the fact that Lord Langley helped me when I fainted? What are they saying, that he ravished me in full view of my aunt and his sister? That would be a scandal indeed."

"That's true," put in Isabelle, finding her voice. "She was never out of our sight. Lady Diana was there too."

Mrs. Hunt was turning increasingly red. "It's not about what happened, it's about what people think happened."

Amelia appeared to think about this. "Ah. So I shouldn't worry about my actions, so much as about people's perception of them? Perhaps I should take out an advertisement in the *Gazette* to reassure the public that nothing improper occurred?"

Mrs. Hunt could tell she was being mocked. "I came here out of kindness," she said. Amelia inclined her head but said nothing.

"I have known the Stone family for years," Mrs. Hunt continued. "We are neighbours in Kent, you know."

"I wonder why you chose to call upon me rather than

upon Lord Langley?" Amelia asked. "If my actions were improper, his must have been equally so. Since you're already acquainted with the earl, it would have been more logical to approach him, as I've never met you before."

"Lord Langley behaved like a gentleman," said Mrs. Hunt. "But your actions have made him a target for gossip and speculation."

"What do you suggest I do?" Amelia asked coolly. "Make him an offer of marriage to save his reputation?"

Mrs. Hunt snorted, and her veneer of politeness slipped. "There's no way he would marry a girl such as you," she said cruelly.

"Certainly not," Amelia agreed placidly. "He knows I would never accept him."

"Miss Fleming, this levity is not becoming," said Mrs. Hunt. "I came to give you a piece of advice."

"Only one?" Amelia asked. "I would have thought you would be good for more than that." Had she been familiar with boxing terminology, she would have said the gloves were off.

Mrs. Hunt did not rise to this. "Go to the country, Miss Fleming. Stay out of sight until the talk dies down."

"Ah," said Amelia, pretending to think about it. "And how long a stay would you suggest? When will my reputation be restored?"

Mrs. Hunt snorted again. "Miss Fleming, your reputation will never recover. But you must think of your sister. She's pretty enough that she just might take. She won't be able to look too high, of course, and she's unlikely to catch a title, but a landed gentleman may be within her reach. But she won't have a hope of a decent match if she can't distance herself from you."

Amelia struggled to maintain her composure. Mrs. Hunt didn't know it, but she was making the only argument that would have any effect.

"No," said Isabelle stoutly. Amelia turned to her in surprise. She had almost forgotten Isabelle was there.

"I don't believe that's true," continued Isabelle, "But even if it is, I'm not ashamed of my sister, and I have no wish to catch the sort of man who would be scared off by my relationship to her."

Amelia stood. "Well, Mrs. Hunt, I believe you have fulfilled your duty," she said coolly. "It seems my sister and I are both beyond help. Allow me to show you out."

After she had bolted the door behind their unwelcome visitor, Amelia returned to the sitting room and collapsed on the sofa with a sigh. She was physically and emotionally spent, and grateful she had managed to hold herself together.

"What a meddlesome busybody," she ranted. "If these sorts of people make up English high society, then I think we're well out of it. Saying it pains her to tell me what people are saying! Any fool could see that she takes great pleasure in repeating malicious gossip."

"I'm sure that's all it is," said Isabelle reassuringly. "She's probably jealous, and worried you'll outshine her daughter."

"Jealous of me?" said Amelia incredulously. "What does she have to be jealous of? I have no dowry and very few feminine accomplishments. Really, I have little more than a broken engagement to my credit."

"Amelia, you have many accomplishments," protested

Isabelle, who thought her older sister underrated her abilities. "Most of them aren't feminine, but think of the way you've kept Cliveden Manor afloat."

"I doubt Mrs. Hunt is jealous of my skills in estate management."

"But Lady Diana has taken an interest in you, and Langley danced with you," Isabelle pointed out. "That must raise your credit."

Amelia sighed. "Yes, but that's only because Langley knows that his best hope of getting his money is to help me make a good marriage," she explained. "I have little hope of catching a man like Mr. Garland unless I look like I belong in high society."

"Yes," said Isabelle dubiously. "Oh Amelia, are you sure there isn't another way?"

"Another way for what?" asked Aunt Lizzie, who had come down the stairs so quietly that neither sister had noticed her.

Seeing that Isabelle looked panicked, Amelia answered her. "Another way to brew tea, that will achieve the same result with half the tea leaves," she said glibly. "Isabelle has heard it can be done, but I don't believe it."

"I should think not," said Aunt Lizzie, giving Isabelle a scandalized look. "My dear Isabelle, I don't think it would be the same at all. And we have not reached the point where we must economize over tea."

"I must have been mistaken," Isabelle said meekly.

Eleven

The door had barely closed behind Mrs. Hunt when another caller arrived at the Flemings' townhouse, and moments later, Barlow announced Mr. George Garland.

Mr. Garland had spent the morning in a lather of indecision. At thirty-six, he had decided it was time he was married, and he had his heart set on marrying into the nobility. He was realistic enough to know that only a nobleman in desperate financial straits would consider marrying his daughter to a tradesman, but Garland still wondered if he could do better than Miss Amelia Fleming. She wasn't unpleasant to look at, but there was still the matter of her red hair, and she seemed to have decided opinions for a young woman.

Diana's ball had swung things in Amelia's favour. The blue gown flattered her colouring, and she had been a pleasant dancing partner. But it was Amelia's apparent intimacy with Lord Langley and his family that had truly piqued Garland's interest. Although Langley was known as the Stoneheart, the Stone family was unquestionably part of the social elite. After Amelia had fainted, Langley had looked at her with such concern that Garland wondered if the earl had an interest there himself. Garland didn't want to offend Langley, but there was something appealing about the idea of winning a girl from under the earl's nose.

Garland bowed to Mrs. Crenshaw and Isabelle, then took a seat on the sofa across from Amelia. "I came to ask after your health, Miss Fleming," he said. "I hope you have recovered from last night's excitement?"

"Yes, I'm quite well."

"I am relieved to hear it," said Garland. "I was worried about you, you know."

"Thank you," said Amelia, who was too weary to make more of an effort. Her eyes were shadowed from lack of sleep, and in her old white muslin gown, she looked particularly young and fragile. Today she had none of the excessive confidence that Garland had found off-putting. His greatest reservation had been that Amelia was too bold, and ironically, her lack of conversation pushed him to a decision.

"Is Lord Cliveden at home?" he asked abruptly. "I would like to speak to him."

Amelia flushed, for she could guess why he wanted to speak to William. "My brother is out, sir."

"What, already?" asked Mrs. Crenshaw, who had still been asleep when William had left the house.

"Yes, he left shortly after breakfast," Amelia explained.

"I see," said Garland, looking a little deflated. "Perhaps I'll wait for him. When do you expect him home?"

"I'm not entirely sure," said Amelia. "But I think he will probably be out until this evening."

Garland debated how to proceed. He had planned to ask Cliveden for Amelia's hand in marriage, as was proper. However, he was not a patient man, and now that he had decided to marry Amelia, he wanted to settle the issue without delay.

He turned to Mrs. Crenshaw. "Mrs. Crenshaw," he said importantly. "I wonder if you would grant me the favour of a few minutes—a very few minutes—alone with your niece?"

As Mr. Garland was clearly the sort of man who placed great stock in proper behaviour, the significance of his request was obvious to everyone in the room. Mrs. Crenshaw knew Amelia had been encouraging his attentions, and although the idea pained her, she was a practical lady. "A very few minutes, Mr. Garland," she emphasized as she rose to leave, signalling to Isabelle to follow her.

After the door closed, Garland moved to sit beside Amelia on the sofa. The knowledge that she was about to receive an offer of marriage had woken her up quickly, and she forced herself to meet his gaze.

"Rest assured, Miss Fleming, that the delicacy of your constitution only adds to your charm," Garland began.

Amelia could not imagine why a man would want a woman who was prone to fainting, but she held her tongue. He took her silence as encouragement.

"I'm sure you have guessed the reason for my call today," he continued. "You must know I hold you in high esteem."

"Thank you," said Amelia, for lack of a better reply.

"And I flatter myself that you are not indifferent to me," he said pompously. "Miss Fleming, the longing in your beautiful eyes has led me to hope for a closer connection." Garland moved closer, so his leg was only inches from Amelia's, and she fought the urge to move away. She told herself she was uncomfortable because she was unused to being alone with a man, but a voice inside her head reminded her she had spent time alone with Langley without wanting to escape.

Garland dropped to his knees in front of her and grabbed her hands. His palms were sweaty and warm.

"Miss Fleming—Amelia—I am a hard-working man, and I think I have a great deal to offer a lady," he said with pride. "Some may view me as a tradesman, but I see myself as a man in service to the nation. As you know, I am preparing to build Garland Castle, which will be one of the finest estates in England. I don't have a title now, but I'm confident the Regent won't ignore my contributions to our country, and I hope that in the not-so-distant future, I will be Lord Garland. My happiness won't be complete without a Lady Garland by my side, and I think you are the perfect lady for the role. Miss Fleming, will you do me the honour of becoming my wife?"

Amelia was gripped by conflicting emotions. She did not love him, of course, and he hadn't claimed to love her. If she married him, she would spend her life on the fringes of society, and she and her marriage would likely be the subject of many a joke. However, as she had told Langley during their first meeting, she was a practical girl. Garland was essentially harmless, and Amelia thought he would treat her kindly. She would never want for money, and more importantly, neither would her brother and sister. William wouldn't be driven to gamble, and he might even be able to invest in improvements for Cliveden Manor. Her marriage to Garland wouldn't do wonders for Isabelle's marriage prospects, but having a wealthy tradesman as a brother-in-law might be better than having a sister with a ruined reputation.

In the end, it was the thought of Langley that tipped the scales. She had told the earl that if he helped bring the Flemings into society, his debt was likely to be repaid. He had played his part brilliantly, and now Amelia would uphold her part of the bargain.

"Miss Fleming?" Garland asked with barely concealed impatience. He was clearly surprised it was taking her so long to give him an answer.

"Mr. Garland, I am honoured by your proposal," she began carefully. "And I would be delighted to accept–" she broke off as he leaned toward her, and for an awful minute, she feared he was going to kiss her. She ducked her head to the side and twisted her hands out of his grasp.

"I would be delighted to accept, but I'm afraid I'm not in a position to marry," she continued. "My brother needs me at Cliveden Manor."

Garland sat down next to her, closer than was comfortable. "I don't understand," he said, looking put out. "Surely your sister can act as hostess until your brother takes a wife."

"There's more to it than that," Amelia explained. "I'm sure you're aware my father's death put my family in a difficult financial position." She wasn't sure how much

Garland knew about her family's circumstances, but she decided he didn't need to know the details of their debt to Langley. "We're deeply in debt, and it is a lot for my brother to cope with. I have had to take an active role in the management of Cliveden Manor."

"Yes, my dear, and I'm sure Lord Cliveden appreciated your help," Garland said with condescension. He secretly thought that this decision reflected poorly on Lord Cliveden, as in his opinion, a gentleman should not ask a lady to do anything more difficult than manage the servants. "But I assure you I won't ask you to do such work when you're married to me."

"I'm afraid you misunderstood," Amelia said. "I don't mind the work, and I like to think I'm helping my family. But I don't imagine you would want me to continue to assist at Cliveden Manor when I am your wife."

"Certainly not," said Garland, much struck. "Miss Fleming, I'm sure your brother would not want you to trouble yourself with his problems. Surely he will hire an estate manager."

"I'm afraid not," said Amelia apologetically. "There is no money to hire anyone else, and I don't think I could be happy in a marriage if I knew I had left my brother to carry the family's burdens alone."

Garland, who assumed that Cliveden had been humouring his sister by allowing her to think herself useful, tried to dismiss her fears. "My dear Miss Fleming, surely you underestimate Lord Cliveden. I'm confident your brother is more capable than you think."

"I don't doubt that William is capable, Mr. Garland, but I fear the debt is too great for one man to manage alone." She looked up at him through her eyelashes. "I just don't see a solution."

She waited expectantly, hoping that he would take the hint so she wouldn't have to make the suggestion herself.

"The settlement!" said Garland, looking very pleased to have come up with the idea. "I had always planned to settle money on you, and I can arrange for a sum to be paid directly to your brother. Would that relieve your worries, my love?"

"Oh," said Amelia, with feigned surprise. "I couldn't expect you to pay a settlement to William."

"Nonsense," said Garland, warming to the idea. "You may not realize it, but this sort of thing is quite commonly done."

"I suppose so." Amelia still looked doubtful. "If you give a settlement to William, I wouldn't expect you to settle anything on me, and I would need very little for pin money."

"Now Miss Fleming," he said with an amused smile, "I think I have the resources to both satisfy your brother and keep you fashionably dressed." He cast a critical eye over her old gown. "I can't have my wife looking like a frump."

Amelia was struck by the fear that he would want input into her clothing, as she imagined his taste ran to bright colours with plenty of frills and feathers. She bravely decided that if she was to be ostracized as the wife of a vulgar cit, she might as well look the part, and it was a small price to pay for her family's financial security.

"You are very generous, sir. I guess all that remains is to discuss terms."

"Terms?" asked Garland, looking surprised. "Oh, I'll hash out the details with Cliveden." He stretched out an arm and let it rest around her shoulders, and Amelia fought a shiver. She stood and turned to face him.

"I'm afraid that's not a good idea," she said apologetically. She had already decided that she couldn't rely on her brother's negotiation skills. "You see, Mr. Garland, my brother is proud. If you approach him with this idea, he's likely to refuse, and it may lead him to refuse his consent to our marriage altogether."

"If you think so," said Garland skeptically.

"I do," said Amelia firmly.

"Well, I don't see how the thing is to be settled," he said peevishly.

"We must present it as a *fait accompli*. I'll work with our solicitor and draw up a contract. If we've already reached an agreement, it will save William the embarrassment of feeling like he's asking for money."

Garland looked taken aback. "Miss Fleming, I hardly think–"

"Oh Mr. Garland, now that you have raised my hopes, I would be so disappointed if William said no." The desperation in her voice was genuine, and she grabbed his hands. "It would be like waking up from a beautiful dream and realizing none of it was real."

He folded her hands in his. "When you put it like that, Miss Fleming, you make it impossible for me to deny you anything."

"Forty thousand pounds," she blurted. She could feel his hands clench around hers. "I heard William say that's what he would need to make the family comfortable." Garland was silent, and Amelia wondered if she had overplayed her hand. "But perhaps it's too much," she said, looking stricken. "No man could be wealthy and generous enough to consider such an amount."

"My dear Miss Fleming, please don't distress yourself," Garland said kindly. "It sounds very reasonable. Have your brother's solicitor draw up the contract."

Amelia was so relieved that she hardly knew what was happening when Garland pulled her towards him and pressed his lips against hers. He smelled like garlic, and she forced herself to stand quietly and not pull away. She wondered if he expected some sort of response.

She had never been more grateful to hear a knock on the door. Garland released her with reluctance, and she turned to face her aunt.

"Mr. Garland has been kind enough to make me an offer of marriage," she said simply.

Mrs. Crenshaw's good-humoured face broke into a smile. "Congratulations," she said warmly.

"Yes, we mean to be married as soon as we can make the arrangements," said Garland jovially.

"Yes, I'm very happy," Amelia said mechanically. She turned to Mr. Garland. "I'll have William's solicitor draw up the contract directly."

Garland was surprised by the businesslike tone of her voice, and for a moment he wondered if he had been outmanoeuvred. But Amelia looked so feminine and fragile, almost ethereal really, that he told himself that there was no way she could have schemed to win a fortune. He reminded himself that the settlement had been his own suggestion, and took the view that he was simply a generous man who had offered a ridiculously large settlement to ensure his future wife's happiness.

They were interrupted by an impatient knock at the front door, and minutes later, a petite lady, dressed in the height of Parisian fashion, swept imperiously into the sitting room.

"Mama!" Amelia exclaimed.

Twelve

"Amelia!" said her mother, crossing the room to her daughter. Amelia was enveloped in a surprisingly strong embrace and a cloud of scent. Her mother took a step back and frowned at the sight of her dress. "*Ma chérie*, what is this thing you are wearing?"

"It's a morning dress, Mama," Amelia said stiffly. "I think you've seen it before."

"Yes, and as I haven't seen you in almost a year, I would have expected you to have new clothes."

Amelia took a deep breath and tried to hide her frustration. "Mama, allow me to introduce you to Mr. George Garland," she said politely. "Mr. Garland, Lady Cliveden."

Garland bowed deeply, seemingly awestruck.

Lady Cliveden barely spared him a glance. "*Enchantée,*" she said, in a tone that suggested she was anything but. She turned back to her daughter. "Amelia, I must have money to pay off the post-boys." She sighed with the air of a martyr. "There was some trouble with my sister-in-law, and it turned my brother into a skinflint. That is the English word, yes?"

Amelia correctly deduced that her mother's decision to return home had stemmed from a quarrel with her sister-in-law and not a desire to help her children in their hour of need. It didn't surprise her that despite having no money, her mother had travelled by post-chaise rather than the less expensive stagecoach.

"I'm sorry, Mama, I have no money for the post-boys," Amelia said without sympathy. "Perhaps you could give them your earrings." The particularly fine pearl drops at her mother's ears had not escaped her notice.

Lady Cliveden turned to Aunt Lizzie, whom she had not yet acknowledged. "I wonder, Elizabeth, if–"

"No Mama, Aunt Lizzie will not pay your charges either," said Amelia firmly.

"Where is William?" her mother asked, suddenly concerned about the whereabouts of her only son. "Surely he will pay the charges for me."

Mr. Garland pulled a purse from his pocket. "Lady Cliveden, it would be an honour to assist with the post charges," he said obsequiously.

She looked at him with approval. "Thank you, Mr.–" she paused, having forgotten his name.

"Garland, my lady," he supplied. "Mr. George Garland." He bustled out to pay off the postilions.

As soon as the door closed behind him, Lady Cliveden turned to her daughter. "Amelia, I see it was a mistake to stay away for so long. I return to find you dressed like a maid, entertaining such a vulgar person as this Mr. Garter–"

"Garland, Mama."

"As you say," agreed Lady Cliveden. "But regardless of his name, he is not at all *comme il faut*. I'm surprised at you, *chérie*." Her gaze swept the room, noting the squares of dark wallpaper where paintings had previously hung. "What has happened to the art?"

"Sold it," said Amelia bluntly.

Her mother surveyed the room thoughtfully. "It may have been a good decision, as your grandfather bought most of the paintings, and to tell you the truth, *chérie*, I never thought much of his taste. When we replace them–" She broke off as Garland returned.

"Ah, but you need not have returned," she told him bluntly, with no thanks for having settled her debt. "You will understand, I have not seen my daughter in months, and we have much to discuss."

Amelia cringed, afraid Garland would be insulted by her mother's careless dismissal, but he didn't seem to take offence.

"It has been an honour to meet you, Lady Cliveden," he said, bowing deeply. He bowed to Mrs. Crenshaw, then crossed the room to Amelia and raised her gloved hand to his lips. "Miss Fleming," he said reverently. "I look forward to a closer acquaintance with your family."

"What a funny man," said Lady Cliveden, as soon as the door had closed. "A closer acquaintance with our family, indeed." She turned to Mrs. Crenshaw. "I wonder at you, Elizabeth, allowing a morning call from a man such as him."

Mrs. Crenshaw, who had always been intimidated by Lady Cliveden, racked her brains for an answer. Amelia leapt to her defence. "It is unfair to blame my aunt, Mama," she said. "I am twenty years old and able to make my own decisions about which callers to receive."

"Indeed, I would hope so, but if Mr. Garland is any example, I fear you are not," said her mother.

Amelia, correctly judging that it was not the right time to inform her mother that not only had she allowed Mr. Garland to pay a morning call, she had accepted his offer of marriage, was relieved when Isabelle arrived to distract her mother.

"Isabelle!" said Lady Cliveden, crossing the room to embrace her second daughter. "I hadn't thought it was possible, but you are even more beautiful than when I saw you last. You take after me, of course."

Isabelle laughed shyly. "Thank you, Mama. I didn't know you had come home." She surveyed the room. "Mr. Garland has gone?" she asked, with a questioning look at Amelia.

"I don't want to hear any more talk about this Mr. Garland," said Lady Cliveden dismissively. "We have wasted far too much time on him already." She looked critically at Isabelle's dress, an old pink muslin that had been made over to make it appear more fashionable. "That dress is a little better than your sister's, but not much," she said with her characteristic frankness. "We must go to the modiste." She looked at Mrs. Crenshaw. "You too, Elizabeth, for although your figure has never been good, I think we can show it to better advantage."

Her daughters and her sister-in-law stared at her. "Mama, we have no money," Amelia said. "And you have told us you have none, so we have no way to buy new dresses."

Lady Cliveden laughed. "The modiste will take credit,

my love," she said airily. "No one actually takes money to the shop."

"But they will send bills, Mama, and we have no way to pay them!" Amelia said, with poorly concealed frustration. She had no intention of telling her mother about her agreement with Garland for forty thousand pounds, as she knew her mother would start spending the money before they had seen a penny.

"But surely William has the income from Cliveden Manor," said Lady Cliveden confidently. "We will have the bills sent to him."

"William needs the income from Cliveden Manor for repairs and investments, without which the estate will fall to ruin and cease to produce any income at all," said Amelia ruthlessly. "Anything that can be spared must go towards our debt to Lord Langley."

"Yes, I remember you wrote to me about that," said Lady Cliveden, with a nod of recognition at the name. "You said he was rude and disagreeable. And *chérie*, if that's the case, I don't see why we're troubling ourselves about this debt to him."

"It's a debt of honour, Mama," Amelia explained wearily.

"Yes, but it was a debt incurred by your father, and your father is dead," argued her mother, with the air of a woman pleased with her logic. "Lord Langley can't expect William to take on his father's debt."

"Perhaps not legally, Mama," agreed Amelia. "But William won't be able to hold up his head in society if he takes that position. None of us will."

"It doesn't make sense," complained her mother.

"Why, this Lord Langley as good as murdered your father–"

"He did not," said Amelia fiercely, her blue eyes sparkling with fury. "Papa made his own choices. If he hadn't lost to Lord Langley, he would have lost to someone else." She didn't point out that if her mother hadn't been so extravagant, her father might not have felt compelled to try to increase his fortune at the gaming tables.

"We don't know that," said her mother. "Me, I think that Lord Langley has blood on his hands."

Amelia found herself too angry to reply.

"Would you like some refreshment, Mama?" Isabelle asked diplomatically. "You must be tired after your journey."

"I am not tired," insisted Lady Cliveden. "I want to go to the modiste." She pulled the bell imperiously, and when Barlow appeared, ordered him to send for the coach.

"I am sorry, my lady," he said apologetically. "The coach and the horses were sold several months ago."

Lady Cliveden let out a deep sigh. "We will walk," she declared. "It isn't far." She rose to her feet and looked expectantly at the others. Mrs. Crenshaw and Isabelle stood to join her, but Amelia remained obstinately on the sofa.

"I'm afraid I have a headache, and will stay behind," Amelia said stiffly.

Once the shopping party had left, Amelia slipped into her brother's study and composed a letter to the family solicitor, instructing him to prepare a contract of marriage between her and Mr. Garland. She had some practice at imitating her brother's handwriting and flattered herself that her note could easily pass for William's. She shamelessly signed her brother's name, then sealed the letter and gave it to Barlow to deliver.

There was a knock on the door not five minutes after Barlow had left. Amelia considered ignoring it, as she felt as though she could happily go several days without speaking to another person, but she remembered that Langley had planned to call. Sure enough, when she opened the door she found the earl on her doorstep, elegantly dressed in a coat of blue superfine, tan pantaloons, and Hessian boots. She thought he looked more cheerful than she had ever seen him.

"Miss Fleming," he said with a smile.

"Lord Langley," she said, meeting his eyes awkwardly. "My lord, with all the confusion last night I can't remember if I thanked you properly. I want you to know how much I appreciated your kindness."

"I really did very little." He looked at her in concern, taking in the dark circles under her eyes. "Are you sure you have recovered? I really wish you had allowed Diana's physician to examine you."

"I am perfectly well, so there was no need," she said firmly. "But I wanted to talk to you about that. I know you sent for the doctor, and I'm sure you paid him for his trouble. I'd like to reimburse you."

"That's not necessary, Miss Fleming," Langley began.

Amelia flushed. "I'm sure the amount is insignificant to you, but it's a matter of principle."

Langley raised an eyebrow. "The doctor didn't ask for payment, because Diana invited him to stay for the ball. I understand he enjoyed himself immensely, so if anything, he's in your debt."

"Oh," Amelia said, discomfited. She realized that she had once again kept the earl standing on her doorstep. "Would you like to come in, my lord?"

He nodded. "I've actually come to see Lord Cliveden."

"He's out," Amelia said bluntly.

"I see," said Langley, looking put out. "That's disappointing. I sent him a note advising him of my intention to call."

"Yes, I know," said Amelia, without thinking. "He left before he received it."

"Ah," said Langley with a knowing smile. "No doubt you are in the habit of opening correspondence on his behalf."

"Sometimes," she admitted truthfully. "In any case, I can meet with you on his behalf."

"All right," Langley said. He had planned to ask William for permission to marry Amelia, but he realized he would rather discuss it with her first.

Amelia had expected an argument and was surprised he agreed so easily.

She showed him to the sitting room. "Shall I ring for tea?" she asked. Tea was literally all they had to serve him, as they had served Mr. Garland the last of the sandwiches.

"What?" he asked distractedly. "Oh. No thank you, Miss Fleming." Langley took a chair across from her, and Amelia found herself wishing he had sat next to her on the sofa. They stared at each other in silence for a moment, and if Amelia hadn't known better, she would have thought the earl was nervous.

"What did you want to discuss with William?" she prompted.

Langley met her eye. "Miss Fleming, I wondered if you were concerned about the possibility of gossip arising from last night's events."

"I try not to worry about gossip."

"No doubt that's wise," Langley said kindly. "But I know how damaging gossip can be to a young lady's reputation, and I would hate to think that my actions had compromised yours."

"You needn't worry. I have received an offer of marriage from Mr. George Garland."

"Indeed," said Langley, trying to hide his surprise. "And have you accepted him?"

"Yes," said Amelia calmly. "There are still some details to discuss, but I expect we will be married within the next few weeks." She realized she hadn't thought about what kind of ceremony Garland might want. She hoped the wedding wouldn't become a circus.

"In that case, I congratulate you," Langley said curtly. "Although I think it might be more appropriate to congratulate Mr. Garland." He knew he should be relieved that he was no longer honour-bound to offer for her, but strangely enough, all he felt was disappointment.

"Thank you," said Amelia. "There will be a settlement, and I believe we will soon be able to pay you most of what we owe. I wish you would tell me the amount of the debt?"

"Miss Fleming, it would not be appropriate for me to discuss it with you. I will take it up with Cliveden. Please tell him to call upon me when he returns."

"But when you first arrived, you seemed perfectly

willing to meet with me instead of my brother," she said, stung. A month ago she had thought that if she could clear her family's debt she would have nothing left to hope for, but for some reason the victory felt hollow.

"I made a mistake, Miss Fleming." Langley rose, bowed stiffly, and left.

Thirteen

Notes from the diary of the Earl of Langley

It seems that whenever I decide to offer marriage to a young lady, she runs into the arms of another man. Miss Fleming fainted at Diana's ball last night, and because I did what any gentleman would, the gossips are saying that she was caught in a compromising situation. It's entirely ridiculous, but gossip isn't fair, and I planned to make her an offer of marriage.

But Garland beat me to it. I must say I was surprised, both that Garland came up to scratch and that Miss Fleming accepted him. I wonder if she doubted I would do the honourable thing and offer for her, which is hardly flattering. The alternative is that she expected me to offer for her and thought she would do better with Garland, which is even worse.

I wonder if she plans to drink champagne every morning to tolerate the sight of Garland across the breakfast table. And every night, to tolerate the sight of Garland—no. Better not to think about that.

If I were so inclined, I'm sure I could profit from this talent of driving women to accept proposals from other suitors. I imagine many men would pay handsomely to have me feign interest in a particular lady, to make them seem attractive by comparison. Stoneheart Matchmaking has a nice ring.

But Mama is right that I will have to marry eventually, and I have come to believe that Miss Fleming would suit me as well as anyone.

~

After leaving Amelia, Lord Langley made his way to Jackson's Boxing Saloon, where he went a few rounds with his old friend, Mr. Lucas Kincaid. When he was in town, Langley visited Jackson's regularly, and he was known as a formidable opponent. Not only did he have a punishing right hook, he had a strong mental game, as he was able to think several moves ahead and was rarely riled by his opponent. But Kincaid thought his friend was fighting hot this evening, with an uncharacteristic lack of discipline and a wild look in his eyes.

"Easy, Robert," Kincaid said, after a particularly violent exchange of blows. "It's only a sport."

"Yes, Lucas," said Langley. "It's a sport. If you want something more delicate, take up dancing."

Kincaid had heard a tale of a young lady fainting in Langley's arms at a ball the previous night, and wondered if it had something to do with his friend's mood. It was not an uncommon ploy, for a young lady to faint in front of an eligible man in the hope of being caught in a compromising position and trapping the gentleman into marriage. He wondered if Langley had found himself trapped, and now felt obligated to make an offer to a scheming young lady.

"I heard there was a bit of fuss at Diana's ball last night," Kincaid began carefully.

"Yes," said Langley shortly.

"A young lady taken ill?"

"Yes."

Kincaid realized the delicate approach was getting him nowhere. "Were you trapped into offering marriage, Robert?" he asked bluntly.

"No," said Langley in a tone that Kincaid couldn't interpret. "It wasn't a trap. Miss Fleming was simply taken ill."

Kincaid raised an eyebrow. "Miss Fleming? Not Cliveden's daughter?"

"Yes," Langley admitted curtly. "Cliveden's daughter."

"Did her brother ever pay the debt?"

"No, but that's irrelevant."

Kincaid thought it was highly relevant. If Miss Fleming could entrap Langley into marriage, she would make it highly awkward for him to collect a debt from her brother. "You don't think she was hoping–"

"Not her style, Lucas," Langley interrupted. "She's more likely to break into my study to try to steal the IOUs, or abduct Adrian and hold him for ransom."

"She would abduct Adrian, but she wouldn't try to entrap you?"

"I have it on good authority that she doesn't want me," said Langley with a wry smile.

"She sounds like an unusual young lady." Kincaid

thought any girl who could faint in Langley's arms without raising his suspicion must be either highly unusual or an excellent actress. "Do you think there will be a lot of talk?"

Langley sighed. "I think it's inevitable. I actually went to make Miss Fleming an offer this morning, but found that George Garland had been before me. Miss Fleming accepted him, so everyone is happy."

Kincaid didn't think his friend looked very happy. "I see," he said thoughtfully. "Miss Fleming will be a rich woman."

"Yes, at the expense of being married to the most vulgar social climber in the country," said Langley scornfully.

"Come on, Robert," said Kincaid, who thought Langley might show more appreciation for the man who had saved him from a disastrous marriage. "I've always respected self-made men."

"Lucas, I have great respect for self-made men. But I have great contempt for a man who inherits a thriving business and considers himself a brilliant businessman, then neglects his business to devote his energies to infiltrating the aristocracy. Especially when he's a ham-handed driver with no understanding of horses."

Before Kincaid could explore the reason for his friend's low opinion of Garland's driving abilities, a footman interrupted with a note for Langley. The earl read it quickly and seemed pleased with its contents.

"I think I've had enough for today," Kincaid said. "Will you join me for dinner?"

"Another time, Lucas," Langley said absentmindedly. "I have business to attend to tonight."

Lucas laughed. "It's nearly eight o'clock, Robert, I can't imagine what business you would have at this hour. If you don't want to dine with me, you can say so, I won't take offence."

"You assume incorrectly, Lucas. I am headed to what is sure to be a very disreputable gaming hell. You're welcome to join me if you wish."

"If you want to gamble, Robert, why don't we go to White's? The food will surely be better."

"I don't want to gamble," Langley said enigmatically. "I am off on an errand of mercy."

Kincaid raised an eyebrow. "An errand of mercy? You, Robert?"

Langley smiled, but his dark eyes were hard. "I daresay it won't appear that way tonight."

"Well, you've piqued my interest, so I think I'll join you."

Langley preferred not to take his horses to what he expected to be a rough part of town, so they took a hackney to the east end of the city. He stared silently out the window, watching the well-kept streets of Mayfair give way to more modest houses, and then to tenements.

"Sure you wouldn't rather go to White's?" asked Kincaid, as they drove past two men having a fistfight on the side of the street.

"If you're nervous, Lucas, you can have the hack take you back to Mayfair as soon as it sets me down."

Kincaid bristled. "I'm not nervous, Robert, but it seems like a deuced odd way to spend an evening."

The coach came to an abrupt stop beside a row of slum housing. After paying off the driver, Langley led them down a dark alley to a ramshackle building. The door was opened by a short but muscular man, whose crooked nose and cauliflower ear suggested he had once been a pugilist.

"Yes?" he asked, staring at them suspiciously.

"We're here to play," said Langley smoothly. The doorman cast a skeptical eye over their clothes, which were far finer than he generally saw at his establishment.

"Ye're sure yer not officers of the law?" he asked.

"I say!" exclaimed Kincaid, looking offended. "Of all the insulting—"

"We're not law officers," Langley interrupted in a conciliatory tone. "We're only looking for a game, but if our money's not good enough for you, we'll take it elsewhere."

The mention of money seemed to settle the issue, for the doorman led them down a flight of shallow stairs to a room that smelled of sweat and desperation. The air was so hazy with smoke that it was difficult to see, and it took Langley a minute to find his quarry.

William Fleming sat at a table with five other men, staring miserably down at the small pile of notes in front of him. He was so absorbed in the game that he didn't notice Langley take the chair next to him.

"Is the luck out tonight, Cliveden?" Langley asked sympathetically.

William jumped. "M-my lord," he stuttered weakly. "I didn't see you arrive." He flushed and looked down at the money in front of him.

"Don't let me distract you," said Langley politely.

William took a long drink from a glass at his elbow and asked for another card. He was dealt a four and came in at nineteen, but as the dealer had twenty-one,

William's stake was swept away. He rose from the table, looking ill.

Langley took a large roll of notes from his pocket and set them casually on the table. "Can I offer you a loan, Cliveden?"

He could see the temptation in William's blue eyes. The play had stopped, as the men listened to the conversation between the earl and the boy.

"N-no, my lord," William said finally. "It wouldn't be right."

"Why wouldn't it be right?" Langley asked.

William looked at him pleadingly. "Because I already owe you money."

"Ah," said Langley. "I thought perhaps you had forgotten. Or perhaps I'd misunderstood when you said you didn't have the money to pay your debt of honour." Although Langley had not raised his voice, it seemed to carry throughout the room.

"It was my father's debt, my lord," said William desperately.

"I see. So you inherited your father's title, his estate, and his townhouse, but not his debts?"

"I intend to pay you," he said defensively.

"Forgive me, Cliveden, but I must say you have done little to convince me that you do." He pinned William with his dark eyes. "I wonder where you found the funds for tonight's little venture? Were you holding out when you told me you were done up? Or perhaps it was an unexpected windfall? Or a moneylender?"

William flushed an even deeper red. "I found a brooch," he explained sulkily. "Diamonds. It had fallen between my mother's dresser and the wall."

"I see," said the earl. "I take it you pawned it. No doubt your mother will be pleased to learn her brooch has funded this evening's entertainment."

"It's not entertainment," said William defensively. "You can't think that I play for enjoyment?"

"You're right that it isn't entertainment," said Langley coldly. "Not for your sisters, your mother, or for the people to whom you owe money. I would call it folly."

"But it's the only way I'll ever be able to pay the debt," argued William.

Langley thought that was a curious statement, since Amelia had just contracted an abhorrent betrothal to rescue her family from bankruptcy. He was tempted to give Cliveden his opinion of a man who would sell his sister to pay a debt, but they had attracted an audience, and he thought it best to keep Amelia's name out of it.

"Unless I mistake the matter, Cliveden, it seems as though your gambling is only adding to your debts," he said in a silky voice.

William turned a deeper shade of red. "The cards haven't been kind to me tonight, but my luck is bound to turn soon. The odds are in my favour."

"Do you think the cards are intelligent beings, Cliveden?" asked Langley, as though he were giving the idea serious consideration. "With a memory of the hands that have come before, and the sympathy to ensure each player has a fair outcome?"

"No, sir," stammered Cliveden, who had long been wishing he had never left his house that night.

"Of course, that would take away the point of gambling," said Langley speculatively. "If there were no winners and losers, and everyone walked away from the table with the same money that they had brought to it. And what would be the point of running a gaming house if there was no hope of any money changing hands? Would gaming house owners provide players with a roof, food, and drink out of charity?"

Cliveden stared at his shoes and said nothing. Silence reigned in the room, and players from other tables walked over to watch the spectacle.

"Come on, Robert," said Lucas, who thought his friend had more than made his point. The boy looked as though he was about to collapse. "The smoke in this room is giving me a headache. Let's go home."

But Langley continued as though his friend hadn't spoken. "And what about a player who loses as a result of his own poor decisions?" he mused. "Would the cards feel obligated to give him better hands to compensate for his lack of skill?"

William stood, goaded beyond endurance. "My lord, you are insulting," he said angrily.

"I am gratified to hear I'm not losing my touch."

William's face had turned white. "Sir, these insults are not to be borne," he said bravely. "I demand satisfaction. N-name your weapon."

The room had fallen silent, and all play had stopped. Langley looked surprised. "Really, Cliveden, there's no need to call me out. If you insist upon a fight, we can go a few rounds at Jackson's. Or if you can't wait, we can step outside now."

"We're far beyond that," said William. He hated that his voice was trembling, but he was powerless to stop it. "You have insulted my honour, and I'll meet you for it. Dawn, the day after tomorrow, in Hyde Park." He turned to the young man seated next to him. "Micklebury will act for me, won't you, Freddie?"

Freddie Micklebury appeared to be incapable of speech, but he nodded loyally.

Langley sighed. "Very well, Cliveden." He turned to Kincaid. "Lucas, you'll act for me?" Kincaid nodded gravely, not sure why his usually cool-headed friend was determined to humiliate a boy who was barely out of short trousers.

"Very well," said William, fuelled by the conviction that he had been badly treated and right was on his side. "I will see you the day after tomorrow."

Fourteen

"William, are you ill?" Amelia asked at breakfast the next morning. "Maybe you should go back to bed. I'll bring up some toast and tea."

"I'm not sick, Amelia," he told her, but the haunted look in his eyes told her something was very wrong.

"Oh. Is it—have you lost something else at play?"

"No," he said defensively. "That is, I pawned a brooch of Mama's and lost the money, but that's nothing to signify."

"I see," Amelia said slowly. She was frustrated that he could describe the loss of a brooch in such casual terms, but she realized he was in no state to listen to a lecture.

They were alone at the breakfast table, and Amelia decided to tell her brother about her betrothal. So far, Aunt Lizzie was the only member of her family to know about it, and Amelia had hoped to find an opportunity to tell her mother and siblings together. But William looked so defeated that she decided not to wait.

"Mr. Garland came to see us yesterday," she began.

William rolled his eyes. "In the purple carriage? What did he want?"

"He asked me to marry him," explained Amelia matter-of-factly. "And I accepted him."

William's jaw fell. "Oh, Amelia, why?" he asked, without thinking.

"You know very well why," she said testily. "He's agreed to pay you a very generous settlement. You knew I was hoping for this," she told her brother, who still looked shocked.

"Yes, but only if there was no alternative."

"There isn't," she said firmly. "And now that we have a solution to the problem, you need to stop gambling. If you keep on like this, we'll end up in an even worse mess than we are now."

As William had very little appetite, he downed a cup of tea and retreated to his bedchamber to escape the conversation. As soon as he was alone, his thoughts returned to the duel. Lord Langley was rumoured to be an excellent shot, and William knew there was a very real chance he would not survive the meeting. Despite its challenges, William loved his life and had no wish to lose it, and he considered trying to back out of the duel. Langley had hesitated to accept his challenge, and William knew if he apologized, Langley would agree to call it off. But that would leave William with the knowledge he lacked the courage to fight for his family's honour, and overall, a valiant death seemed preferable to a continued existence as a coward.

William decided to write a will, but quickly realized that he had very few assets of which to dispose. The title and estate were entailed upon a distant cousin, and when the dust settled on everything else, there would be little left but debts. He wondered if the cousin would become guardian to his sisters, and took comfort in the thought that Amelia was engaged, so her future was secure. In all likelihood, Isabelle would live with Amelia and Mr. Garland until she married.

Dinner was a miserable affair. Their mother did not come home for it, and William was tense and jittery. Amelia had to ask three times whether he wanted a second helping of soup, and he had nothing to add to Aunt Lizzie's prediction that they would have a mild spring. Amelia was disappointed that the news of her betrothal had done so little to ease her brother's worry. For his part, William marvelled at the dispassionate nature of the women in his family, who were content to discuss such mundane topics as the weather.

Amelia was too anxious to sleep well, and in the early hours of the morning, her worries crystallized into the fear that William had gone out gambling again. She peeked into his room shortly before dawn and was alarmed to find his bed empty and a letter on the pillow.

To My Beloved Family,

By now, you know I challenged Langley to a duel, and if you are reading this letter, you know I met my End. Suffice it to say that Langley insulted me, and our family, in a way that could not be borne.

I hope you will take comfort in the knowledge that I died a Noble Death.

*Your loving brother,
William*

Amelia stopped only to put on her boots and throw an old pelisse over her nightgown before running madly out of the house. She thought of trying to intercept Langley at his townhouse, but knew he had likely already left, so she turned and ran toward Hyde Park. Amelia ran until her feet ached and her lungs burned, with little thought of what she would do when she arrived.

When she was finally forced to stop to catch her breath, Amelia realized that her chance of stopping the duel was slim. William's note had not included the location of the meeting, and although she had assumed Hyde Park, they could equally well have gone to some other park or field completely unknown to her. Even if they were in Hyde Park, she didn't know their location, and she wouldn't be able to search the entire park on foot.

The situation seemed hopeless, and Amelia felt betrayed. Given William's attitude, she wasn't surprised that Langley had insulted him, but she would not have expected the earl to accept his challenge. Langley had seemed a coldly rational sort of man, and she would have expected him to see that William was little more than a boy. A very foolish boy, perhaps, but one whose actions were driven by ignorance, desperation, and the wish to look after his family. Amelia had no doubt that Langley was a skilled marksman, and no one would have faulted him for laughing at William's challenge. But for some incomprehensible reason, he had accepted it, and they were to meet this morning. Perhaps they had already met.

She attempted to slow her breathing and consider the matter rationally. The sky over the trees in Hyde Park was streaked with pink, but it was still too dark to see well, and regardless of William's wishes, she couldn't believe Langley would be foolish enough to conduct a duel in the dark. She hitched up her skirts and started running again. If they had gone elsewhere, the situation would be out of her hands, but if they were in Hyde Park she might have a chance.

As Amelia was desperately trying to find the duel, Lucas Kincaid was making a last-ditch effort to convince Lord Langley not to go through with it.

"This is madness, Robert," he said anxiously. "He's just a boy, and after what happened to his father! Apologize to the child and let's go home."

"He's a boy who is old enough to gamble away what few resources remain for his family, and old enough to call me out. It was his challenge, Lucas, not mine, and it is for him to withdraw if he chooses."

"Well, we should postpone it then," tried Kincaid. "I couldn't get a reputable surgeon to come, and I visited three yesterday. They were concerned about the risk of prosecution and said you couldn't pay them enough."

"I doubt they understood what I could pay them," said Langley dryly. "It's no matter, Lucas. I don't imagine we'll need a surgeon."

Kincaid looked troubled. "I don't like this, Robert."

"Neither do I."

A similar conversation was playing out at the opposite end of the field.

"William, I don't like this," said Freddie Micklebury. "It's not too late to withdraw your challenge. Langley's said to be a brilliant shot, but I daresay he doesn't want to fight you. You know, after your father and everything."

William's face was pale, but his expression was determined. "Freddie, this is a matter of family honour," he said staunchly. "I owe it to the memory of my father."

Micklebury and Kincaid met to inspect Langley's pair of duelling pistols, then measured out twelve paces. The duellists took their places. William was pale and trembling, but Langley appeared remarkably calm.

Amelia reached the field in time to see Kincaid drop the handkerchief. Langley jerked his arm up and fired into the air, at the same time that William shut his eyes and resolutely pulled the trigger. There was a heavy pause, then both men staggered and fell.

Amelia reached her brother first.

"What were you thinking, you idiot?" she cried. "Such a stupid, stupid thing to do. First Papa, now you."

"But I didn't die, Amelia," William said, as though amazed by the fact. He sat up and took an inventory of his person. "I don't even think I was hit."

"Of course you weren't hit, Langley fired in the air," she said impatiently. "But you hit Langley, you imbecile. And if he dies, you may hang for murder!"

William's face turned white. "Amelia, 'twas an affair of honour. These things are understood among gentlemen."

"William, he's an earl!" she exclaimed. "Do you really think it will be dismissed as an affair of honour? There was nothing honourable about it."

"We could say that he shot himself," suggested Micklebury, who had walked over to join them.

Amelia gave him a scathing look. "So you mean to spread the story that he came to the park at dawn and shot himself? A man of rank, fortune, and family, who had everything to live for? And the friend who is with him, what do you think he will say?"

"Could say it was an accident," tried Micklebury lamely. "Or that he was set upon by footpads."

Amelia did not deign to reply to that. "Lord Langley must not die," she said firmly.

William got to his feet and looked across the field to where Langley lay on the ground, eerily still. "I'm sorry, Amelia," he choked out, before running to Micklebury's phaeton, untying the horses, and driving away.

Amelia ran across the field to Langley. Kincaid knelt beside him and was carefully removing his coat, and Amelia saw an ugly red stain under the earl's left shoulder. She felt dizzy for a moment, seized by a fear too great to put into words.

Langley noticed her standing over him and winked. "You always wear the most unconventional clothes."

Amelia looked down and saw that her pelisse had fallen open, exposing her white cotton nightdress.

"Have you no conscience?" she asked angrily. "Are you hoping to exterminate the entire Fleming line?"

Langley managed a smile. "Lucas, I'm not sure if you're acquainted with Cliveden's sister?" he asked, as though they were meeting in a drawing room. "Miss Fleming, Mr. Lucas Kincaid."

Amelia nodded impatiently at Kincaid. "Pleasure to

meet you." She turned back to Langley. "You know that if you die, William will probably be tried for murder?"

"I have no intention of dying, Miss Fleming. Can you imagine Adrian as the earl? Fate would not allow it."

"You're right. You aren't going to die, because I'm going to nurse you."

Langley's eyes widened. "You most certainly are not."

Amelia nodded. "I certainly am." She turned to Kincaid. "Do you have a pocketknife?"

Langley's shoulder was starting to hurt a great deal, and he allowed his eyes to close for a moment. When he opened them, Amelia was kneeling over him with a knife in her hand.

"Planning to finish the job?" he teased.

Amelia flushed. "It's not funny! I thought it would be obvious, but I will need to remove your shirt."

He raised an eyebrow. "You can't simply undo the buttons?"

"This will allow me to expose the wound without moving your shoulder."

"Ingenious. It's also more dramatic," Langley agreed. "But Miss Fleming, I'm not sure this is proper."

"Nonsense. I will not let William hang for you." She sliced open his shirt. "Besides, I saw William's chest many times growing up. It's the same thing."

"First your brother wounds my shoulder, then you attack my pride," he complained. Amelia looked down at his chest, which was all sculpted muscle, and looked nothing like William's adolescent chest.

"Well, I've seen statues in museums," she amended. "This is not the time to be missish."

MISS FLEMING FALLS IN LOVE

"I'll try very hard not to be missish," Langley promised.

Amelia laughed. "You know that wasn't what I meant."

She removed Langley's shirt, exposing a wound where his left shoulder met his upper arm. An inch to the left and it would have missed him completely; a few inches to the right and he would have been dead. She could not see a bullet, and although she didn't want to move him to check for an exit wound, she suspected the bullet had passed through the muscle.

"I don't think it has hit any vital structures," she said cautiously. "It looks to have missed the shoulder joint, and I think the ball passed through."

"So a scratch," said Langley. For all his apparent unconcern, he was quite relieved to hear her favourable assessment of the situation, for the entire left side of his body was now in considerable pain.

Amelia used the pocketknife to cut a strip off the bottom of her nightgown, which she folded into a pad and pressed over the wound. "Hold this, please," she instructed Kincaid, who was starting to feel a bit dazed. It took a great deal to shock Lucas Kincaid, but the events of the morning had done it. Not only had his best friend been shot in a duel, but the opponent's sister had taken charge of the situation with the confidence of a military surgeon.

Amelia cut another strip off the bottom of the nightdress. Langley lifted his head and raised himself on his good elbow to see what she was doing.

Amelia frowned at him. "Lie back. We'll need to lift your injured shoulder, just a little, to bind it."

With Kincaid's help, she wrapped the makeshift bandage around Langley's shoulder, securing the pad against the wound, and tied it tightly.

"There," she said. "It may feel a little tight, but that's to better stanch the blood."

"Perfectly comfortable," said Langley.

Amelia sighed. "The question is, what are we going to do with you?"

Fifteen

"You aren't going to do anything with me, Miss Fleming," Langley said firmly. "You are going to go home. I wish I could escort you, but I'm afraid I don't feel equal to it. Lucas will drive me home, where I think I'll need a short rest before resuming my usual activities."

Amelia looked over at his curricle, and the beautiful pair of horses that were tied to a post. "Mr. Kincaid will have to drive, and those horses look quite spirited," she said. "Someone will need to support your shoulder and apply pressure to the wound."

"Thank you for the offer, Miss Fleming, but I assure you that Lucas and I will manage without your help."

Kincaid looked worried. "I don't know, Robert. I think she may have a point."

Langley looked at him in disgust. "All right, Lucas. We'll bring Miss Fleming. Although I don't know how we'll all fit in the curricle, as I refuse to sit on your lap."

Amelia was struck by a new fear. "And people will talk." The sun had fully risen now, and London would be coming to life. In Langley's aristocratic Mayfair neighbourhood, most of the gentry would still be asleep, but the servants would be awake, and they spread gossip more quickly than anyone.

"She's right," said Langley. "I can't go to the townhouse, the talk would be dangerous." Even though his servants were among the best disciplined in the city, they were not immune to the temptation of spreading a scandalous story.

"Could say you shot yourself," suggested Freddie Micklebury, who had crossed the field to join them. Since William had driven off in his phaeton, Micklebury found himself without transportation. "Or you were set upon by footpads?"

Kincaid and Amelia turned and glared at him.

"I'll have to go to Stonecroft," Langley said, as though Micklebury hadn't spoken.

Kincaid stared at Langley in disbelief. "Are you mad? The drive to Stonecroft would kill you!"

"I have a very comfortable coach," said Langley decisively. "I can lie in a coach just as easily as I can lie on a bed."

"Don't be ridiculous," said Amelia. "All that bouncing? You would be in agony, and the movement would increase the bleeding from the wound."

"I'll be fine," Langley said firmly. "The coach is very well sprung. Lucas, I must ask you to drive the curricle back to my house, then instruct my coachman to pick me up here. Come to think of it, Timms will come with us. Have him pack enough gear for a month."

"Robert, you can't go to Stonecroft with only your

valet for company," Kincaid said firmly. "If you insist on going to the country, I'll come with you."

Langley looked up at him with gratitude. "You're a good friend, Lucas."

"I'm coming too," said Amelia resolutely.

"No, you are not," said Langley.

"Yes, I am. William's future depends upon your survival, and I'm not going to leave it to chance. Who would change your dressings if I didn't come? Mr. Kincaid? Mr. Timms?"

"I thought we might consult a doctor," said Langley sarcastically.

"Even worse!" Amelia exclaimed. "Most of them are ignorant bloodsuckers. I'm coming with you. You don't have the strength to keep me out of your coach, and I suspect Mr. Kincaid is too much of a gentleman to do it."

"You don't consider me too much of a gentleman to forcibly remove you from the coach?" Langley said with a small smile.

"I know you too well," Amelia said.

"I suppose I could come too," suggested Micklebury dubiously. "If another gentleman is needed."

"That won't be necessary," said Kincaid curtly. "In fact, your presence in the park is entirely unnecessary."

"Right," said Micklebury, but he made no move to leave. "It's just that I've realized I have no way to get home. Cliveden took my phaeton, you see."

"You're not injured. You can walk," said Kincaid unsympathetically.

"Yes, but if you leave to fetch the coach, Lord Langley and Miss Fleming will be without protection," Micklebury said. "I told Cliveden that if anything happened to him this morning, I would look after his family. I think honour demands I stay and stand guard until you return."

"Lucas, you'd best take him with you," said Langley in disgust. "Just be sure you don't bring him back."

Kincaid helped Langley walk off the open field to a cluster of trees, where he would be less visible to passersby. Although Langley tried to walk unassisted, his face was white by the time Kincaid helped him to lie back down. Amelia directed them to a gentle slope and told Kincaid to position the earl so that his head was about a foot higher than his feet.

"This way your shoulder is elevated to minimize the bleeding, but you'll be flat enough that you shouldn't be dizzy," she explained.

Kincaid looked impressed by this logic, and left to fetch Langley's chaise with the confidence that he was leaving his friend in capable, if slightly unconventional hands.

"Quite an extraordinary female, Miss Fleming," commented Micklebury, after Kincaid had grudgingly taken him up in the curricle. "My sister would have had the vapours. But she's cool as a cucumber, that one."

Kincaid didn't reply, but resolved to set Micklebury down as soon as they reached the edge of the park.

Amelia knelt beside Langley and examined his shoulder. Blood was seeping through the improvised bandage. Kincaid had left her the pocketknife, and she cut another strip off her nightgown, wadded it up, and held it firmly against the wound.

"It would have been better to have brought the coach

MISS FLEMING FALLS IN LOVE

to the duel in the first place," she remarked conversationally.

"I didn't expect to get shot," Langley admitted. "I underestimated your brother."

"No, you didn't," Amelia said. "William is a terrible shot. I doubt he could repeat that shot if you gave him a hundred attempts."

"No doubt you shoot better than he does?"

"No," said Amelia regretfully. "I don't know how to shoot."

"I'm surprised to hear it, Miss Fleming."

"I wanted to learn, but Papa refused to teach me," she confessed. "He said it wasn't ladylike."

Langley had a wild impulse to offer to teach her, but recollected himself before he spoke. He looked up to find Miss Fleming deep in thought.

"You're right-handed, are you not?" she asked abruptly.

"Yes."

"Then although it's fortunate the injury is on the left, William should never have been able to shoot your left shoulder," she chastised. "You're supposed to turn your body sideways to present a smaller target. Had you done so, you likely wouldn't have been hit."

He smiled. "I'll remember that next time."

Amelia's eyes widened angrily. "Don't even talk about the next time! You men are all dull-witted *idiots!* To duel once is bad enough, but to talk about doing it twice! It's beyond anything! I've never been so afraid–" she broke off as she realized she was on the verge of saying too much.

"Were you afraid, Miss Fleming?" Langley asked curiously.

"Yes," she admitted. "The sight of you and William facing each other across the field—it almost stopped my heart."

"He's lucky to have you for a sister," Langley said quietly.

Instead of replying, Amelia threw herself on top of him and kissed him. She kissed with more enthusiasm than skill, pressing her lips against his with desperation. Langley, who had been feeling dizzy but had not wanted to admit it, wondered if he had passed out and fallen into one of the most pleasant dreams of his life. Almost unconsciously, his body began to respond.

It was over almost as quickly as it had begun. Amelia suddenly pulled herself off him and returned her attention to his shoulder. As he came to his senses, he heard hoofbeats fading in the distance.

"A gentleman on horseback," Amelia explained. "I didn't want him to stop and offer help, and I figured if he thought we were lovers he would pass on. I'm sorry I didn't have time to warn you." She blushed. "I hope it looked realistic. I wasn't sure how to do it properly, as I've never done it before."

Langley was now thoroughly disoriented. He wanted to reassure Amelia that she had done it very well, but found himself unable to form the words. The kiss had been the fulfilment of a fantasy that he had hardly allowed himself to acknowledge, and its abrupt ending left him feeling bereft. He realized he was cold, and he shivered involuntarily.

"Oh, you should have said something," Amelia said

reproachfully. She removed the pelisse from her shoulders and draped it carefully over his chest. He still had sense enough to know he should refuse it, but he couldn't bring himself to do so. It was warm from Amelia's body and smelled faintly like vanilla, and although he would have preferred to be warmed by her body, her pelisse was the next best thing.

"Chivalry be damned," he murmured, and closed his eyes, hoping that someone else would pass by and necessitate a repeat of Miss Fleming's charade.

Langley's coach arrived shortly after. The sight of Langley lying on the grass shocked his coachman, who almost drove the coach off the path in his distraction. Langley had always seemed larger than life to his servants, and most of them considered him invincible. Morgan jumped down from the box, hurriedly tied the horses to a tree, and rushed to Langley's side.

"My lord!" he exclaimed.

"I'll be all right, Morgan," Langley said with a forced smile. Kincaid joined them, and he and Morgan helped Langley into his coach. Langley lay on his side on the bench, well-supported by pillows, while Amelia and Kincaid sat opposite.

"I forgot—Miss Fleming will need a chaperone," Langley said firmly. "Tell Morgan to stop for Diana."

"This truly is madness," protested Kincaid. "This trip is already likely to kill you, without adding a detour to pick up your sister."

"Lucas, if I die you can take comfort in the knowledge that you fulfilled my final wish," Langley said philosophically. "We'll stop for Diana. Tell her to pack clothes for a couple of weeks, and to bring things for Miss Fleming too." He looked at Amelia and raised an eyebrow. "Unless you would prefer to borrow from the servants?"

Kincaid shook his head, but he leaned out to tell the coachman to stop for Langley's sister. When they reached the Templetons', Amelia stayed with Langley while Kincaid went to get Diana. The earl closed his eyes, and Amelia worried his breathing was shallow. She picked up his hand to feel his pulse.

Langley's eyelids fluttered open. "Holding my hand for comfort, Miss Fleming?"

"Something like that, my lord."

"How is the pulse? Am I still alive?"

Amelia smiled in spite of herself. "I believe so."

"How is it, Miss Fleming?"

There was a slight hesitation before she answered. "Strong and steady."

"The truth, Miss Fleming."

"Faster than I would like," she admitted. "My lord, I wish you would reconsider your plan to go to Stonecroft. Bouncing along the road will increase the bleeding."

"Don't forget, I'll have you to look after me," he said. "It is a scratch, Miss Fleming. You said you didn't think any vital structures were affected. We'll go to Stonecroft. Now I will sleep."

With that pronouncement, he closed his eyes. Several minutes later his breathing slowed, and Amelia believed he had, in fact, fallen asleep.

"How could you?" she murmured quietly. "And just when I was starting to believe–" She broke off when she realized that his dark eyes were open, and fixed intently on her face.

"What were you starting to believe, Miss Fleming?" he asked curiously.

She shook her head. "It doesn't matter. I was wrong."

But the answer in her eyes must have pleased him, for when his eyes drifted closed again, there was a smile on his lips.

Diana was at home, and Mr. Kincaid assisted her into the chaise within fifteen minutes of their arrival at her house. Amelia was nervous that Diana would be angry with her, as Langley had been wounded in a duel with Amelia's brother, but Diana quickly set her fears to rest.

"Oh Robert, it's too bad of you," she said, taking Langley's hand. "What were you thinking, fighting a duel? Of all the foolish things to do."

"Yes, thank you, Diana," he said. "You'll be glad to hear that Miss Fleming shares your feelings on this subject and has already treated me to a lecture."

Diana hugged Amelia tightly before turning back to her brother.

"Are you badly wounded?" she asked him anxiously.

"Just a scratch to the shoulder, really," he said dismissively. "Miss Fleming has examined it and doesn't think any vital structures are involved. So I shall be as good as new after a few days in the country."

"I'll want to check the dressing as soon as we arrive," Amelia said.

"How do you know about dressings?" asked Diana curiously.

"Don't tell me, you used to impersonate a doctor," said Langley dryly.

"Of course not," said Amelia. "It was a midwife, actually, and I didn't impersonate her. I assisted her, and she taught me. She said I had an aptitude for nursing."

"A midwife?" asked Kincaid, startled. "Did you attend confinements?"

"No," Amelia admitted. "She didn't think it would be appropriate. But she treated many of the tenants and villagers for various complaints, as they didn't have the money for a physician. I once helped her care for a man in the village who was kicked in the chest by a horse. There was no one else to help, so she sent for me. You would be surprised at the number of people who fall to pieces in a crisis."

"How did the patient do?" asked Langley conversationally.

"He survived," said Amelia, smiling at the memory. "For several days we thought he wouldn't, but he pulled through. It was remarkable."

Diana turned to face Amelia. "I'm glad you were there this morning, but how did you know? Surely your brother didn't tell you he was planning to fight a duel?"

"William left a letter in case he didn't survive," Amelia explained. "I found it on his pillow this morning. Can you believe, he wrote he hoped we would take comfort in the knowledge that he died a Noble Death?"

Diana shook her head. "Men can be very stupid."

"I didn't know of the duel until I found the letter this morning," Amelia said. She spoke to Diana, but it suddenly seemed terribly important that Langley believed it. "If I had known, I would have done everything in my power to stop it."

"What would you have done?" asked Langley curiously. "Called the Runners?"

"I don't think so," said Amelia thoughtfully. "That might have led to charges against William."

"And against me," Langley pointed out.

"Possibly, but I'm not sure I would have worried about that," she lied. "While William has the excuse of youth and inexperience, you should have known better."

Kincaid burst out laughing, and Langley raised an eyebrow. "Do you consider me very old, Miss Fleming?" Langley asked her.

"Oh, not *very* old," she reassured him. "It's just that compared to William . . ." She trailed off when she saw the teasing gleam in Langley's eye.

"You're quite right," Langley agreed. "Compared to your brother, I must seem positively ancient. And on the subject of your brother, you still haven't explained how you would have tried to stop the duel."

"I might have locked William in his bedroom," Amelia said thoughtfully. "But that would have left the problem of Mr. Micklebury, who would have come looking for him, so I would have had to incapacitate him too."

"Miss Fleming, I believe you're quite as dangerous as your brother," said Langley.

"Oh, likely more, my lord," she said matter-of-factly. "There are no limits to what I would do to protect the people I love."

Sixteen

"Oh, it's beautiful!" Amelia exclaimed impulsively when a curve in the lane gave her a look at the earl's country estate. Langley met her eyes and smiled. He had similar thoughts whenever he returned to Stonecroft after a stay in town. The original house had been destroyed by fire a century earlier, and Langley's great-grandfather had rebuilt in the Palladian style. Amelia didn't know its history, but she admired the mansion's elegant proportions, and how well it seemed to fit against the backdrop of wooded hills.

Although Langley's housekeeper, Mrs. Prescott, boasted of keeping Stonecroft in such good order that it could be ready to receive him on a moment's notice, the claim had never been tested before. Langley was not a capricious man and wasn't in the habit of arriving unannounced. So when Higgins, the second footman, saw the chaise and four sweeping up the drive, his first thought was that a member of the social climbing merchant class had come to beg a tour. He was preparing to deliver a crushing snub when he recognized the chaise as that of his master, and he rushed back into the house to alert the rest of the staff. The servants flew through the house, removing dust covers from furniture and chandeliers, airing linens, and wringing their hands.

By the time the carriage stopped in front of the house, two footmen were waiting to meet it. Mr. Kincaid descended first and told the footmen their master had suffered an injury and would need assistance to get into the house. After the footmen recovered from their initial shock, both declared themselves eager to help, and proposed to remove a door from its hinges to use as a stretcher. As they debated which door in the house was most suitable, Langley emerged from the carriage, white about the lips, but able to walk under his own power.

"Nonsense, I'm perfectly able to walk. Lucas, I'll just borrow your arm."

He was an unusual sight. His shirt had been left behind in Hyde Park, and as Miss Fleming's pelisse was far too small to accommodate his broad shoulders, he had draped it around himself like a cape. The colour and trim were still undoubtedly feminine, but he moved with such dignity that his staff barely noticed.

After Kincaid assisted the earl to a sofa in the drawing room, Amelia introduced herself to Mrs. Prescott and requested hot water and clean linens for his dressing. The housekeeper had been inclined to look askance at Amelia, who was still wearing nothing but her thin cotton nightdress, but Diana's claim that Amelia was a close friend gave her respectability. Amelia realized that Langley had been right to insist that Diana come, as she would have had a difficult time at Stonecroft without the respect of his staff.

"I need to check your bandages, my lord," she told Langley in her matter-of-fact way.

Langley put his good arm protectively over his injured shoulder. "Thank you, Miss Fleming, but I'll wait for the doctor. We've sent a footman for him."

"You must have been a difficult patient as a boy," Amelia said. "I don't envy your nurse. I imagine you were a robust child, and rarely ill, and that is always the type that kicks up a fuss over every minor ailment."

"This is hardly a minor ailment, Miss Fleming," he said through gritted teeth.

"Why, in the park you said it was only a scratch, and there's no knowing when the doctor will arrive. I just need to have a look, and I don't think it should hurt too badly."

Langley glared at her. "If it will get you to stop talking, I'll allow it." He moved his good arm to allow her to examine the injury.

Amelia was pleased with what she found. The bandages she had applied in the park were saturated with blood, but it appeared to have dried, and she elected not to remove the dressing. Mrs. Prescott had found a bottle of laudanum, and Amelia gave Langley a small dose.

A commotion in the entrance hall heralded the arrival of Matthews and Timms, who had been instructed to follow Langley to Stonecroft but had not been told the reason for the sudden trip. A loose-lipped housemaid met them at the door and told them that his lordship had been shot, and had just been carried into the sitting room half dead.

Timms rushed frantically into the sitting room. "My lord, I am beside myself!" he exclaimed. "When Mr. Kincaid told me you were going to Stonecroft I feared something was badly wrong, but I never dreamed you were hurt. So to hear you were shot! I have sweats! Palpitations! I can barely speak!"

"We've already sent a man for the doctor, Timms," said Langley dryly.

"That's very kind of you, my lord," he said. "And it shows great foresight, too. Although how you would know I would need one–"

"The doctor is for Lord Langley," said Mr. Kincaid impatiently.

"Oh! Oh yes, of course," said Timms. "Excellent idea. He should attend to Lord Langley first."

"You're very considerate, Timms," said Langley, with a twinkle in his eye.

"But I don't understand what happened," Timms said. "Who shot you?"

Langley cast a speaking glance at Kincaid. "Footpads. How many were there, Lucas? Six?"

"I recall at least eight," said Kincaid mischievously.

"These miscreants were trying to relieve a lady of her jewels," Langley continued. "And despite being outnumbered, Mr. Kincaid and I felt obliged to intervene. You'll be happy to hear that the lady, and Mr. Kincaid, escaped unharmed."

Timms was wide-eyed. "Did you call the Runners, sir?"

"You know, Timms, in all the excitement, I believe we

forgot," Langley said. "The affair must be kept secret. A lady's reputation is at stake, you understand."

"Yes, of course." Timms paused, looking puzzled. "But why?"

"She wouldn't want word to get out that she was walking in the park at dawn wearing jewels," Langley said vaguely. "So we mustn't speak of it. I know I can trust your discretion."

Timms nodded proudly. "You can rely on me, my lord." He looked at Miss Fleming and Diana, who were talking quietly in the corner. He lowered his voice to a whisper. "Is one of those ladies the lady in question?"

"Certainly not," Langley said. "The lady in question is suffering from nervous shock, and we escorted her home to her family. That is my sister, Mrs. Templeton, and her particular friend, Miss Fleming."

"I see," said Timms, who didn't understand why Langley had brought the ladies to Stonecroft but thought it best not to say so. His gaze fell on the earl's upper body. Although Langley's chest was covered by Amelia's pelisse, which he had spread over himself like a blanket, his bare arms were visible.

"My lord, our shirt," Timms said in a pained voice.

"Yes, Timms," acknowledged Langley. "I'm afraid the shirt was a casualty of this morning's adventure. The waistcoat, too."

"If I recall, that was the blue waistcoat," said Timms mournfully. "You always looked so well in it." He brightened. "Perhaps it can be repaired."

"I don't think so. It was forgotten in Hyde Park."

"Oh. I suppose you had other things to think about," said Timms kindly, although he privately thought he would never have forgotten a waistcoat in the park, no matter the circumstances.

"You could say that," agreed Langley.

"How remiss of me, my lord," said Timms, remembering his job. "I will find you a fresh shirt and coat immediately."

"No shirt, Timms," murmured Langley, who was suddenly feeling exhausted. "I apologize, but I'm very tired, and I would like to rest upstairs."

Kincaid assisted him to stand and gave him his arm. Both Timms and Amelia followed them to the stairs.

"I don't need a nursemaid, Miss Fleming," Langley said. He was feeling lightheaded and wasn't confident that he would make it to his room under his own power. The last thing he wanted was for Miss Fleming to see him carried up the stairs by his friend and his valet.

"Considering your recent actions, I believe you do," Amelia said lightly, for she still hadn't forgiven him for duelling with her brother.

"Come now, Miss Fleming, no gentleman would stand by and watch a lady be robbed of her jewels," he rallied, reminding her that the servants were still ignorant of the true cause of his injury. They reached the top of the stairs, and he felt like he had climbed a mountain.

"And no lady would stand by and watch a gentleman suffer when she had the means to relieve it," Amelia replied.

Langley turned to look at her and saw she was holding the bottle of laudanum and a teaspoon.

"Give it to Timms," he instructed.

"I'm afraid I can't," she said resolutely. "I'm sure I don't need to remind you of my motivation to see you get well." She noticed his face was grey and his breath was coming quickly after the exertion of climbing the stairs, and she fought to hide her anxiety. Despite her claims, her first concern had never been William's risk of prosecution.

"Have you always been this stubborn?" Langley complained.

"Yes," Amelia said simply. "You should save your breath for the walk." She looked down the long, richly carpeted hallway and sighed. "I suppose your bedchamber is at the very end of this corridor?"

Langley nodded, gritted his teeth, and made his way carefully down the hall. By the time he reached his doorway, he was leaning heavily on Kincaid's arm, and he was relieved to collapse onto his bed. He meekly accepted a spoonful of laudanum from Amelia, and allowed Timms to tuck the covers around him. Under the watchful eyes of his best friend, his valet, and Miss Amelia Fleming, the Earl of Langley fell asleep.

~

When they were confident their patient rested comfortably, Amelia and Kincaid returned to the sitting room, where Diana had been unsuccessfully trying to distract herself with a novel.

"How bad is it, really?" Diana asked. She had very little experience with sickness, and the sight of her brother's bloodstained bandages had shaken her more than she cared to admit.

"Really, Diana, I think he'll pull through," Amelia said reassuringly. "The bleeding appears to have stopped, and so long as the wound doesn't turn putrid, I think he'll do very well."

Diana let out a breath. "I'll help you nurse him."

"He may not need very much care," Amelia said optimistically. "Just the dressing changed every day, and someone to prevent him from exerting himself before it's safe to do so." She turned to Kincaid. "You may need to help with that, as Lord Langley strikes me as a stubborn man."

Kincaid laughed. "Miss Fleming, I have known Langley since he was a schoolboy, and I could never convince him to do anything he didn't want to do."

"I believe it," said Amelia seriously. "Mr. Kincaid, why were they duelling? William wrote he challenged Langley, but I can't imagine what provoked him to do so?"

"And what on earth could have induced Robert to accept his challenge?" Diana asked. "That doesn't seem like him at all."

Kincaid looked from Amelia to Diana uncomfortably, but knew he would have no peace until he gave them an answer. "Two nights ago, we came across Lord Cliveden in a gaming establishment," he explained. "The luck was not running his way."

"Where did he get the money to stake?" Amelia interrupted anxiously. "Don't tell me he went to a moneylender!" She could not imagine how she would cope with another debt.

"I don't think so," Kincaid hastened to reassure her. "He said something about a brooch of your mother's."

Amelia's brow cleared. "That's right, he mentioned the brooch. I remember the fuss Mama made when she thought she had lost it. All right, so William sold Mama's brooch and went gambling. I understand why Langley was upset to find him gambling while our debt is unpaid, but I can't understand why William would challenge him?"

"Langley tried to point out the folly of continuing to play when he was already—er—on the rocks," explained Kincaid apologetically.

Amelia stared at him. "But that sounds quite sensible," she said slowly. "I'm sure I've told him the same thing many times, and he never saw the need to challenge me to pistols at dawn."

At this inopportune moment, Matthews opened the door to announce Dr. Carter, and both the doctor and the butler heard the end of her sentence. Matthews' eyes widened, and the doctor's face assumed a mask of disapproval.

Dr. Carter was a young and earnest physician who had recently moved to the county after completing his medical training at St. Bartholomew's Hospital in London. He was not yet acquainted with the Stone family, and although he knew that Langley's good opinion was essential to the success of his practice, he was inclined to resent him for it. As the son of a solicitor, Carter had strong opinions on a class system that judged people on their birth rather than their achievements.

"Pistols at dawn!" Carter said in disgust. "So it was a duel. I couldn't understand why your footman refused to explain how Lord Langley was shot."

The three occupants of the room rose to their feet.

"Miss Fleming was speaking of an unrelated matter," said Diana. "It's no concern of yours."

"I concern myself with both the physical and spiritual

health of my patients," Carter said. "It is impossible to have one without the other, Mrs.–"

"Lady Diana Templeton," she interrupted coolly. "I am Lord Langley's sister. This is Miss Amelia Fleming and Mr. Lucas Kincaid, both close friends of our family."

Carter nodded gravely. "Well, Lady Diana, I must say that duelling is a barbaric practice. There is truly nothing honourable about settling one's differences with pistols."

"Dr. Carter, if we wanted a sermon we would have sent for the vicar," said Diana impatiently. "We summoned you to give medical advice. If we erred, please tell us now and stop wasting our time." Diana wished for Dr. Ballantyne, the hearty country doctor who been both a physician and a friend to the family at Stonecroft, but Ballantyne had passed away two years earlier.

"Well," said Carter, shaking his head. "This is a terrible business, but if you would be kind enough to take me to the patient, I'll do what I can for him."

"Lord Langley is upstairs," said Amelia, who had taken the doctor in instant dislike. "But he just fell asleep and he can't be disturbed."

"Can't be disturbed? After I've been urgently summoned to attend him?" Carter said incredulously. He blinked at the red-headed young lady who appeared to be wearing a nightgown with a torn hem and grass stains. She spoke with such authority that he had initially wondered if she was the countess, but had quickly dismissed the idea. He knew that if Langley had gotten married he must have heard about it, as the villagers would have talked of nothing else for a month.

"That's right," Amelia said, nodding. "He's had a difficult day."

Kincaid made a strangled noise that was halfway between a laugh and a snort.

Dr. Carter had had a difficult day himself, at the home of a squire in the neighbouring county whose wife was subject to nervous attacks. He turned to Kincaid. "Sir, you understand I must see Lord Langley immediately. I may need to remove the bullet."

Amelia answered before Kincaid could. "I have examined the wound, and I'm quite certain the bullet passed through."

"You examined the wound?" Carter asked her in disbelief. Despite her dishevelled appearance, Miss Fleming's accent was that of a gently-bred young lady, and in his experience, the sight of blood brought on the vapours in ladies of her class.

"Yes," said Amelia. "I had to know if the bullet was still there before I bandaged it. I don't think it would have been safe for him to travel from London with a bullet in his shoulder."

Carter gaped at her. "He travelled here from London? After he was shot? The bouncing of the carriage could have been fatal!" He would never understand the decisions of the aristocracy.

Diana's face turned white, and Amelia looked at Carter reproachfully.

"Yes, well, clearly it wasn't, so that's hardly a helpful observation," she said testily. "Really, Dr. Carter, what did you think had happened? You seem to be convinced that he was shot in a duel, so where did you think this affair took place? Did you imagine that Lord Langley and his opponent travelled into Kent for their confrontation? Or perhaps Lord Langley quarrelled with a guest at a house party, prompting a meeting in one of the fields?"

Carter decided it would be beneath his dignity to reply to this, but Amelia's speech had its intended effect, which was to make Diana smile.

Carter turned back to Kincaid, whom he judged to be the most rational person in the room. "We have strayed from the point. Lord Langley will need to be bled."

Amelia intervened again. "I've never understood the logic of that. He has already bled a great deal today, I don't see how further blood-letting would help."

"I suppose the medical school you attended did not teach bloodletting?" Carter asked sarcastically.

"You know very well that I did not attend medical school, which is why I must rely on common sense," Amelia said patiently. "And it doesn't make sense to treat blood loss by removing more blood. That would be like saying we will distract him from the pain in his left arm by shooting him in the right. Completely irrational."

"I will not be able to explain the theory to you," Carter said condescendingly.

"No, I didn't think you would," Amelia agreed. "What I suggest is that you join us for dinner, which should be ready soon. Then, I'm sure Mrs. Prescott can find a room for you so you can be on hand when Lord Langley wakes up."

"And what do you propose I do when he wakes?" asked Carter. "You've already told me there is no need to examine the wound, and that you don't believe in bloodletting."

"I don't know," Amelia said bluntly. "But Lord Langley wanted you sent for, and I expect he'll want to see you."

She paused. "He won't want any sermons. If you've brought any laudanum, you could leave us some of that."

Carter faced a dilemma. Langley was greatly respected in the county, and Carter was curious to meet him and learn about the duel that had led to his injury. But he deeply resented the houseguest who had the audacity to tell him how to practice medicine. He had his professional reputation to consider; he had no doubt that word would spread that he had treated Langley, and he truly believed that in cases of serious injury, bloodletting was necessary to ensure a good outcome. Despite his resentment of the aristocracy, he aspired to one day build a practice in London, and having Lord Langley die under his care would not be an auspicious beginning.

Carter looked at Kincaid again. "If I attend Lord Langley, I'll treat him as I think best. I cannot in good conscience withhold medical treatment because one of his houseguests doesn't understand it."

Amelia nodded. "Then I think you should leave."

Carter raised an eyebrow. "I'm the only doctor in the county, you know, and if I leave I won't come back tonight. You won't find anyone else to attend to him until tomorrow. By then, the inflammation will have spread, and it may be too late."

Amelia shrugged. "I'm sure we could find an apothecary willing to assist us." In her experience, physicians were notoriously jealous of apothecaries who tried to encroach on their territory.

Carter turned red. During the year between the death of Dr. Ballantyne and the arrival of Dr. Carter there had been no physician in the county, and the apothecary had become, in Carter's opinion, rather uppity.

"I don't think the apothecary will want to perform bloodletting on an earl," said Carter.

Amelia smiled. "He sounds like a sensible man."

Carter gritted his teeth and turned to Diana. "Is that your decision, Lady Diana?"

Diana nodded. "Thank you for coming, Dr. Carter," she said firmly. "Please send us a bill for your time."

Dr. Carter bowed stiffly. "Good evening, Lady Diana." He nodded to Amelia and Kincaid and walked out.

As soon as the door closed behind him Amelia collapsed into a chair, suddenly exhausted and unsure of herself. Although the final decision had been Diana's, her arguments had swayed the issue.

"He'll come back if we send for him," Diana said reassuringly. "In fact, he's probably hoping we will."

Seventeen

Langley spent the next three days in a feverish dream. Amelia and Diana took turns nursing him, feeding him spoonfuls of broth when he was alert and small amounts of laudanum when he was agitated. Amelia cleaned his wound and changed the dressing every day, and although the area from his neck to his upper arm was red, the redness never spread further. The earl was restless much of the time, and called out nonsensical things. At one point he called out, "Amelia—understand—had to teach him a lesson."

"Yes, yes," Amelia said reassuringly. "I understand," although she didn't know what he was talking about.

Amelia thought the sound of her voice seemed to soothe him, and she spent many hours reading aloud at his bedside. She alternated between *Gulliver's Travels*, a small volume of Byron's poetry, and *Practical Management of the Modern Estate*, a large tome she had found in the library. At times, she wondered if Langley even knew she was there, but there were occasional moments when he seemed rational. On the second day, she distinctly heard him say "no more farming," so she obligingly set down *Practical Management* and picked up *Gulliver* again. In another lucid moment, he commented: "beautiful voice."

Amelia hated to leave him in Diana's care, for although she knew Diana was capable, she feared disaster would strike while she was away. But she recognized that too many days without sleep would make her sick herself, so she let Diana take her place for a few hours in the morning while she napped. When she woke, she hurried to Langley's room to assure herself he still breathed.

On the third night, Langley was particularly restless. He was sweaty, and his pulse was tumultuous, and Amelia knew his illness had reached a critical point. She second-guessed her decision to send Dr. Carter away, and considered sending for him and humbling herself. But the die had been cast; she had decided against bloodletting, and she knew in her heart that it was too late to try it now. She dipped a cloth in an ewer of water and wiped Langley's brow. His dark hair was in disarray, and she brushed it back from his face with her fingers.

"You have the loveliest hair," she whispered softly. "I've wanted to touch it since the first day we met."

Her touch seemed to settle him, for he stopped thrashing and seemed to breathe more easily. Encouraged, Amelia leaned over and took his hand. He seemed to like that, and the slow, even breathing continued. After half an hour she developed a cramp in her arm and tried to pull her hand away, but Langley gripped it firmly, and she fell forward onto the bed. After three days of very little sleep, Amelia was almost delirious herself, and she stretched out beside him and fell into the deepest sleep she had enjoyed since the duel.

Amelia woke with the dawn, and was alarmed to find herself in bed next to Langley, with her head resting on his good arm. By some miracle, she managed to get out of bed without waking the earl, and she tiptoed back to her chair to keep watch.

An hour later, Langley awoke with a clear head and a searing pain in his left shoulder. He turned and saw Timms standing at his bedside.

"Timms," he croaked, in a voice so feeble he barely recognized it as his own.

"My lord," said Timms anxiously. "You are awake, my lord!"

"I'm aware of that," said Langley tartly. "Not only am I awake, I'm in agony. I feel like my shoulder is being stabbed with a poker."

"But this is wonderful!" exclaimed Timms.

"I'm glad it pleases you," said Langley sarcastically. "Nonetheless, I need something for the pain."

"I mean, it's wonderful that you're lucid. We weren't sure you would ever be yourself again."

"What do you mean?"

"Just that, for the past three days, you've been–" Timms paused, sensing that Langley would not appreciate being told he had been confused. "Not yourself."

"I'm not in the mood for riddles, Timms," said Langley. "Please tell me the doctor has left something for pain."

Timms moved quickly to the bedside table and picked up the bottle of laudanum. Langley watched incredulously as he poured a small amount into a teaspoon.

"I need a proper dose, Timms. That's hardly enough to drug a flea."

Timms swallowed. "Miss Amelia said not to give you more than a teaspoon at a time," he said bravely.

Langley stared at him in amazement, not sure whether he was more surprised that his valet had referred to Miss Fleming by her given name, or by his suggestion that her instructions might supersede his own.

"Who is master in this house, Timms?"

"It's just that you were so very sick, my lord," Timms said apologetically. "We were all so worried, and Miss Amelia seemed to know what to do. She just popped down to the kitchen to help prepare your broth, but she'll be back shortly."

"My broth?"

Timms nodded. "Yes, it's Miss Amelia's own recipe, especially for invalids."

"I'm hardly an invalid, Timms!" Langley tried to prop himself up on his good elbow but stopped when the movement worsened the pain in his injured shoulder.

"Of course not, my lord," Timms agreed. He held the teaspoon of laudanum to Langley's lips. "When Miss Amelia comes back, she'll change your dressing, which will help ease the pain."

Langley gaped at him. "She certainly will not!" he said emphatically. "It's not a task for a young lady. She shouldn't even be in my bedchamber."

"Miss Amelia has been looking after your dressings

since you arrived," Timms explained. "She said she had a knack with bandages, and she does."

"And what about the doctor? Has he been too busy to assist me?" Langley asked sarcastically.

Timms looked pained. "Not exactly, sir."

"Please tell me that someone in this house had the wit to send for the doctor!" Langley exclaimed.

Timms quailed. "The doctor came and left the laudanum, but Miss Amelia sent him away."

"Was Miss Fleming hoping I would succumb to the wound?"

"Miss Fleming would not allow you to be bled," said Amelia as she swept into the room carrying a bowl of broth on a tray. "You lost so much blood from the shoulder wound, the idea of further bloodletting was completely nonsensical. Dr. Carter had a different opinion, so I told him his services weren't needed."

"And none of my staff thought to overrule you?" Langley asked in disbelief. He looked over at Timms, who was walking quietly towards the door.

"Timms! Where are you going?" Langley was quickly learning that it was hard to keep command of a conversation while lying in bed.

"I wanted to give you and Miss Amelia the opportunity to discuss the matter in private," Timms explained. "I'll return later to help change the dressing."

"I won't have any further discussion with Miss Fleming in my bedchamber," Langley said decisively. "And I don't understand why you're calling Miss Fleming by her Christian name. It's disrespectful."

"Oh, I asked him to call me Amelia," she explained.

"We've had to work so closely together over the past few days that I consider him a friend."

"I see," said Langley. "And do you invite all your friends to call you Amelia?"

"Almost all of them," she admitted.

"And what do you consider me?" Langley asked with a gleam in his eye.

"Right now, I consider you a stubborn man with a wounded shoulder and a dressing that needs to be changed." She met his eye and smiled. "I've been told I have a light touch. I'll be as gentle as I can, and it shouldn't cause you much pain."

Langley's face turned red. "I'm not concerned about the pain, Miss Fleming," he said through gritted teeth. "I'm perfectly able to cope with that. But this situation is highly improper." Not only was it improper, Langley knew he wouldn't be able to handle Amelia's touch on his bare skin. The effort of controlling himself would make him delirious again.

Amelia's brow furrowed. "I suppose I could send for Diana, but I don't think she's ever dressed a wound before," she said doubtfully.

"No. I'll have to make do with Timms' gentle hands," Langley said. "And I'll need a proper dose of laudanum, because the pain is intolerable."

The corner of Amelia's mouth lifted. "I've heard it's a good sign when a patient becomes fractious. I think you've turned the corner. But I don't think it's a good idea for you to have more laudanum. Too much will have you vomiting, and you'll never get well if you don't drink your broth."

"Miss Fleming, if you don't leave this room immediately I will forcibly remove you from it," said Langley, forgetting that he lacked the strength to sit up in bed.

She smiled again, which he found infuriating. "Very well. Eustace, please send for me if you need help."

Langley let out a long exhale after Amelia had left the room, then turned to his valet. "Your Christian name is Eustace?"

Timms nodded.

"If it's all the same to you, I'll stick to Timms." Langley ran a hand across his face and grimaced. "Timms, haven't I been shaved?" he asked.

"No, my lord," his valet said apologetically. "You were restless, you see, and we weren't sure it was safe."

"Well, I'd like to be shaved immediately."

"Yes sir," said Timms. "I'll get the shaving gear, and we can also get your hair in order." He peered doubtfully at Langley's messy black locks. "I'm afraid your hair's quite tangled, and some of it may need to be cut off."

"No, Timms," Langley said. "You will not cut my hair."

∼

Notes from the diary of the Earl of Langley

I am clearly employing fools. I don't understand why none of the staff had the sense to keep a young lady out of my bedchamber. A man doesn't want female company when he hasn't shaved in days and has barely enough strength to lift his head from the pillow.

But I'm feeling stronger today, and I think I'll get out of bed. I need to rebuild my strength, for I would hate for my impromptu houseguests to think of me as an invalid.

⁓

The earl spent the next two days in his bedchamber, trying to regain his strength. On the first day he was exhausted by the walk from his bed to the door, but on the second day he made the trip four times. Kincaid sat with him in the afternoons, but the earl would not allow Amelia or Diana to enter his bedchamber.

Despite his efforts to threaten and cajole Timms, all that came up for him from the kitchen was bread, butter, and broth.

"Can't you bring me something from your own fare, Timms?" he asked at lunch on the second day. "I realize I haven't exactly been in the habit of sharing my meals with you, but I must beg for your pity. I won't get well eating nursery pap."

Timms looked miserable. "It's not so easy, my lord," he began. "You see, Miss Amelia expected you to be—er—unhappy with the menu, and she guessed you would appeal to me for more substantial fare. She inspects the trays herself before they're brought up to you, and she's enlisted several of the footmen to ensure that no other food leaves the kitchen."

"And they obey her?" he asked in disbelief.

"Yes, my lord," Timms admitted. "She has a way with her, you know. She's convinced everyone it's in your best interests, and that failure to follow her orders will sabotage your recovery. Everyone downstairs has been very anxious about you, my lord."

Langley wasn't sure whether he was more surprised by his staff's willingness to follow Amelia's orders, or by their concern for his health.

"I see. I'm going downstairs for dinner today, Timms," Langley said resolutely. "Fetch my evening wear."

"Miss Fleming thought you might say that, sir," Timms said apologetically. "And she gave strict instructions that you are not to wear anything but a dressing gown for at least a week."

Langley's eyes widened. "Now she wishes to control my attire?"

"She's concerned that your clothing is particularly close-fitting, and fears that a shirt or jacket will irritate your wound."

Langley glared at his valet. "I won't go to dinner in a dressing gown. Bring me a shirt."

Half an hour later, Langley made his way cautiously down the stairs, dressed in his loosest shirt, a forest green waistcoat, and buckskin breeches. Timms hovered anxiously behind him.

Dinner was in progress when he reached the dining room, and Diana dropped her spoon in surprise when she saw her brother. "Robert," she said anxiously. "Are you sure you should be out of bed?"

Amelia turned to look at him. "I think it's time he got up," she said thoughtfully. "If he spends too much time in bed, he'll just get weaker. But I'm not sure it was wise to try the stairs."

"Nonsense," said Langley. "I was shot in the shoulder, not in the leg."

"Yes, yes," Amelia said soothingly. She gave Timms a reproachful look. "I thought we discussed the question of his clothing? A dressing gown is really the most practical thing for at least another week." She turned to Langley. "I wish you would let me look at your wound."

"No," Langley said succinctly. "And I'll thank you not to talk about me as though I'm not here." Kincaid rose to assist him into a chair, but Langley waved him off and seated himself without mishap. He stared at the meal in disbelief. "Don't tell me you're having broth," he said in disgust.

"There's bread and butter with it," Amelia said cheerfully.

"We thought that since you were subsisting on broth, we would too," said Kincaid, with the air of a martyr.

Langley's eyes narrowed. "Tell me the real reason."

"Your staff weren't expecting you to arrive with a party of friends, so they weren't prepared to feed us," Amelia explained. "The kitchen staff have gone to a great deal of trouble to feed Mr. Kincaid, Diana, and me over the past few days, so we thought they deserved an evening off. This broth is really quite delicious."

"Never mind my shoulder, at this rate I'll die of starvation," Langley said sourly.

"Oh no, my lord, the broth is very nourishing," Amelia assured him. "And I think we could safely progress to poached eggs at breakfast tomorrow."

Langley cast a reproachful look at Mr. Kincaid, who was staring down at his broth. "Lucas, you had nothing to say to this?"

"Robert, we're close friends, but I don't think it's my place to interfere in your kitchen," Kincaid said, looking very pleased to have come up with this answer.

Langley sighed in resignation. "Broth it is." A footman

brought him a bowl, and Langley helped himself to a large helping of soup.

"I'll need a drink," Langley said.

"Of course," said Amelia. "We're having orgeat lemonade."

Langley rolled his eyes. "I'm not surprised. Timms, go down to the cellar and find us a bottle of wine."

"If you're sure," Amelia said hesitantly.

"Of course I'm sure," said Langley testily. "Do you think I want to sit here and drink lemonade like a child in the nursery?"

"It's just that you lost quite a lot of blood, and you've had very little solid food for close to a week," Amelia said calmly, as though he was indeed a small child. "You may have lost your tolerance for alcohol."

"A glass or two of wine will not knock me out," said Langley, who was reaching the end of his patience.

"I know many people think wine is medicinal, but I've never been convinced of that," said Amelia, undaunted by the murderous look in his eyes. "If you become intoxicated, you may need help to get back to bed. However," she mused thoughtfully, "if you fall into a stupor, I'll be able to examine your wound."

Langley gritted his teeth and gestured to a footman. "I'll have the lemonade."

After they finished the broth and bread, Amelia walked to the sideboard and retrieved a large bowl of rice pudding.

"I've always disliked rice pudding," Langley complained.

"Oh, I think you'll like this," said Amelia cheerfully.

"It's my own recipe, and I made it myself. Mrs. Prescott was kind enough to show me around the kitchen."

"Don't hesitate to treat my house as your own," Langley said dryly.

As Amelia spooned the pudding into bowls, Langley saw her exchange a satisfied smile with Diana. They looked far more content than anyone had a right to be after a dinner of bread and broth.

"You knew I was coming down for dinner!" he said in disbelief. "And the story about giving the staff the evening off is nonsense!"

"Oh no, they had the evening off," Amelia assured him. "The broth was already prepared, and I made the pudding myself. We didn't know you would be joining us."

Langley stared at her through narrowed eyes.

"I guessed you would be down tomorrow, but I knew there was a chance it would be tonight," Amelia admitted. "Diana told me you have a robust constitution."

"Miss Fleming, you are fortunate that I have an injured shoulder and that we're in the presence of my sister," Langley said.

"Oh, I don't consider your injury fortunate in the slightest," said Amelia, at the same time that Diana said, "Don't hold back on my account."

Eighteen

Letter from Miss Isabelle Fleming to Miss Amelia Fleming

Dear Amelia,

It was such a relief to get your letter and learn you're safe at Stonecroft with Lady Diana. At first, I couldn't understand why you went with the earl, but now I see it makes sense. The best thing we can do for William is to ensure Lord Langley gets well.

William blames himself for the duel, and he's understandably distraught. He's been fighting with Mama, as we can't seem to make her understand there is no money. Mama blames William for losing the townhouse, and he blames her extravagance for getting us into this mess. As you can imagine, Mama enjoys the argument, but I think William is weary of it. This morning he announced he was going to Cliveden Manor, to try to put things in order there.

And oh, Amy, I was shocked to hear of your betrothal to Mr. Garland! Mama and I did not learn of it until yesterday, *when William's solicitor called to discuss the settlement contract. He seemed to think William had written to him about it, but William later told me he had not. I can hardly believe Mr. Garland agreed to give William forty thousand pounds, it seems a veritable fortune! But Mr. Garland, Amy, are you sure?*

Mama is quite upset about your betrothal. She does not approve of the match, and although we've told her it is not her place to approve or disapprove, we can't convince her of it. She intends to call upon Mr. Garland to discuss the matter.

Your loving sister,
Isabelle

∽

True to her word, Lady Cliveden called upon Mr. Garland that afternoon to discuss his betrothal to her daughter. When Garland's butler, Hargreaves, opened the door, she swept past him into the hallway in a swish of silk skirts.

"I must speak with Mr. Garland," she demanded imperiously. "Where can I find him?"

"Mr. Garland is dressing for dinner, Ma'am," said Hargreaves, cowed by the tiny but formidable lady who, despite her rude manners and French accent, was clearly a member of the nobility. "If you would like to wait in the sitting room, I will inform him–"

"I didn't ask what he was doing, I asked where he was," she interrupted impatiently. "But if he is dressing for dinner, I suppose he is upstairs, yes? *Bien,* I will go to him." She stepped neatly around the butler and made for the staircase.

By the time Hargreaves had recovered his wits, Lady Cliveden was halfway up the stairs.

"Ma'am, you may not go up—he's dressing for dinner–" he stammered, but he might as well have been talking to himself. Lady Cliveden ignored him and continued up the stairs to the third floor, where she correctly guessed that Mr. Garland's apartments were at the far end of the hallway.

Lady Cliveden threw the door open without knocking and found Garland in the process of being shaved by his valet. His valet jumped in surprise, and Garland came very close to having his throat cut.

"Mr. Garland!" Lady Cliveden said contemptuously. "I have heard the most disturbing report. My son told me you are betrothed to my daughter, and I find this utterly ridiculous. I have come to tell you that you cannot marry her."

The valet quickly rubbed the soap from Garland's chin, and Garland stood to address his visitor. She was a sight to behold, in a gown of dark blue silk and a sapphire necklace and earrings. Her blonde hair was swept up in an elaborate coiffure that had taken her maid an hour to achieve. Garland thought she looked like a queen preparing to lead men into battle.

He bowed deeply. "Lady Cliveden," he said reverently. "It's an honour to see you again." He paused and surveyed her figure appreciatively. "My lady, you must allow me to compliment you on your dress. I have never seen such an exquisite gown. I must beg you for the name of your dressmaker, for I believe something in that style would suit your daughter very well."

Her sapphire eyes flashed fire. "Mr. Garland, the

dressing of my daughter is no concern of yours, nor will it be your concern in the future."

Garland took a step towards her. "My lady," he said obsequiously. "Let me assure you that your daughter has consented to the match. Indeed, I believe she desires it."

"My daughter is not of age, and she does not know her mind."

"Ah," said Garland. "But I understand we have the consent of her brother, Lord Cliveden. His solicitor has already been in contact with mine, and we are close to finalizing the marriage contract. You'll find the terms very generous."

Lady Cliveden stamped a dainty foot. "Mr. Garland, my son is but a boy! I am Amelia's mother, and I will not permit such a *mésalliance!* Why, Amelia is the daughter of a viscount, the sister of a viscount, and the granddaughter of a duke! She will not marry a man with one foot in the shop! It is madness! An obscenity!"

Her words seemed to have no effect on Garland. "But you are magnificent," he said, staring at her in admiration.

"Yes!" she said emphatically. "That is the point I am trying to make! Amelia is from a very old and noble family, and she cannot marry one such as you. *C'est impossible!*"

"As to that, Lady Cliveden," he began confidently. "I have bought an estate and intend to build a castle. Your daughter will be mistress of one of the grandest estates in the country." He lowered his voice, as though imparting a secret. "And Lady Cliveden, you may not have known that I studied at Cambridge."

"Yes, so you should understand English when it's

spoken to you plainly. I am telling you that you can't marry my daughter."

Garland did not appear daunted by her plain speaking. "I've reached an agreement with Lord Cliveden. I am to pay him forty thousand pounds for the honour of your daughter's hand."

"Mr. Garland, I have no objection to you giving my son money," she said, as though she were speaking to a particularly slow child. "But you will not marry my daughter."

"Lady Cliveden, I am a businessman–"

"Yes, that is the problem!"

"And I understand you may see this as only a starting point for negotiation," he continued, as though she hadn't spoken. "I am perfectly willing to continue negotiations with you and Lord Cliveden. If you permit, I will call upon you tomorrow to continue this discussion."

She let out a frustrated sigh. "It seems I am wasting my time," she said. "You are not hearing a word I say."

"I assure you, Lady Cliveden, that I hang upon your lips," Garland said. But the viscountess did not hear him, as she had already marched out of the room.

∼

Notes from the diary of the Earl of Langley

I am growing increasingly convinced that Miss Fleming's strategy is to make life as an invalid so unpleasant that my mind will trick my body into believing it is well. Every time I reach for something substantial, or think of having more than a single glass of wine with dinner, she gives me a look of such disappointment that I give it up, as I know I won't have any pleasure in it. I thought I could count on Diana for help, but she seems to find the situation amusing. It is altogether such a frustrating way to live that I barely think of the pain in my arm.

I thought of sending for Dr. Carter, as I know it would irritate Miss Fleming, and if she continues to insist that I retire to bed by eight o'clock I may be driven to it. But from everything Kincaid said, Carter sounds like an unpleasant, self-important sort of man, and I have no desire to talk to him. Perhaps I could arrange for Timms to talk to him in my bedchamber while I hide elsewhere, say, in the wine cellar. Timms might enjoy it, Miss Fleming would be driven mad wondering whether Carter was playing the vampire, and I would be in the wine cellar.

I wish I had seen Miss Fleming argue with Carter. I expect she was magnificent.

∽

When Amelia came down to breakfast the next day she found Langley already there, fully dressed in riding gear and eating poached eggs with apparent contentment.

Amelia's eyebrows rose at the sight of his riding clothes.

"My lord, you must think this is a joke," she said indignantly.

"Yes, and not a very good one," he agreed, gesturing to the dishes on the sideboard. "I never thought I would see breakfast served at Stonecroft with nothing more substantial than poached eggs."

"I'm not referring to the breakfast," she said in frustration. "My lord, you're wearing riding clothes!"

"Do you not like the coat?" asked Langley curiously. "I admit I had doubts myself. I've been thinking of changing my tailor."

Amelia let out a deep breath. "Aside from the risk of putting your injured shoulder into a shirt, a waistcoat, and a riding coat, the thought of riding is ridiculous. Imagine if you fell, you could reopen the wound–"

"I can't imagine it," he said, cutting her off. "I don't think I've fallen from a horse since I was a boy." He smiled at her. "That's a lovely dress."

"Thank you," said Amelia, momentarily distracted. "It belongs to Diana."

Langley nodded. "I guessed as much. Have some eggs. If you put enough butter on the bread, you can almost convince yourself that you're eating a real breakfast."

"Why did you assume that the dress belonged to Diana?" she asked, sensing an insult. Amelia knew pale pink wasn't her colour, but as Diana had been kind enough to share her wardrobe, she hadn't complained.

"Because I know you didn't have a chance to pack before we left town."

"Oh," said Amelia, mollified.

"Also, it's an inch too short, and not the colour I would have chosen for you," Langley continued shamelessly.

"I see. I guess you would have chosen powder blue?" When she had discovered that Diana's dresses were all an inch too short for her, Amelia had realized that the pale blue ballgown she had worn to the ball hadn't been one of Diana's castoffs.

"Blue or green," Langley agreed. "Although the pink suits you better than I would have expected."

"I don't dress to please you," she said tartly.

"And I don't expect you to," he said reasonably. "But it does seem rather unfair, since you expect me to dress to please you."

"What!" exclaimed Amelia. Her cheeks flushed. "I would never comment on your clothing!"

Langley's lips twitched. "Miss Fleming, I can't believe your memory is as poor as that. Not five minutes ago you criticized my riding clothes."

"I criticized your decision to wear riding clothes, not the clothes themselves. I think that's a very handsome jacket, and it fits you very well . . ." she trailed off when she realized he was teasing her.

"Thank you, Miss Fleming. Tell me, was someone sent to fetch your things from town?"

She nodded. "Yes, Matthews sent a man to town, and Isabelle packed a trunk. It arrived yesterday, so I no longer need to wear Diana's gowns. But I like them," she admitted.

"They suit you, even if they are an inch too short."

Mr. Kincaid chose that moment to enter the breakfast parlour, and when he saw Langley and Miss Fleming engaged in a spirited conversation, he turned around, intending to make a quiet retreat.

"Come in, Lucas," said Langley hospitably. "There are plenty of eggs to go around."

"Mr. Kincaid," said Amelia persuasively. "Try to make your friend see reason. He plans to go riding!"

"I never said that," Langley objected.

"You are wearing riding clothes!" said Amelia in exasperation. "And you said–" she broke off as she realized he hadn't actually said he intended to ride.

"I said I couldn't imagine falling from a horse."

"So you don't intend to ride?" Amelia asked suspiciously.

"I haven't decided yet. Perhaps we should send for Dr. Carter and get a medical opinion on whether it's safe for me to ride."

Amelia took a deep breath. She thought that between Dr. Carter and riding, riding was likely the lesser evil. "My lord," she began in a conciliatory tone. "Perhaps if you went for a short ride, on a quiet horse–"

"Miss Fleming, I fear I would not do well on a quiet horse," Langley interrupted. "I might fall asleep and fall off."

Kincaid burst out laughing, and Amelia looked at him reproachfully. "As the two of you seem to share the same sense of humour, I'll leave you to entertain each other," she said, rising to leave.

"But you haven't eaten anything," Langley protested.

"I'll eat in the kitchen," Amelia said. "I have to find Mrs. Prescott to discuss the menu for the rest of the day." She gave Kincaid a speaking look. "I am trusting you to keep him off a horse."

The eyes of both men followed her out the door.

When she had left the room, Langley looked at Kincaid. "Now that you're here to assume nursemaid duties, she takes off for the kitchen, where I'm sure the food is better."

Kincaid smiled, but the look in his eyes was serious. "We were all very worried about you, Robert," he said. "You probably don't remember, but you were nonsensical for the better part of three days. And that girl damn well held this household together."

"She keeps her head in a crisis, I'll give her that," Langley acknowledged.

"It's more than that, Robert. You owe her a debt."

"I know it," Langley said quietly, his expression suddenly thoughtful.

Matthews entered with a small stack of letters on a tray. Langley flipped through them with little interest until he came to one addressed to Kincaid.

"Here, this one's for you," Langley said, picking it up. It was addressed in a decidedly feminine hand, and the sender had written URGENT in capital letters under the direction. "Shall I open it for you?"

Kincaid reached across the table and plucked the letter from Langley's hand. He broke the seal with his butter knife and skimmed the page, his eyes alight with amusement.

"Well?" asked Langley curiously. "If you're going to read your letters at the breakfast table, it's only fair to share the joke."

"It's from my ward," Kincaid explained. "She writes to complain about her new governess."

"I didn't know you had a ward, Lucas."

"A man doesn't like to advertise such a misfortune," said Kincaid dryly. "This is the third governess Felicity has had this year. She has a talent for driving them away."

"How infelicitous," said Langley with a smile.

"It is, rather," agreed Kincaid. "It's a far bigger responsibility than I expected. I suppose I should return to London."

"By all means. Morgan will drive you."

Kincaid looked his friend in the eye. "Are you well, Robert?"

"Yes, yes, very well," Langley assured him. "Twas the merest scratch, as I said from the start."

"Don't make light of it, Robert," Kincaid said reproachfully.

"No," said his friend. "To be honest, it was the most painful thing I've ever endured in my life. I have no memory of the time I was off my head, which is probably a good thing for my pride. But now I feel much better, and Timms tells me the wound is healing beautifully. You can return to London, and your troublesome ward, with a clear conscience and my gratitude. You're a good friend, Lucas."

"You'd have done the same for me." An awkward silence fell between the men, for whom the discussion of emotions was an unfamiliar thing.

Kincaid spoke first. "I suppose it's a good time for me to return to town. I would hate for you to feel obligated to entertain me."

Langley raised an eyebrow. "I wouldn't. Lucas, for the next few weeks, I intend to entertain no one but myself. I plan to laze about, eating, sleeping, and rebuilding my strength. I will be a very demanding convalescent, and I'm sure I'll drive my servants to distraction." He paused. "That is, if Miss Fleming ever relinquishes the management of my household."

Kincaid smiled mischievously. "In any case, you'll do better in that department without my interference."

"What do you mean?"

"Oh, come on, Robert, it's clear that you have an interest in the girl."

Langley choked on a mouthful of coffee. "An interest? In that redheaded termagant? Lucas, I've known you to have some crazy ideas, but this is beyond anything!"

"If you say so," Kincaid said with a knowing smile. "But I can't imagine you allowing another girl to talk to you the way Miss Fleming does. Nor have I known you to look at a girl the way you look at her."

"How do I look at her, Lucas? As though I wish she would go away?"

Lucas shook his head. "I know you better than that, Robert. I predict you'll lead her to the altar before the year is out. Or, more likely, she will lead you."

"To the altar?" Langley asked incredulously. "You know that she's engaged to George Garland? Even if I found her less objectionable than the other young ladies of my acquaintance, you can't imagine I would interfere in her engagement?"

"To a lesser man, that might be an obstacle," Kincaid mused. "But I think the challenge will be good for you. Add a bit of spice to the affair."

Nineteen

"In the study, you think? No need to announce me, Matthews, I know the way." Moments later, Adrian Stone came through the door of his brother's study, looking travel-stained but happy.

"Your staff told me you had gone to the country, Robert, but I wasn't sure I believed it," Adrian said.

Langley lifted an eyebrow. "Did you fear they were conspiring to keep me from you?" He sighed. "Unfortunately, I fear they lack the intelligence for that."

"What? No, it just seemed like a deuced odd thing to do, in the middle of the Season."

"So you've come to investigate?"

"Something like that," Adrian agreed.

"Would you believe I came to the country to escape the rigours of the Season? All the balls can get quite tiresome."

Adrian laughed. "I know that's nonsense. I'd be surprised to hear you'd been to a ball this year besides Diana's."

"Diana's was the second," Langley admitted. "Tell me, Adrian, what exactly did you hear in town?"

"Oh, there are several stories making the rounds. Corky heard you got shot protecting a lady from footpads in Hyde Park." Adrian laughed. "There was even talk of a duel, but I knew that couldn't be right, as it's not like you to do something so reckless."

"No, I suppose not," Langley agreed. "When did you notice I was missing?"

"Oh, a couple of days ago," Adrian said vaguely. "And some of the rumours were disturbing, so I thought I should look for you. I figured if you were in trouble, I might be able to help."

Langley smiled at his brother. "You are very kind to me, Adrian. How was your journey?"

"Well, I'd planned to come by post-chaise, but I remembered your lectures on economy, and I thought that rather than waste money on a post-chaise, I would buy a vehicle. It took me a couple of days to find one, but Robert, I've bought the most bang-up curricle you've ever seen."

"Indeed." Langley looked at his brother skeptically. "Did you make it here without damaging this vehicle?"

"Of course!" Adrian looked affronted.

"I congratulate you. Have you set up your own stables?"

"Well, as to that, Robert," Adrian said cautiously, "I intended to buy horses, but I ran out of money, and I was wondering if you could give me an advance on my next quarter's allowance?"

"But how did you get the curricle here?" asked Langley, fearing he knew the answer.

"I borrowed your chestnuts," he admitted sheepishly. "And oh Robert, I've never driven such sweet-goers! You wouldn't believe how beautifully they handle."

"I'd believe it, they're my horses," Langley said dryly. "Are you telling me they made it here without injury?"

"Of course," said Adrian. "Really, Robert, just because I had one accident, it isn't fair–"

He stopped in mid-sentence when Amelia strolled into the room without knocking, as had become her habit. She paused when she saw Adrian.

"Good afternoon, Mr. Stone," she said politely, before turning to Langley. "I beg your pardon, my lord. I didn't realize you had company."

Adrian bowed to her. "Afternoon, Miss Fleming," he said before turning back to his brother. "You could have simply told me it was a lovers' tryst, Robert," he said. "I won't judge."

Langley's lips thinned. "Miss Fleming is a friend of Diana's," he said sternly. As if on cue, Diana joined them.

Adrian looked surprised. "You're here too? Have you left Templeton?"

"What?" asked Diana, turning red. "Of course not. Why would you think that?"

"Oh, you're always so polite when you speak to him. Noticed it at the ball," Adrian said frankly. "It isn't like you, and it isn't natural!"

Diana's look of distress prompted Langley to intervene.

"Stop talking nonsense, Adrian," he said firmly. "Diana has joined me at Stonecroft to enjoy the countryside in the springtime. Miss Fleming has come along as her companion. It's as simple as that." He rose from his desk. "Let's go see if you were swindled in the purchase of this curricle."

Later that day, Langley and Diana found themselves alone in the sitting room before dinner.

"You know, Diana, I would hate for your stay here to cause any awkwardness between you and Templeton."

Diana flushed. "There is no awkwardness, I assure you. I left him a note, explaining I was going to Stonecroft, but I'm sure it makes no difference to him, as he has gone to Vienna. Even when he's at home, he hardly notices I'm there, and he rarely speaks to me unless he has something to criticize."

"Ah," said Langley, thinking that he was finally getting somewhere. "And what does he criticize?"

"He tried to forbid me to ride by myself in the park. As though I was a child, unable to look after myself. Or maybe he thought I was carrying on an affair in the early hours of the morning. Either way, it's ridiculous!"

"So he forbade you to ride?"

"Well, not exactly," Diana admitted. "He insisted I take a groom. But Robert, I used to ride by myself all the time before I was married, and you were never concerned about it."

"That's because I had you followed by a groom," Langley told her unrepentantly.

Diana's mouth fell open in shock. "What! Robert, you couldn't have. I would have noticed."

The earl shrugged his shoulders. "If you say so."

This nonchalant answer only aggravated his sister.

"I'm sure I would have seen him; he would have had to keep me within sight. I'm not completely oblivious when I ride."

"He knew to keep his distance, and he was very discreet," Langley told her. "Sometimes when I was in town I followed you myself. It's a peaceful time of day to ride."

"I can't believe you didn't trust me," Diana exclaimed.

"It's not a matter of trust, Diana," her brother explained. "The fact is, you're a very beautiful woman." His lips twitched. "And you never know when you might run into footpads in the park."

Notes from the diary of the Earl of Langley

If my mother truly wanted me to get married, she would not have given me so many siblings. I know I asked Diana to come to Stonecroft, but now I wish she would leave, and she shows no inclination to do so. And now Adrian has arrived. There really isn't much more to say about that. Really, Mary is the best of my siblings. Not only has she moved to Scotland, she's even drawn my mother north to assist with her confinement.

If a man's house is his castle, Stonecroft needs better defences.

"I have been thinking, my lord, that it's time for me to go home," Amelia said to Langley as they played chess one afternoon.

"What?" asked Langley. "So soon?"

"It's been two weeks, my lord, and your shoulder seems to be healing nicely. And now that your brother and sister are both here, I thought you might appreciate some time alone together as a family."

"I assure you, I would not," Langley said firmly.

"Oh," said Amelia slowly. "Well, I feel guilty leaving my family to manage without me. Isabelle wrote that William was going to Cliveden Manor, so she and Aunt Lizzie will have to deal with the creditors on their own. Mama won't be any help, she'll just be trying to spend money we don't have." She chewed her lower lip anxiously. "At least William will have fewer opportunities to gamble at Cliveden. I just hope he doesn't do something foolish."

"You mean more foolish than challenging me to a duel?" Langley said in a teasing tone. "Miss Fleming, even your brother could hardly top that. We have to trust he'll be satisfied with the folly he has already achieved."

"I suppose," she said dubiously. "But it hardly seems right for me to stay here, eating delicious food and playing chess."

"But Miss Fleming, my shoulder is far from healed," said Langley. "It will be weeks before I can return to my usual activities."

Amelia frowned. "I wish you'd let me look at it." Langley had not let her see his shoulder since he had woken from his delirium and banished her from his bedroom. "There must be something wrong if it's still causing you pain."

"I'm sure it's healing as it should," he reassured her. "But these things take time. The most frustrating part of it is that under normal circumstances I'd be busy advising my land agent and meeting with my tenants."

Amelia wrinkled her brow. "Does your land agent need that much help?"

"Pettigrew's a good man, but he's young, and he needs guidance. It's the most distressing thing about this injury."

"And you can't advise him from your study?" she asked, in some confusion.

"Well, I can," Langley agreed. "But I like to get out in the fields, to look at the new machinery and talk to my tenants. There's no substitute for seeing the situation for oneself."

Amelia acknowledged the truth of this, for she had observed it at Cliveden Manor. She chewed her lip for a minute. "Perhaps I could help, sir," she suggested.

"Oh, I couldn't ask that of you," he said. "And it's not a role for a lady."

She bristled at the suggestion that she wasn't up to the task. "But that's exactly the sort of thing I do on our estate," she exclaimed. "William isn't entirely happy about it, but he admits that I'm good at it, and the estate is better for it."

"Well, if you really wouldn't mind . . ." said Langley hesitantly.

"Oh, I'd be happy to," said Amelia. "The only problem is, I don't have the right clothes. I have an entire set of work clothes at Cliveden Manor, things that William has outgrown. At the start I tried to work in my dresses, but the skirts got in the way." She paused. "Maybe we could send someone to Cliveden Manor–"

"You will find a way to work in your dresses, Miss Fleming," Langley said firmly. "If you damage your dresses, we will replace them."

She nodded doubtfully. "If you think that's best, my lord."

"I do," said Langley firmly. If he knew Amelia was roaming around his estate in men's clothing, he wouldn't be able to focus on anything else.

Langley sent a footman to fetch Thomas Pettigrew, and his land agent presented himself half an hour later. Mr. Pettigrew was in his mid-twenties, with fair hair, blue eyes, and a tan that spoke of hours spent in outdoor work. The son of a vicar, he had been educated at Cambridge and had worked at Stonecroft since his graduation. He lived in a cottage on the estate and enjoyed a good relationship with the earl. Langley frequently invited him to dine, and had been heard to say that Pettigrew was one of the few men of his acquaintance who could talk politics sensibly.

"You wished to see me, my lord?" Pettigrew asked politely.

"Yes, Pettigrew," Langley said. "I'd like to introduce you to Miss Amelia Fleming." Pettigrew bowed to the young lady sitting opposite the earl and tried not to let his curiosity show. In the three years that Pettigrew had worked at Stonecroft, Langley had never held a house party or invited a woman outside of his family to come for a visit.

"I'm pleased to meet you, Mr. Pettigrew," Amelia said warmly.

"I have just been telling Miss Fleming that you're in need of an assistant," Langley said.

"Oh, no sir," said Pettigrew quickly, concerned that Langley thought he was struggling with his job, or worse, that he had complained about his work. "What made you think . . . " He let the sentence trail off as he caught the look in Langley's eyes.

"I meant to say, sir, that I have long been wishing for help, but I am resigned to the current situation," he corrected. A glance at his employer confirmed that this was the right answer.

"Well, Mr. Pettigrew, your wish is about to be granted," said Langley. "Miss Fleming has some expertise in estate management, and she has volunteered to assist you while I recover from my injury. She has knowledge of crop rotation, ploughs, and all that sort of thing, as she has played an active role in managing her brother's estate."

To his credit, Pettigrew took this without a blink.

"That's wonderful news, Miss Fleming," he said. "When will you start?"

"I thought tomorrow," she said.

"Mind you, Miss Fleming will only be available for several hours each day," Langley cut in quickly. "She will still play chess with me before dinner, and she will want to spend some time with my sister."

"Naturally," said Pettigrew. "I'll be grateful for any time Miss Fleming can spare."

Twenty

Letter from Miss Isabelle Fleming to Miss Amelia Fleming

Dear Amy,

Finally, some good news! Yesterday the funniest little man came to call. He told us he was the agent for a noble family that had fallen on hard times and been forced to sell almost everything they owned. This family has since regained their fortune, and wished to buy back the heirlooms they had sold. Amy, he wanted our brass candlesticks, and he gave me three hundred pounds for them! I almost fainted on the spot. I told him they were brass, and unlikely to be worth a fraction of that amount, but he insisted they were of great sentimental value to his employer. At first I wondered if it was some sort of joke, but he pulled out the banknotes then and there. I've never seen such a large sum of money in my life.

William is still at Cliveden Manor, but Aunt Lizzie and I found a stack of bills in his study, and we have settled those that seemed most pressing. Even so, there is a very good sum remaining. I have set some aside to buy meat and fruit, as I am heartily sick of potatoes.

Mama was out when the man came for the candlesticks and I haven't told her of our good fortune. If she knows there is money, she will spend it. I don't think she can help herself; it's an illness, just as gambling was for Papa.

Despite our desperate financial situation, Mama still insists that you can't marry Mr. Garland. He visited yesterday to discuss the matter, and they had quite a spirited conversation.

I hope you are well, and the earl's shoulder is mending.

Your affectionate,
Isabelle

―

"Something amusing you, Miss Fleming?" Langley asked across the breakfast table. Diana and Adrian had not yet come down, so Amelia and Langley were enjoying a quiet meal together.

"It's the strangest thing, my lord," Amelia said with a laugh. "Isabelle writes that a man showed up wanting our brass candlesticks! He gave her three hundred pounds for them. It's bizarre, but he said they were of great sentimental value to his employer."

"That's unusual," Langley remarked.

Amelia nodded. "Imagine spending a fortune on brass candlesticks! I don't think he can be a sensible man, do you, sir?"

Langley's lips twitched. "I'm almost certain he is not, Miss Fleming."

"Well, I'm grateful. Although I suppose it's his employer we have to thank. He must have more money than wit."

"I'm sure you're right, Miss Fleming."

Amelia sighed happily. "It's certainly a weight off my shoulders, as the money has allowed Isabelle to settle the most pressing obligations. And even though it feels fraudulent, it was honestly obtained."

"I imagine both parties were pleased with the transaction," Langley agreed.

They finished their meal in companionable silence. When Amelia rose to leave, Langley handed her a box that bore the name of the same London dressmaker who had made the powder blue gown she had worn to Diana's ball.

"I ordered this last week, and Timms brought it up from town yesterday," Langley said casually.

Amelia's eyes widened. "Timms travelled to town for this?"

"He was in London on some other business."

Amelia stared at the box and fought a battle with her conscience. "I couldn't accept this; it wouldn't be right. And Diana's already been so generous in sharing her wardrobe."

"Open it," Langley insisted. "I don't think it's improper, as it replaces something you were kind enough to give to me."

Amelia reluctantly lifted the lid to find a beautiful green silk pelisse, with elaborate ruching and pearl buttons down the front. She couldn't believe it had been made in a week, and realized that Langley must have paid a fortune to have it done so quickly.

"I couldn't," she protested weakly, but she already knew that she couldn't give it up. "But oh, it's exquisite."

Langley looked pleased. "Well, if you don't accept it, I won't have any other use for it," he said lightly. "Timms has made it very clear that green does not flatter me."

―

Amelia knew she owed Mr. Garland an explanation for her departure from London, and she reluctantly sat down to write him a letter. After several drafts, she settled on the following communication:

Dear Mr. Garland,

As you may have heard, I have accompanied my friend, Lady Diana Templeton, to Stonecroft, her brother Langley's estate in Kent. I know it may seem like my departure was sudden, but I felt weary after the excitement of the Season, and I am finding the fresh air and slow pace of country life restorative.

I expect to return to London soon and look forward to seeing you then.

Yours,
Miss Fleming

After reflecting that she had never written a more insipid letter in her life, Amelia addressed it and took it to Langley, who franked it without comment.

The reply arrived five days later, hidden in a pile of

letters that Matthews brought to Langley at the breakfast table. The earl handed it across the table to Amelia.

"You have a reply, Miss Fleming," he said politely.

Amelia flushed and tucked it into the pocket of her dress.

"Feel free to read it, Miss Fleming, we don't stand on ceremony at breakfast," Langley said.

Amelia flushed. "It's all right, my lord, I'm in no rush."

She opened her letter later that morning in the privacy of her bedchamber.

My Dearest Amelia,

It gives me pleasure to use your given name, as it signifies a degree of intimacy that can only lead to greater intimacy in the future. If I may be so bold, it would make me very happy to have you call me George.

Although London is dull without you, I can well understand how the rigours of the Season would tax the nervous sensibilities of a gently bred lady. I am pleased you are enjoying yourself at Stonecroft, and your close acquaintance with Mrs. Templeton certainly does you credit.

I have always wanted to see Stonecroft, as I've heard it is a great estate. If my responsibilities permit, I will pay you a visit there. As you know, I am interested in noble estates, as I am always looking for inspiration for Garland Castle. I find myself facing a dilemma. Do you think I should call it Garland Castle or Castle Garland?

Yours,
George

Amelia was glad that she had read the letter in private, as it threw her into a panic. Garland's innuendoes of intimacy made her queasy, and his suggestion that he might come to visit made her feel frankly sick. After the initial stress of Langley's injury, her stay at Stonecroft had turned into a sort of holiday, and Garland's intrusion would bring reality crashing back.

After careful consideration, Amelia composed a reply that bore even less resemblance to the truth than her previous missive. She took it to Langley to be franked, and if he was surprised by the speed of her reply he made no mention of it. He certainly would have been surprised had he been able to read the contents:

Dear Mr. Garland,

Thank you for your letter.

I fear you have heard inaccurate reports of Stonecroft, as I think it's more like a large cottage than a noble estate. I find it restful, as there is no formality or ostentation, and it is charmingly rustic. The roof in my bedroom leaks, which is tiresome, but we have had surprisingly little rain. As I mentioned, we are very informal here, and we often assist the staff with the housework. The cook is quite old, and the fare is somewhat old-fashioned, but I'm sure she does her best.

So although it has been a diverting experience, I don't think Stonecroft would do as a model for Garland Castle.

Sincerely,
Miss Fleming

My Dear Miss Fleming,

Your insistence on formal address is charming.

I am surprised to hear you find Stonecroft rustic, as I have often heard it described as a splendid estate. But I suppose that might explain why the nobility keep to themselves; they don't want outsiders to know they've exaggerated their assets!

But a leaking roof, Miss Fleming! I can scarcely imagine. I must beg you to return to London immediately so you don't fall ill.

I have made inquiries into the availability of St. George's church for our wedding ceremony next month. I have been told they are fully booked, but I know this is only a starting point for negotiation. Rest assured, Miss Fleming, I will not take no for an answer.

Ever your devoted,
George

∽

Amelia, impatient to learn whether Garland still planned to visit Stonecroft, made the mistake of opening this letter at the breakfast table under the curious eyes of Langley and Diana. Her relief that Garland did not mention a visit gave way to dismay when she read he was looking for a church for their wedding. She turned as pale as a ghost, and the letter slipped from her fingers and onto the floor.

"Are you all right, Miss Fleming?" asked Langley solicitously. He hoped she would leave the letter on the floor so that he could collect it later, but to his disappointment, she picked it up and tucked it into her pocket.

EMMA MELBOURNE

"Yes, I'm perfectly fine," she lied.

"So there is no need to send for Dr. Carter?" Langley persisted.

"Certainly not," said Amelia firmly. "But on that subject, I found a medical book in your library yesterday, and read something that I wish to discuss with you."

Langley sighed. "Really, Miss Fleming, I have very little medical knowledge. You would do better to discuss it with Carter. I would be happy to have him summoned."

"But it relates to your injury, my lord," Amelia said persuasively. "The authors of the book recommend exercise for those recovering from an injury to bone or muscle. Without regular use, the muscles may contract and stiffen, making it more difficult to regain function in your arm."

"I see," said Langley, who privately agreed with Amelia's opinion on the value of exercise. His favourite horse, North Star, had been brought up from London, and for the past week Langley had been riding in the early mornings before the rest of the household was awake. In the afternoons he performed strengthening exercises for his arm while his household thought he was napping. "What sort of exercise would you recommend?"

"Well," Amelia said thoughtfully. "As it is now three weeks since the injury, and you've been limited to sedentary activities, I would expect you to be deconditioned. You would have to start slowly."

"I quite agree," said Langley. "Did you have any specific activities in mind?"

"Pall-mall," Amelia said earnestly.

Diana burst out laughing. "We haven't played Pall-mall in years!" she exclaimed. "I hate to discourage you,

Amelia, but I doubt you could find the equipment, and even if you did, you'll never convince Robert to do it."

"I found a very nice set of mallets and balls in the back of one of the old gardening sheds," Amelia said. "And I thought Lord Langley would be open-minded. It would be gentle exercise, and should not put significant stress on his arm."

"Would you join me, Miss Fleming?" Langley asked with a twinkle in his eye. "I would think such exercise should be supervised."

"Yes, of course," Amelia replied. "Will you play, Diana?"

"No, thank you," Diana declined with a smile. "I've been neglecting the pianoforte, so I think I will take the morning to practise."

Amelia and Langley were about halfway through their course when Adrian arrived.

"What freak is this?" Adrian asked his brother.

"I thought it was obvious," said Langley. "We are playing Pall-mall."

Adrian stared at his brother in concern, then turned to Amelia. "I thought you said he was shot in the shoulder, not the head. The next time he wants you to play a child's game, come and find me. I'll try to talk some sense into him."

Amelia laughed. "It's good for his shoulder," she explained. "If he doesn't exercise the joint it will stiffen."

Adrian gave his brother a pitying look. "You're getting old, Robert."

"It's certainly preferable to the alternative," Langley said.

"I think I'll join you," Adrian announced.

"It's a game for two people," Langley said in a discouraging tone.

"What do you mean?" asked Adrian. "The four of us used to play as children. As I recall, Mama used to help me, because I was so much younger than the rest of you. So technically, we were five."

Langley sighed. "You may start at the beginning of the course," he said, gesturing across the field to the first wicket, which was about a hundred yards away.

"Oh, don't be ridiculous, I'll start here. I don't suppose you brought an extra mallet and ball?"

Amelia had left the extra mallets and balls by the first wicket, so Adrian was able to quickly collect his equipment and join the contest. He was surprisingly good at Pall-mall and quickly took the lead.

"At last, we have learned where Adrian's talents lie," said Langley. "He's tremendously skilled at hitting a ball through a wicket."

"Yes, well, don't feel too bad about it," Adrian said kindly. "You can't be the best at everything."

"When do you go back to Oxford?" Langley asked casually.

"Not until the fall."

"Ah," said Langley. "I thought they might have started a summer term."

"No," Adrian said cheerfully.

"And they don't want you for any additional tutoring, since you missed all that time while you were rusticated?"

"No one has mentioned it."

"I see," said Langley, taking a particularly violent swing at the ball. It missed the wicket by inches and rolled a further ten feet down the field.

"Now you'll have to hit it back," Amelia pointed out with satisfaction.

"I understand the rules," Langley said sourly before turning back to his brother.

"Do you mean to make a long stay at Stonecroft, Adrian?" he asked, just as his brother was about to hit a particularly difficult shot.

The shot went wide, but Adrian barely noticed. He gaped at his brother. "A long stay? Robert, I live here!"

Langley nodded. "Yes, of course. I just thought you might want to go back to town to see another play, or perhaps visit a friend."

"Actually, I was thinking I might invite Corky here," Adrian said slowly. Now that his brother was behaving so strangely, he was reconsidering his plan. If he didn't know better, he would almost think Langley wished him to leave.

"But you wouldn't want to invite a friend to Stonecroft in the spring," Langley said. "It's quite the wrong season for it."

"Well, I don't know, I've always thought Stonecroft is quite nice in the spring," Adrian said. "The weather is perfect for riding and fishing. We might drive the curricle around." The more he thought about it, the better it sounded. Stonecroft was really beautiful in the spring.

"I'm sorry, Adrian, but I must ask you to postpone Corky's visit," Langley said apologetically. "My shoulder is still troubling me, and too much noise and excitement might impair my recovery."

Amelia looked at Langley anxiously. He was looking so fit, so much like his usual self, that it was easy to forget he had been shot in a duel less than a month before. He was a proud man, and she knew it must have been hard for him to admit his shoulder still troubled him. Perhaps the Pall-mall had been too much, too quickly.

"I'm sorry, my lord, but I am suddenly tired," Amelia lied. "I wonder if we could stop and resume the game another day?"

"Of course," Langley said, looking at her with concern. He worried she was exhausting herself trying to assist Pettigrew, but feared that if he put a stop to that scheme, she would decide to leave.

"Admit it, Miss Fleming, you've realized it's a lost cause," Adrian teased her. "Neither you nor Robert is a match for my skills at Pall-mall."

"Oh, we freely admit that," said Langley. "There's no point even trying to compete with you. Next time Miss Fleming and I will just play ourselves. But for today, we agree that you're the winner and you've earned the right to put away the balls and wickets."

Langley offered Amelia his arm and she took it, noting that he didn't seem weary, and they returned to the house together.

Twenty-One

On a beautiful sunny afternoon, Langley and Amelia were playing their daily game of chess and listening to Diana play the pianoforte. Langley was in a particularly mellow mood, as he had just captured his opponent's queen. So when Matthews informed him that Lord Cliveden had arrived, Langley simply raised an eyebrow.

"Is he armed?" he asked casually.

"I don't believe so, my lord. Would you like me to inquire?" After several months as the earl's butler, Matthews still didn't understand many of the things Langley said, but he prided himself on having learned to hide his confusion.

Amelia, who had been cast into a froth of anxiety by the news of her brother's arrival, gave Langley a reproachful look. She wasn't sure how much the servants knew about Langley's injury, although she suspected that few of them believed his ridiculous story about footpads in Hyde Park.

"That won't be necessary, Matthews. Show him in and send for tea. Don't forget clotted cream for the scones."

"Very good, my lord." Matthews had noticed that Langley had seemed much happier during the past few weeks at Stonecroft than he had ever been before; getting shot seemed to agree with him.

William entered, looking nervous but resolute. He bowed stiffly to Langley.

"My lord," he began. "I hope you will forgive my unexpected appearance. I'm here to apologize. You had every right to question my gambling, and I had no right to demand satisfaction. I'm sorry the duel ended the way it did. The truth is, I didn't expect to hit you. Amelia wrote you were recovering, but I wanted to come and see for myself."

Langley felt a rush of compassion for the man, who was really little more than a boy.

"Your sister is right. The shoulder is almost back to normal." He saw Amelia's surprised look and corrected himself. "It will eventually be back to normal," he amended. "I don't think you have caused lasting damage."

"As for the rest of it," William continued, "I mean to pay the debt. Upon my honour, the gambling is done. I will repay you, in instalments, as quickly as I can."

"I'm pleased to hear it," said Langley, then fell silent as Matthews entered with the tea tray. "Have a scone," he offered, gesturing to the tray.

"Oh," William said, surprised at the change of subject. "No, thank you." His nervous energy had robbed him of his appetite.

"Go on," Langley encouraged him warmly. "You must be hungry after your journey. Matthews will get you a drink." He took a scone and spread it lavishly with clotted cream.

"Thank you," said William. He wasn't sure what to make of this new side of Langley, but he found his hospitality almost as disconcerting as his cutting remarks had been at their first meeting.

After William had been given a drink, Amelia had selected a cake, and Matthews had withdrawn, William returned to the heart of the matter.

"I've been doing my best to make sense of things at Cliveden Manor," he explained. He turned to Amelia. "I didn't realize how much work you were doing there. We're barely breaking even right now, but there's a lot of room for improvement, and I expect to make it profitable within two years at the most."

"Excellent," said Langley.

"There will still be a significant delay in repayment," William admitted. "But I'd like to pay you back with interest."

"Nonsense," said Langley dismissively. "A gentleman doesn't charge interest on a debt of honour."

"Because a gentleman doesn't delay payment of a debt of honour," said William with a rueful smile. "I wish you would tell me the exact amount of the debt, so I know what I'm facing."

"Of course, of course," said Langley vaguely, but he made no suggestion of the sum.

"Very good," said William. "And now, if you don't mind, I'd like to speak with my sister."

"Certainly," said Langley kindly. "I'm in no rush to return to our chess game, although I think I am ahead. Incidentally, Cliveden, did you know your sister is remarkably good at chess? I frequently find myself outmanoeuvred."

"What?" asked William. "Oh, yes. Amelia's always been good at that sort of thing."

"Well, go ahead," encouraged Langley, looking at him expectantly.

William flushed. "Oh. The thing is, I was hoping to speak to Amelia privately."

"My dear Cliveden, you should have said. You must use my study." Langley rose to show them the way.

When the Flemings were alone, Amelia threw her arms around her brother. "Oh William, I'm so pleased to see you. I was worried you might do something foolish after the duel."

William smiled sheepishly. "I can understand why. I owe you an apology, Amelia. I know that since Papa's death—even before Papa's death—I haven't been facing up to my responsibilities, and I mean to change that. I'm the head of the family, and from now on, I mean to act like it."

"I always believed you could do it, you know."

"I'm not sure I can, but I mean to try," he said earnestly. "The duel forced me to face reality in a way I never had before. I almost went to France, so that if Langley–" he broke off, not wanting to put the fear into words. "If the worst happened, at least I'd save my neck. I had everything packed, but then I asked myself how it would end. I don't want to live out the rest of my life in France." He rolled his eyes. "With Mama's relations, you know, a little goes a long way." His expression turned serious again. "I've lived in fear long enough. So I went to Cliveden Manor, planning to do what I could to turn things around. I decided that if charges were brought, I would face them."

"I'll help you with Cliveden Manor, of course," Amelia assured him. "I wish I had gone with you, I could have explained the new system of record keeping, and the plan for crop rotation, and oh, so many things. It will be so much easier with two of us. I'll leave with you today."

"Well, that's the other thing I wanted to talk to you about," William said slowly. "I thought you might want to return to London to get ready for your wedding."

Amelia's face fell at the mention of her wedding.

"You don't have to marry him, Amelia," he said gently. "I know you don't care for him, and you only accepted him because we need his money. But we'll manage without it."

"But the debt," she protested. "Even apart from the debt to Langley, we don't have the money for the improvements that are needed at Cliveden Manor. You'll need capital to turn the estate around."

"I don't think things are as desperate as that," William said. "It will take time, but that might not be a bad thing. I'll learn as I go. And we'll have to decrease our spending. Before I left town, I had a frank talk with Mama and explained how things stand. Told her that if she runs up more bills at her dressmaker, milliner, and the like, I won't pay them. Once the townhouse is packed up, she'll have to move back to Cliveden Manor, where she'll have fewer opportunities to spend money."

Amelia laughed. "How did she respond to that?"

"Oh, as well as you might expect. She kicked up a fuss, of course, but I told her if she kept it up, I'd banish her to the Dower House. And I wouldn't put up the funds for a staff."

Amelia's eyes widened. "But she has no money of her own."

William nodded. "Exactly. But I would do it. Her extravagance ruined our father, and I won't allow it to ruin me." He sighed. "To tell the truth, I don't feel quite right about taking Garland's money. Not when you have to marry him for it."

Amelia laughed. "He's not so bad. A little obsessed with appearances, perhaps, but so are many people. I think he will be kind to me."

William looked at her searchingly. "But you don't love him."

"William, I don't think I'm made to fall in love. I love you, of course, and Isabelle, and even Mama. But romantic love–" she shook her head. "I think I'm too practical. Certainly practical enough to know it makes sense for me to marry."

"You don't have to," William assured her. "You'll always have a home at Cliveden Manor."

She smiled at him, reflecting that at least one good thing had come from the duel. Her brother had grown up.

"Thank you, William," she said sincerely. "That is a great comfort to me. But I expect—indeed I hope—that you will get married, and have your own family, and although I will delight in being an aunt–"

"Not for many years yet," protested William, looking surprised by the suggestion.

"Maybe not," she agreed. "But I think I will enjoy having my own household."

"It doesn't have to be Garland. You're young, and you will have plenty of other opportunities."

"But I accepted Mr. Garland's proposal."

"Yes, and I know you don't like to go back on your word," William said. "But this is your entire life, Amelia. You know, you wouldn't even have to tell him. As your guardian, I could refuse to consent to the match."

"I understand from Isabelle's letters that Mama has already tried that."

"Yes, and for some reason it has only made him more determined," William admitted. "But he wouldn't be able to ignore me."

"I'll be of age in six months."

"True," William acknowledged. "And there's a chance that he'll want to wait for you. But I think he will probably be so insulted that he'll want to move on."

Amelia chewed her lip with indecision. She didn't want to marry Garland, but she couldn't see a better alternative. If she let William break the engagement, she would have two failed engagements to her name, and although few people knew about her betrothal to Percy, the betrothal to Garland was widely known. She thought her looks were passable, but she knew she didn't have the sort of beauty that could prompt a man to overlook two past engagements, a family scandal, and the complete absence of a dowry. If she didn't marry Garland, she would most likely end up a spinster in her brother's household, and rather than adding to her family's resources, she would be a drain on them.

She stood and embraced her brother. "Thank you, William," she said. "But I wish to marry Mr. Garland. I believe I will be happy with the situation." It was as far as she could stretch the truth. "Perhaps I'll even get involved in running his business."

"If you're sure," he said doubtfully.

"I am. Have you heard from Mr. Wells about the marriage settlement?"

"I heard from Wells, yes. He seemed to think I had written to him." William gave his sister an amused look, and Amelia had the grace to blush.

"Well," said Amelia. "Then you know that Mr. Garland is to pay you forty thousand pounds, free and clear, upon our marriage. I am to have five hundred pounds a year as pin money. We're unlikely to do better."

Although William was impressed by the sum she had negotiated, he was unsettled by the dispassionate way she spoke of the deal.

"I would think the forty thousand pounds will go a long way to settling the debt," Amelia continued. "Maybe even clear it with some left over. Did Langley ever tell you the amount?"

"No, he didn't," William said in frustration. "And as you know, Papa had his accident immediately after he lost to Langley, so no one had the chance to speak to him about it. I assume it was a large sum, to drive him to act the way he did." He sighed.

"And Langley never mentioned anything, even a rough figure?"

William shook his head. "He's a funny man."

"What do you mean?"

William shrugged. "When I first met him, I could see why people call him the Stoneheart. He was colder than ice, and made me feel about the size of a bug. But today, he was like a different man. You heard what he said when

I asked about the amount of the debt. Brushed it off, almost as if it was of no consequence."

"Some men are happier in the country than in town," Amelia suggested thoughtfully.

"Perhaps. Or perhaps he was suffering from an attack of gout." William smiled. "Do you remember the fuss great-uncle Clarence used to make when he had an attack? He could hardly speak a civil word on any subject."

Amelia laughed. "Oh William, Lord Langley's not old enough to have gout."

"Maybe not," he agreed. "But it could explain why he's so capricious. Have you been comfortable here? I've been so busy at Cliveden Manor that I haven't given much thought to your situation, but I realize you may have been put in an awkward position."

"Oh no," Amelia hastened to reassure him. "I've become excellent friends with his sister, it's as though I've known her all my life. And Langley has been an excellent host. In fact, he invited me to treat his house as my own."

"I'm glad to hear it," said William. "In any case, I can escort you back to town today. We still have several weeks before we must give up the townhouse, so you can work on your wedding arrangements, and help Mama and Isabelle with the packing."

"Oh," said Amelia thoughtfully. Now that she had the opportunity to leave, she found she didn't want to go. "Do you know, William, I think perhaps it's my duty to stay here a little longer."

"What?" asked William in confusion. "But Langley seems so much better, I don't understand why you want to stay. Surely you must find it awkward?"

"Well, Langley is better, but he's not entirely healed, so he hasn't been able to advise his land agent as he usually would. There is also the matter of his rehabilitation exercises, to ensure he regains full use of his arm and shoulder."

"What kind of rehabilitation exercises?" William asked suspiciously.

"We have been playing Pall-mall," Amelia explained earnestly. "And if the weather is fair tomorrow, we may walk down to the river for a picnic. I really think, William, that I should stay another week. Perhaps two."

"Whatever you think, Amelia," said her brother, who privately thought the whole situation was dashed peculiar. He decided that if his sister claimed to be happy, he wouldn't push the matter further.

Twenty-Two

Notes from the diary of the Earl of Langley

Miss Fleming seems to be wedded to the idea of wedding Garland. Cliveden visited yesterday and surprised us all by behaving like a man. He assured me he is doing his best to set his estate to rights, and will pay the debt as soon as he is able. He then requested to speak to Miss Fleming privately, so I put them in my study and listened at the door. Unfortunately the door is very solid, so I missed parts of the conversation, but the gist of it was clear. Cliveden offered to refuse his consent to her marriage to Garland, which I think is the most sensible thing he has ever said. I had to respect the boy, even if he later called me a funny man and compared me to his gouty great-uncle.

But Miss Fleming spouted a lot of rubbish about having given Garland her word, which was to be expected. She certainly places a great deal of importance on honour, as I guess I know better than anyone. But when she claimed she didn't think she was made to fall in love—that I didn't believe.

A woman who kisses the way she kissed me after the duel is certainly made to fall in love. She may argue it was a charade to prevent us from drawing the attention of passersby, but there was nothing practical about that kiss, and I've been dreaming of a repeat performance ever since. Preferably without having to be shot first. But maybe I'm deluding myself.

Garland agreed to give Cliveden forty thousand pounds as a marriage settlement, which he apparently plans to use to pay the debt to me. I can't decide whether I'm witnessing a tragedy or a farce, but the devil of it is, I can't see a way to enter the scene without appearing like the villain.

Is it dishonourable to wish that a lady would behave dishonourably?

~

The residents of Stonecroft had barely finished their breakfast when Matthews announced they had morning callers.

Langley sighed. "Who is it this time, Matthews?"

Matthews swallowed nervously. "Mrs. Hunt and her daughter, my lord."

"No doubt you explained I don't receive callers at the breakfast table?"

"I thought I could put them in the sitting room, my lord?" Matthews asked hopefully.

Langley fixed his poor butler with a stare.

"He means it's too early in the day to deal with that harpy," Adrian put in helpfully.

Matthews swallowed again and turned back to the earl. "I tried to explain that your lordship was not at home, but Mrs. Hunt was most insistent. She said that if you were unable to receive her now, she would come back later."

Langley nodded in resignation. "I understand, Matthews. Show her into the sitting room and fetch Mrs. Prescott."

"Very good, my lord," said Matthews, plainly relieved that he would not have to turn Mrs. Hunt away.

Mrs. Prescott arrived, and Langley spoke to her briefly before leading the party to the sitting room to receive the Hunts.

Mrs. Hunt was dressed in an elaborate gown in a vibrant shade of blue. As usual, her hat was trimmed in feathers that had been dyed to match her dress. Beside her, in a cream muslin gown, her daughter looked washed out.

"Lord Langley," Mrs. Hunt said, evidently delighted to see him. Langley sketched a bow to her and her daughter before taking a seat at the opposite end of the room.

"I am so pleased to see you looking well," Mrs. Hunt continued. "As close neighbours, Letitia and I felt obliged to come and assure ourselves you were not seriously ill. There are the strangest stories circulating in London."

"I try not to listen to gossip, Mrs. Hunt," Langley said lightly.

"I quite agree with you, Lord Langley. It is a vulgar habit." She turned to Adrian with a gracious smile. "Mr. Stone, it is a pleasure to see you. Lady Diana," she acknowledged with a nod. She addressed Amelia last. "And Miss–" she broke off, as though she had forgotten Amelia's name.

"Miss Amelia Fleming," Langley supplied. "A close family friend."

Mrs. Prescott silently entered the room, and Langley gestured her to the sofa next to Miss Hunt.

"Mrs. Hunt, Miss Hunt, I would like to introduce you to Mrs. Prescott," Langley said smoothly. "Mrs. Prescott, Mrs. Hunt and her daughter, Miss Hunt."

Mrs. Prescott stood and curtsied. Mrs. Hunt wasn't sure whether she was being insulted, as she recognized Mrs. Prescott as the housekeeper, but she lacked the courage to challenge her host and gave Mrs. Prescott a condescending nod.

"What brings you to the country, Mrs. Hunt?" Langley asked politely.

She blushed faintly. "Oh, there was a slight problem on the estate that Mr. Hunt wished to see to personally. So tedious to leave London in the middle of the Season, but it couldn't be helped. Being a landowner is a big responsibility, as I'm sure you know, my dear Lord Langley."

Langley, whose estate was ten times the size of the Hunts', nodded gravely. "Indeed it is, Mrs. Hunt."

"It is unusual to see you at Stonecroft at this time of year," Mrs. Hunt remarked.

Langley simply nodded, so Mrs. Hunt was forced to try again.

"Was there something particular that brought you here from London?"

"I believe it was the society, Mrs. Hunt," Langley said, with the ghost of a smile.

Mrs. Hunt didn't know what to make of that answer, so she decided to turn the subject. "At the risk of sounding like a proud mama, Lord Langley, I must tell you how fortunate I am in my daughter," she boasted. "Letitia can entertain herself equally well in the country as in town."

"She certainly can't entertain anyone else," Adrian muttered under his breath. Langley cast him a reproachful look.

"She doesn't like to put herself forward by speaking of her accomplishments, so I'm forced to do it for her," Mrs. Hunt continued. "She is a most accomplished needle-woman, and she also plays and sings."

"Indeed," Langley said politely. "We have a pianoforte in the next room, which I believe is quite good. Perhaps she would care to play for us now?"

Miss Hunt blushed. "Oh. Oh no, I couldn't. I haven't brought any music."

"I am fond of the pianoforte myself, and I have a wide selection of music," Diana contributed, with a mischievous twinkle in her eye. "I'm sure I could find a piece that you know, and I would be happy to turn the pages."

"Oh no, I couldn't," Miss Hunt said miserably. "I am not used to performing for strangers."

"But we are not strangers, Miss Hunt," said Langley gently. "We are close neighbours."

Mrs. Hunt turned to Mrs. Prescott. "I find I am thirsty after the drive. I wonder if we could have some tea?"

"Certainly," said Mrs. Prescott, and she rose to pull the bell before returning to her seat on the couch. A housemaid appeared, and Mrs. Prescott requested the tea. Mrs. Hunt looked at her in disbelief, at a loss to understand why the housekeeper was sitting on the sofa like a member of the household.

Tea arrived quickly, and Diana politely but firmly declined Mrs. Hunt's offer to pour it out.

When she had finished her tea, Mrs. Hunt walked to the window. "You have such a beautiful garden, Lord Langley." She turned to Diana. "Lady Diana, I wonder if you and Miss Fleming would care to take a walk with me?"

Diana looked at Amelia, who nodded. Although Langley had been perfectly polite, Amelia had learned to read his body language, and she could tell Mrs. Hunt was grating on his nerves.

"Yes, we will join you," Diana answered. "Miss Hunt, will you come too?"

Mrs. Hunt answered before her daughter could. "Thank you, Lady Diana, but Letitia's skin is so fair she can't tolerate more than a few minutes in the sun. It is such a bright day, she should not take the risk of a sunburn."

"Surely Diana could lend her a hat and a parasol," suggested Adrian, who was bored with the Hunts and couldn't understand why Mrs. Hunt would suggest a scheme that would leave her daughter alone with him and his brother.

"Oh, we wouldn't wish to put dear Lady Diana to any trouble," said Mrs. Hunt. "Don't worry, Mr. Stone, we won't be gone long." She swept out of the room with Amelia and Diana.

Langley, Adrian, and Miss Hunt were left staring at each other. Mrs. Prescott remained on the sofa next to Miss Hunt, quietly drinking tea.

Langley broke the silence. "I hope the problem that

brought your family back to the country was not a serious one, Miss Hunt," he said politely.

Miss Hunt blushed. "Oh, no, I don't think—I mean, Papa handles the estate business, of course, so I am not aware of the details. But I don't think it was serious, my lord."

"I am pleased to hear it," Langley said, with a gleam in his eye. "So you don't assist your father with the management of his estate?"

Miss Hunt, who suspected she was being mocked, turned an even deeper shade of red and fidgeted with the folds of her skirt.

"No, my lord," she finally answered.

"I suppose that would be unusual for a young lady," Langley mused.

"Yes, my lord," Miss Hunt answered. Adrian thought she looked like a trapped animal.

Langley took pity on her. "My sister has left several books on the table if you would like to do some reading while we wait for your mother to return."

Miss Hunt had never had a host suggest she read a book during a morning call, but after a moment's indecision, she saw the advantages of the idea. She picked up a book at random and opened it to a page in the middle. Langley leaned back against the sofa cushions and closed his eyes.

"Lady Diana, I'm ashamed to say I am fatigued," said Mrs. Hunt, after a single turn around the garden. "I think I'll return to the house."

"Certainly," said Diana politely. "I think we're all ready to go in."

"Oh no, Lady Diana," Mrs. Hunt protested. "It's such a beautiful day, I would hate for you to feel obliged to come indoors on my account. When I was your age, I was never indoors in the springtime." She turned and walked purposefully towards the house, at a brisk pace that belied her claim of fatigue.

"Insufferable woman!" Diana exclaimed when Mrs. Hunt was out of earshot. "I wish Robert would throw her out."

Amelia laughed, pleased to learn that Diana shared her opinion. "Why does Lord Langley tolerate her?" she asked curiously.

"I think it's partly habit," said Diana thoughtfully. "When Robert and I were growing up, Mama insisted that we be polite to the Hunts. But in the past few years, Mrs. Hunt has gotten worse, and even Mama wouldn't expect us to be civil to such a spiteful, scheming cat!" She shook her head. "Robert would deny it, but I think has a soft spot for Miss Hunt."

"I see," said Amelia, trying to keep her emotions from showing on her face. It made sense, really; how else could one explain Langley's tolerance for such an obnoxious visitor as Mrs. Hunt? She reflected that his feelings for Miss Hunt must be powerful if they induced him to tolerate her mother. Amelia thought Langley would quickly grow bored with a woman who agreed with everything he said, but she reminded herself that Lord Langley's choice of wife was none of her business. Miss Hunt was an attractive young lady, and if Lord Langley wanted an insipid wife, that was certainly his right.

When Mrs. Hunt returned to the sitting room, she was annoyed to find her host's eyes closed and her daughter staring at a book. Mrs. Prescott remained on the sofa, quietly drinking a cup of tea.

"Mrs. Prescott, I wonder if you could assist me with something?" she asked imperiously.

"What would that be, Mrs. Hunt?" Mrs. Prescott asked politely.

Mrs. Hunt lowered her voice. "It is a feminine matter, Mrs. Prescott," she said apologetically. "If you could just step into the hallway, I can explain."

"I'm sorry, Mrs. Hunt, but I can't do that," Mrs. Prescott said firmly.

"I beg your pardon?" asked Mrs. Hunt incredulously.

"I am unable to step into the hallway with you."

Mrs. Hunt turned toward Langley in disbelief, expecting him to instruct his housekeeper to assist her, but Langley still sat with his eyes closed. Adrian appeared to be trying hard not to laugh, and Mrs. Hunt knew better than to expect any help from him.

"My lord," she said loudly to Langley. The earl opened his eyes. "Ah, Mrs. Hunt, you have returned," he said politely. "Without Diana and Miss Fleming, I see."

"They are enjoying your beautiful garden, my lord," she told him. "But I have a small problem of a private nature, and I asked Mrs. Prescott to step into the hallway to assist me with it."

Langley nodded. "I see."

"She has refused to do so, my lord," Mrs. Hunt said,

expecting him to be shocked at his housekeeper's refusal to assist his guest.

"Well, it seems you have your answer."

"But my lord," Mrs. Hunt protested, unwilling to give up. "Surely she would help me if *you* asked her to do so."

"She might," said Langley. "But I'm afraid we'll never know, as I have no intention of asking her any such thing." A smile tugged at his lips. "Perhaps I could help you?"

Mrs. Hunt stood and acknowledged defeat. "No, my lord, I don't believe you could. I think it is time for Letitia and me to take our leave." She curtsied to Langley, who pulled the bell for Matthews.

When Matthews had closed the door firmly behind the ladies, Mrs. Prescott rose, nodded to Langley, and left the room.

"I say, Robert, that was unusual," said Adrian. "Did you instruct Mrs. Prescott to annoy her?"

"Mrs. Prescott was playing the critically important role of chaperone," Langley explained. "She knows that if I'm trapped into marriage with Miss Hunt, she will be forced to seek a new position."

Adrian looked surprised. "Is that what Mrs. Hunt was trying to do? Trap you?" Understanding dawned. "And you told Mrs. Prescott not to leave your side, so you wouldn't be caught in a compromising situation. That's very clever, Robert."

Langley shook his head. "I told Mrs. Prescott not to leave Miss Hunt. Don't forget, Adrian, Mrs. Hunt might try to entrap *you*."

Adrian's mouth fell open. "You're right," he said, much struck. "Thank you, Robert. But really, you couldn't have told Mrs. Prescott that you would dismiss her if she failed. That's too harsh, even for you."

"Oh, I wouldn't dismiss her, Adrian. But can you imagine what her position would be with Miss Hunt as mistress of Stonecroft? Mrs. Hunt would try to interfere in everything, and Mrs. Prescott doesn't suffer fools. I have no doubt she would seek employment elsewhere."

"Do you know, Robert," said Adrian thoughtfully. "I doubt there was ever a problem at the Hunts' estate. Mrs. Hunt probably just used it as an excuse for coming to the country. Why, she might have come to Kent just to see you!"

"Quite likely," Langley agreed.

"You knew this?" asked Adrian, surprised.

Langley sighed. "I suspected it, Adrian."

"But why do you tolerate it?" asked Adrian, looking confused. "Surely you could give her a setdown that would send her the message. Tell her that her daughter is an antidote with the personality of a doorknob, and that under no circumstances will you offer her marriage."

"I fear I lack your eloquence, Adrian."

Adrian snorted. "You could send a message by raising an eyebrow and staring at her through your quizzing glass. That would unsettle anyone."

Langley nodded. "It might be kinder, but I can't bring myself to do it. Mrs. Hunt would blame her daughter. Completely unjustly, of course." He sighed. "Perhaps I'm too soft-hearted."

Adrian laughed. "You, Robert? Soft-hearted?"

Langley raised an eyebrow and stared at his brother through his quizzing glass. "Do you find it humorous, Adrian?"

"Maybe a little," said Adrian bravely. "So, how do you mean to deal with it? Are you just going to tolerate these visits until she gives up?"

Langley smiled. "Maybe I'll send her a message by marrying someone else."

Twenty-Three

Notes from the diary of the Earl of Langley

I think I've had more visitors at Stonecroft in the past week than I had in London in the past month. The next time I'm shot, I intend to recuperate on the Continent.

The following afternoon, Amelia was enjoying the afternoon sunshine that streamed through the sitting room window and finding it hard to focus on *Practical Management of the Modern Estate*. A commotion in the entrance hall was a welcome distraction.

"Please. I just want to see him, and then I'll go." It was a young woman's voice, clear and determined, with a French accent.

"The earl is not at home," Matthews said in damping tones.

"Then I will wait."

"I'm afraid that won't be possible," said Matthews, who had a poor opinion of young women who showed up at Stonecroft without invitation or chaperone.

"Please," she said again. "Just tell him Celestine is here. If he doesn't want to see me, I'll go."

By now, Amelia had abandoned the pretence of reading and crept to the door of the sitting room. When she heard the name Celestine, she decided to take a role in the drama and strode forward to find Matthews confronting a stylish young woman wearing a fashionable rose-pink pelisse. Despite her appearance of fragility, there was a steely look in her fine blue eyes, and she appeared to be contemplating a dodge around Matthews to gain entry into the house.

"Celestine," Amelia said warmly, as though greeting a long-lost friend. "What a lovely surprise."

Celestine had the presence of mind to smile, nod, and remain silent.

Amelia turned to Matthews, who was looking at her suspiciously.

"Matthews, Celestine is a dear friend of Lady Diana's, and of mine," she said confidently. "We will take tea in the blue sitting room."

Matthews, who had a good idea that Celestine's acquaintance had been with the earl and not with his sister, reflected that he had the most difficult position of any butler in England. Not only had Langley's mistress shown up on the doorstep, but his unorthodox houseguest was now claiming acquaintance with her, and Matthews didn't know what his capricious employer would want him to do. Langley's recent behaviour had been positively eccentric.

As Matthews dithered, Amelia took action. She took Celestine by the arm, towed her to the sitting room, and closed the door.

"*Je m'appelle Amelia,*" she began kindly, and Celestine brightened at the sound of her mother tongue. When Matthews brought in the tea tray ten minutes later, he was surprised to hear them conversing in French.

"Tell me the truth, is he very ill?" Celestine asked anxiously.

Amelia smiled reassuringly. "He was quite unwell, but he's recovering." She wondered what sort of gossip was circulating in London. "What have you heard?"

"So many things," Celestine exclaimed. "People are saying he was thrown from his horse, which is *incroyable,* because I've never seen a better rider. I also heard he was shot while single-handedly defending a lady from a gang of footpads."

Amelia mentally cursed Freddie Micklebury, who she guessed had been the source of that particular fable. "That sounds very silly," she said dismissively.

Celestine nodded. "I've even heard he was shot in a duel, and that is the most ridiculous story of all."

"Why is it ridiculous?" asked Amelia curiously. "Because he's such a good shot?"

"Oh, I'm sure he's an excellent shot, for he's a magnificent sportsman," Celestine agreed. "But it's absurd to think of him taking part in a duel in the first place. He is not a man ruled by emotion."

"I suppose not," Amelia said thoughtfully.

"So you must understand how worried I've been. I wish you would tell me what happened."

"He was shot in the shoulder," Amelia said carefully. "I am not at liberty to explain how it happened, but it's healing, and he gets stronger every day. The shoulder still pains him, but you would never know it to look at him."

Amelia could see the relief in the other woman's eyes.

"He is special to you," Amelia said. It was a statement rather than a question.

"Yes," said Celestine. "He didn't love me, but he was kind to me. Respected me, and that's unusual in my situation." She gave a funny little laugh. "I loved him."

"But you and he–" Amelia broke off, searching for the words. She knew the conversation was highly inappropriate, but she couldn't stop herself.

"He said goodbye," Celestine explained. "I wondered if there was someone else, but he may have just grown bored with me. *C'est la vie.*" She smiled wistfully.

They were so absorbed in their conversation that they hadn't heard the doorknob turn, or noticed Langley standing frozen in the doorway. It wasn't until Adrian came along, clapped his brother on the shoulder, and said, "Lord, Robert, why are you standing in the doorway like a statue?" that the ladies looked up in dismay.

Langley sighed in resignation, then walked over to Celestine, who had quickly risen from her chair. After the initial relief of seeing Langley, who was looking perfectly fit, she recalled the awkwardness of her position, and stood staring at her feet. Langley set her fears to rest by kissing her on both cheeks in the French style, and giving her a warm smile.

MISS FLEMING FALLS IN LOVE

Adrian walked over with a gleam in his eye. "Robert, I humbly request an introduction to our beautiful guest."

Langley rolled his eyes. "Mademoiselle Dubois, this is my brother, Mr. Adrian Stone."

Adrian made an exaggerated bow. "Pleasure to meet you, Mademoiselle Dubois." His gaze fell on the delicate pearl necklace at her throat, and his eyes narrowed. "I say, Robert, that looks an awful lot like the string of pearls you bought for Celestine."

"It is the string of pearls I bought for Celestine," Langley said, with a speaking look at his brother.

Adrian flushed and stared at Celestine, who was smiling at Langley with quiet dignity. "Forgive me," she said. "I know I shouldn't have come, but I heard such stories that I had to reassure myself that you were well. Now that I see you are, I'll take my leave."

"How are you travelling?" Langley asked her. Despite the awkward situation that she had created, he was touched that she had cared enough to come.

"I came by stage, then hired a chaise at the Bull and Bear," she explained. "I asked the post-boys to wait."

"Send them back to the Bull," said Langley. "Morgan will drive you back to London."

"No, thank you, my lord," she said simply, with a little smile. "You are very kind, but I prefer to manage on my own."

Langley saw her safely installed in the hired chaise. When he returned to the sitting room, he found Adrian teaching Amelia to make card houses.

"Putting your time to good use, I see," he remarked.

Adrian smiled at him. "Robert. Don't think you'll get

away without explaining yourself. Why did your bird of paradise come to Stonecroft?"

Langley glared at him and inclined his head in Amelia's direction. Adrian flushed. "Beg your pardon, Miss Fleming. You seem so much like one of the family that I sometimes forget you're a lady."

"I'm not sure if that helpful comment was more insulting to Miss Fleming or to our family," said Langley wryly.

Amelia was looking at them in confusion. "What is a bird of paradise?"

Langley sighed. He had hoped that the expression would pass unnoticed, but figured he should be thankful that Adrian had not said worse. He knew that if he didn't answer, there was a good chance that Amelia would ask Diana to explain the term, and he could only guess what Diana would say.

"Adrian was referring to the fact that I enjoyed a close relationship with Mademoiselle Dubois for several years," he said, wondering if the vague explanation would be enough.

Amelia's brow cleared. "Oh. You mean she was your mistress," she said matter-of-factly. "Yes, I guessed that at the outset."

Adrian burst out laughing. "As I said, Robert," he said when he caught his breath. "Miss Fleming is just like one of the family."

"She is very beautiful," Amelia said frankly. "But you said you enjoyed a close relationship with her. Does that mean you no longer do?"

Adrian roared with laughter, and Amelia blushed with embarrassment. "I'm sorry," she said contritely. "I shouldn't have asked you that, my lord. I spoke without thinking." She took a step toward the door.

"There's no need to apologize, Miss Fleming," Langley said kindly. "If you hadn't asked, Adrian would have. To answer your question, I respect Celestine, but I no longer enjoy a close relationship with her."

"Why did you break it off?" Adrian asked curiously. "I mean, with her looks–"

"None of your business," said Langley curtly, before his brother could say something else indiscreet.

~

In a ballroom in London, Lucas Kincaid found himself cornered by a diminutive lady in a plain red gown. She was in her early fifties and plump, with greying dark hair and merry brown eyes.

"Good evening, Lucas," she said warmly. She didn't stand on ceremony, for she had known him since his boyhood when he had played with her son at Stonecroft.

"Lady Langley," he said, in some surprise. The last he heard, she had been in Scotland visiting her daughter.

"Yes. I was hoping to find you here."

"Ah," said Kincaid noncommittally. "I hope Mary is well?"

"She is very well, and so is the babe," Lady Langley said proudly. "They have another boy, and have named him John Henry."

"Congratulations," said Kincaid, wondering how long he could keep her on the relatively safe subject of her grandson.

"Thank you." Lady Langley smiled. "I have been hearing some very interesting stories about my son."

"Adrian?" Kincaid dissembled.

She smiled. "I hear so many interesting stories about Adrian that they are no longer remarkable. I am referring to Robert, as I think you know."

"Ah," said Kincaid again. "Yes, Robert was obliged to go to Stonecroft. I believe he's still there."

"What obliged him?"

"Estate business," Kincaid improvised. Lucas Kincaid had been on the *ton* for over ten years and was generally held to be a clever fellow. He couldn't understand why Lady Langley, with her laughing eyes and gentle smile, made him feel as green as a stammering schoolboy.

"I see," she said. "I hope it's not a serious matter. Mr. Pettigrew is so capable, I can't imagine a problem that he couldn't handle."

"Nothing serious," said Kincaid reassuringly. "But Pettigrew wished to consult him, and I believe Robert wanted a change of scenery. So he went to Stonecroft."

"I see. And Diana is there too?"

"Yes," said Kincaid miserably, wondering why Lady Langley bothered to ask questions to which she already knew the answers.

"Did Pettigrew wish to consult with her as well? Or did she also want a change of scenery?"

"I'm not sure."

"And she's taken a friend," Lady Langley mused. "Miss Fleming, is it?"

Kincaid nodded.

"That must be an interesting house party, given Robert's history with her family," she remarked.

"Rational or not, many women would hold a grudge. Miss Fleming must be a remarkable lady."

"She certainly is."

Lady Langley looked him in the eye. "Does Robert think so?"

Kincaid could tell that she was circling near the truth, and knew the last thing Langley would want was his mother meddling in his love affair.

"He hardly mentioned her," he said dismissively.

Lady Langley raised an eyebrow. "That's interesting. Perhaps he doesn't find her as offensive as the other young ladies of the *ton*."

Kincaid was starting to sweat. "As I said, ma'am, he rarely mentioned her. The last I heard him speak of her, he described her as a red-headed termagant."

"I see," she said. "I would like to meet her. Do you think she's planning a long stay at Stonecroft?"

"I don't know," said Kincaid honestly.

Lady Langley smiled. "Well, Lucas, it's always a pleasure to see you. I won't keep you from the dancing any longer."

Twenty-Four

Notes from the diary of the Earl of Langley

I'm not sure whose idea it was to have Amelia spend time with Pettigrew, but I'm beginning to think it was a mistake.

For one thing, he's far too good. I'm afraid he will corrupt her with his goodness. Miss Fleming has an unusually lively mind, and she needs a companion who will appreciate it. I would hate to see her become as boring as the other young ladies of the ton.

Miss Fleming also needs a man who won't allow her to run roughshod over him. Pettigrew is far too young. Why, he's barely older than Amelia herself! Amelia should be guided by a man with more experience and maturity.

She and Pettigrew seem to spend hours discussing such topics as farm machinery and crop rotation, and I don't understand how they can find so much to say about it. I've always thought of myself as a knowledgeable landlord, but this is far beyond me. I know it's Pettigrew's job, but that seems like a poor excuse. They will improve the productivity of my estate, but I can't bring myself to care.

Also, Pettigrew's eyes are too blue and his hair is too blond. I don't know how Amelia tolerates his company.

∽

"This is truly a magnificent estate," Amelia said to Pettigrew as they returned to the stables after a morning spent meeting with the earl's tenant farmers. Stonecroft looked beautiful in the spring sunshine. The fields were green, leaves were budding on the trees, and tulips and crocuses were starting to bloom in the well-tended gardens that bordered the house.

Pettigrew nodded. "I'm fortunate to have the management of it."

"It's remarkable to think that one man owns all of this," said Amelia, who couldn't help but compare Langley's estate to Cliveden Manor. Much as she loved Cliveden Manor, Stonecroft was on a completely different scale.

"I think Lord Langley appreciates it." There was something about Amelia that invited confidences, so Pettigrew continued. "You know, Miss Fleming, when I first came to work here, I didn't know what to expect. I mean, people call him the Stoneheart."

"People who don't know him," said Amelia, a little defensively.

"Yes, exactly," agreed Pettigrew. "I was nervous he would be unreasonable, but I had no alternative, and positions for land agents aren't easy to find. But I've found Langley to be one of the most sensible men I've ever met. Generous too. He looks after his people, and never quibbles about the cost of repairs to the tenants' properties, or the bill from the apothecary when one of his staff is sick. When he's here alone, he often asks me to dine with him, and talks to me like an equal. There's no pretension."

"You make him sound like a paragon," said Amelia lightly.

Pettigrew smiled. "He's not a paragon. But I think he's a good man."

Langley watched them through the window as they emerged from the stables, still deep in conversation and apparently in perfect understanding. As he watched Amelia smile up at his land agent, his opinion of Mr. Pettigrew was far less charitable than Pettigrew's was of him.

~

Later that afternoon, Pettigrew found Langley in his study. "My lord, I wonder if I might have a word," he asked bravely.

"Yes, of course, Pettigrew. What's troubling you?"

"It's about Miss Fleming, my lord."

"I thought it might be," said Langley.

Pettigrew swallowed. "Well, you must appreciate, sir, that her situation here is quite irregular. I don't really understand why she came in the first place."

"Her brother put a hole in my shoulder, and she felt obligated to patch it up," Langley explained bluntly.

"Yes. But your shoulder has healed."

"Hardly healed, Pettigrew. It still pains me if I exert myself."

Pettigrew cast his eyes over Langley, who sat behind his desk and appeared to be the picture of health. Unbeknownst to the earl, Pettigrew had seen him riding early that morning, and he had handled his spirited horse with his usual ease. "Yes, my lord," he acknowledged. "But fortunately, you are out of danger. So I don't understand why Miss Fleming is still here."

"She feels guilty about the injury, and is trying to make reparation by helping with the management of my estate."

"Have you been dissatisfied with my performance, my lord?" asked Pettigrew.

"You're doing an excellent job, Pettigrew, but there's always room for improvement."

"I also wondered about her fiancé, Mr. Garland," Pettigrew continued.

"Now we reach the heart of the matter," said Langley.

"I beg your pardon?"

"Nothing. What were you wondering, Pettigrew?"

"From some of the things Miss Fleming has said, I'm concerned that Garland doesn't value her as he should. She's spent the better part of a month at your country estate, with only your younger sister for a chaperone. Why, if she were mine, I would have dragged her away long before now, hole in your shoulder or no!" He flushed. "I'm sorry, my lord, but it's the truth."

"No apologies necessary, Pettigrew. I would have done the same."

Encouraged, Pettigrew continued. "My lord, I fear Mr. Garland is a fool."

"Undoubtedly," Langley agreed.

"And it seems wrong for a lovely young lady like Miss Fleming to be promised to a man like him. If she were released from her engagement, I–"

"Pettigrew, your sentiments do you credit," Langley interrupted. "You may safely leave the matter in my hands."

Understanding finally dawned on Pettigrew. He gave the earl a penetrating look. "So it's like that, is it?"

Langley nodded. "It's like that, Pettigrew."

Amelia, who had come to ask if Langley was ready for their usual game of chess, heard their voices and stopped outside the study door.

"To tell you the truth, Pettigrew, Miss Fleming is driving me to distraction," Langley confessed. "I can't focus on running the house or the estate, but it doesn't really matter because she's taken over their management. I won't be able to focus in the House of Lords, but that's unlikely to matter either because she'll insist on writing my speeches." He shook his head. "I'll end up spouting a lot of liberal claptrap in defence of the working classes."

Pettigrew hid a smile. Although the Stones were a prominent Tory family, Pettigrew had long suspected that Langley held liberal views himself.

"She's turned my life upside down," Langley continued. "In short, she's the most mischievous, meddlesome, *maddening* female I've ever met!"

Outside the door, Amelia decided she had heard enough. She rushed off down the hall, thereby missing Langley's next sentence.

"I don't think I can live without her." Langley raked a

hand through his hair with all the confusion of a man in the thrall of a violent emotion for the first time in his life.

Pettigrew smiled sympathetically at his employer. "Good luck, my lord."

∼

Amelia was unusually quiet at dinner and went to bed early, but found herself unable to sleep. The knowledge of Langley's true opinion of her weighed heavily upon her spirit. She knew she wasn't a conventional young lady, and her mother had always complained she had a tendency to be bossy, but she had always seen herself as someone who did what had to be done. She had thought Langley appreciated her efforts to help with his estate, and hearing him describe her as mischievous and meddlesome wounded her deeply.

It was clear that she would have to leave Stonecroft, but she had no easy way to do so. Amelia had no money of her own, and her pride would not allow her to ask Langley to fund her transportation. She decided to write to William at Cliveden Manor and ask him to bring her home. It would take several days for a letter to reach him and at least two days more for him to travel to Stonecroft, but there was nothing else to be done.

Amelia had noticed that Lord Langley was often the first to arrive at the breakfast table, so the next morning she deliberately came down late, hoping to avoid a tête-à-tête with her host. She was dismayed to find Langley there alone, drinking coffee and sorting through the morning post. He appeared to be absorbed in his task, and Amelia tried to retreat quietly.

"Good morning, Miss Fleming," Langley said pleasantly. Amelia froze in the doorway.

"G-good morning, my lord," she stammered.

Langley gestured to the chafing dishes on the sideboard. "There's plenty of food left, Miss Fleming, but if you would prefer to have something made fresh, it can be easily done." She searched his words for sarcasm, but found none.

"Thank you," she said, and quickly put a slice of toast on a plate before taking a seat across from him.

"You slept late this morning," Langley remarked.

"Not as late as Adrian and Diana."

"Would you believe that they have already breakfasted? They have gone off to play Pall-mall."

Langley had expected that news to bring a smile to her face, but she continued to stare at her plate, listlessly spreading jam on her toast.

"You didn't want to join them, my lord?" Amelia asked.

"I have other plans for the day." Amelia had the uncomfortable suspicion that he had been waiting for her.

Langley handed her a letter. "This came for you, Miss Fleming." She opened it immediately, grateful for the distraction.

Miss Fleming,

I have recently heard some shocking news about your stay at Stonecroft, namely, that you have been engaging in an improper relationship with the Earl of Langley.

I'm sure you understand that my wife must be a model of

decorum and a lady of unimpeachable virtue. I therefore regret to inform you that I consider our betrothal to be at an end.

Sincerely,
George Garland

Despite her efforts to trick herself into thinking that marriage to Garland was a desirable thing, Amelia's first reaction was a feeling of relief. As the implications of the message sank in, however, her relief was replaced by despair. She had now been jilted twice, and not only was her future uncertain, she had no way to pay the debt to the earl. William's visit had cast Langley's actions in a new light, and she now believed that he had treated her family honourably; indeed, with far more kindness than they deserved.

Had Langley renewed his offer to forgive the debt, William would probably still be gambling, and before long, his gambling losses would have exceeded their father's. The duel had shocked William into taking responsibility for his actions, and Langley had paid the price for it, with a wound to his shoulder that had threatened his life. At one time Amelia had tricked herself into thinking he had done it because he cared for her, but the conversation between Langley and Mr. Pettigrew had put an end to that fantasy. It seemed that Langley was just an honourable man.

"Anything of importance, Miss Fleming?" Langley asked. He could see she was miserable, but didn't know the reason for it.

"No," she said slowly, barely able to think. "Yes. I don't know." She looked up and met his eyes, expecting a look of mockery at her incoherent response, and saw only kindness there.

Amelia took a deep breath. "Mr. Garland has written to end our engagement."

"I see." A smile flickered across Langley's face before he schooled his features into a sympathetic expression. "This is a surprise. Did he give a reason?"

Amelia realized that if Langley learned her stay at Stonecroft had compromised her reputation, he would likely make her an offer of marriage. He was an honourable man, and he would see it as his duty. At one time she had let herself hope Langley was coming to care for her, but that fantasy had ended when she overheard his conversation with Pettigrew. Amelia was determined she wouldn't let his sense of honour lead him into marriage with a woman he considered mischievous and meddlesome. Lord Langley had done enough for the Fleming family.

"He decided we wouldn't suit," she lied. "I think he may have found someone else."

"Ah," he said. "It seems it wasn't meant to be. Shall I find Diana for you?"

"No," she said. "If you'll excuse me, my lord, I have a headache." She went up to her room to consider what to do next.

～

That afternoon, Amelia decided to talk to Diana. The end of her engagement gave her an excuse for wanting to return to her family, and she hoped Diana could lend her enough money to get to London. She knew Diana would likely suggest that she go in Langley's carriage, which would force her to think of a reason why she wished to go by stage instead, but she resolved to deal with that problem when it arose.

She had hoped to find Diana alone, and was disappointed to find her in the sitting room with both Langley and Adrian.

"Miss Fleming," said Langley, rising to greet her. "I hope you're feeling better?"

"Yes, thank you, my lord," she said dully. His concerned expression made her uncomfortable, and Amelia felt as though he could read her thoughts.

Distraction arrived in the form of Mr. Templeton, who walked purposefully into the room with Matthews hot on his heels. Templeton's eyes swept the room until they landed on Diana, and he rushed toward her, oblivious to the interested stares of the others in the room.

"Come back to me," he said simply. "I know you don't love me, and I know I don't deserve you, but I've missed you terribly. I need you."

Diana stared at him in shock.

"Giles?" she whispered softly. "I thought you were in Vienna."

"I never went to Vienna," he told her. "I would have been useless there, just as I've been useless in London. I haven't been able to think of anything but you. Come back to me."

Diana looked like couldn't find the words to express her emotions, and she threw herself into her husband's arms.

"This is as good as a play," Adrian remarked. "Reminds me of *The Taming of the Shrew*."

Templeton looked up and glared at him, but Diana had no attention to spare for anyone but her husband.

Langley sighed. "Nice to see you, Templeton," he said dryly. "Would you care to make use of my study?"

Templeton was so focused on his wife that he didn't hear the earl's question. He released Diana from his arms so he could look her in the eye.

"Will you come back to me?" he asked hopefully.

"Giles, I never left you!" she said with a joyful laugh. "You see, Robert got shot, and then he needed a chaperone, and–"

"You're here to chaperone Robert?" Templeton asked incredulously.

"Better than a play," commented Adrian.

"Of course I'm not here to chaperone Robert," said Diana impatiently. "But Robert was shot in a duel, and Miss Fleming was worried the wound would turn putrid, so she came along to tend to it. She needed a chaperone, of course, so they stopped on the way to Stonecroft and asked me to come."

Templeton still looked confused. "I'm not sure I'll ever understand this affair, but as long as you haven't left me, I don't care," he said. "But you've given enough of your time to your brother. Langley looks well enough to manage his own affairs. You're *my* wife, and I need you. Let's go home."

"Yes, Giles," said Diana meekly, as Templeton put an arm around her shoulder and led her to the door.

Langley turned to Matthews, who was still standing inside the door to the sitting room.

"Did you enjoy the performance, Matthews?" he asked pleasantly.

"I'm sorry, my lord," said Matthews apologetically. "He just swept by me and was inside before I knew what was happening. But if I understood correctly, he is Lady Diana's husband, so you would not have wanted me to deny him entry."

Langley sighed. "I'm beginning to think it's impossible to deny anyone entry. I thought this was a private estate, but it seems I'm running a social club."

"Quite so, my lord," Matthews agreed.

Twenty-Five

The following day, Langley asked Amelia to join him for a picnic by the river, and although Amelia found his company uncomfortable, she couldn't think of a good reason to turn him down. She was adamant, however, that Langley's shoulder was still not up to the weight of the picnic basket, and since Langley refused to let her carry it herself, they reached an impasse. In the end it was Timms, who had been up at sunrise to dress the earl for his morning ride, who was enlisted to carry the basket to and from the picnic spot. It was a beautiful day, Langley was in good spirits, and Amelia was almost able to forget that he thought her mischievous and meddlesome.

They walked back from the river at a leisurely pace, and were on the front steps when they saw a purple travelling carriage sweep up the drive. Amelia's heart sank when she recognized the carriage as Garland's, and she was gripped by the fear that he had changed his mind and wished to resume their engagement. She had become resigned to the idea of life as a spinster, and she didn't think she could bring herself to marry Mr. Garland.

Langley recognized the carriage at the same time that Amelia did, and his first impulse was to hide Amelia and throw Garland off his property. He feared Garland had realized the obvious, that ending his engagement to Miss Fleming had been a colossal error, and he should do anything possible to win her back.

"You don't have to talk to him if you don't want to," Langley assured Amelia. "In fact, it might be better if you don't. Why don't you go inside and let me deal with him?"

For her part, Amelia feared that Garland might challenge Langley to a duel, and that Langley might oblige him. She couldn't bear the thought of Langley taking part in another duel, especially as he hadn't fully recovered from his shoulder injury.

"No, my lord," she said resolutely. "I'm sure he's here to talk to me, and it will be simpler if I tell him we have nothing to discuss."

"Miss Fleming, I insist," Langley said firmly. "Please go inside, and I'll join you shortly."

The appearance of Matthews put an end to their debate. "I didn't know you were expecting a guest, my lord," Matthews said blithely.

Langley glared at his butler. "I wasn't expecting this visitor, Matthews," he said caustically. "If he had informed me of his intention to come, I would have told him to stay away. But if you think you can chase him away with an unhappy look on your face, you have my permission to do so. Miss Fleming and I will go inside, and you can inform the visitor that we are not at home. Come,

Miss Fleming." He took Amelia's arm and gently turned her toward the front door.

"But my lord, that will be awkward," protested Matthews. "He is getting out of his carriage, and he must have already seen you–"

"Matthews, I employ a butler to deal with precisely this sort of awkwardness," said Langley over his shoulder. "If you are unequal to it, I will ask Timms."

Although jealousy of Timms gave Matthews a strong incentive to do as Langley instructed, he still hesitated to turn the travellers away. "My lord, they appear to be people of quality, and they must have had a long journey to get here. Shouldn't we allow them to refresh themselves?"

"People of quality, Matthews?" Langley asked, surprised to hear that there were more than one. He could not fathom why Garland would bring a friend on such an errand.

"Yes, my lord," affirmed Matthews. "A gentleman and a lady."

Amelia turned and saw Mr. Garland, resplendent in a many-caped travelling coat and yellow pantaloons. On his arm, in a scarlet gown more suited to a ballroom than a carriage, was her mother.

Amelia ran to her mother and embraced her nervously. She assumed her mother had heard the rumours of impropriety between her and Lord Langley, but she didn't know whether her mother hoped to salvage the betrothal to Garland, or to shame Langley into offering Amelia marriage. If her objective was a match with Langley, Amelia had no doubt her mother would succeed. Once Langley heard that Amelia's reputation had been compromised at Stonecroft, his sense of honour would do the rest. Amelia decided she had to get her mother and Garland away from Stonecroft before they could speak to the earl, but she couldn't think of a way to do it.

Seconds later, Langley joined them, and Amelia realized the situation was out of her control.

"Lord Langley, may I present my mother, Lady Cliveden," she said politely.

"Oh no," Garland interrupted proudly. "She is Lady Marguerite Garland now. We were married by special licence yesterday."

After the events of the past month, Amelia had thought that nothing could ever shock her again, but her mother and Garland had proven her wrong. She stood staring at her mother, bereft of speech.

Langley broke the silence. "It's a pleasure to meet you, Lady Marguerite," he said smoothly, appearing genuinely pleased with the news. "Garland, you have my heartfelt congratulations."

Adrian, who had seen the carriage from the window, came out to investigate the newcomers. He stared at Garland suspiciously before recognition dawned.

"I remember you from the ball," Adrian said. "You're the one who's betrothed to Miss Fleming!"

"He is no longer betrothed to Miss Fleming," Langley said curtly.

"Then why is he here?" Adrian asked bluntly.

"Because I am married to her mother," Garland announced proudly, without a trace of embarrassment. "We are on our way to Paris for our honeymoon."

"You know, *chérie*, this is quite a charming estate,"

Amelia's mother commented. "Obviously nothing to compare with what Garland Castle will be, but there is definite potential." She gave Langley a measuring look. "If the earl wasn't so rude and disagreeable, you could marry him."

Amelia wished she could disappear. "Mama," she said in embarrassment.

"I say," said Adrian, insulted on his brother's behalf.

"What?" asked her mother. "I'm sure that's how you described him. As I recall, you sent a letter begging me to come home because the fishmonger was cheating you and you needed help to deal with the rude and arrogant earl."

Amelia could hardly bear to meet Langley's eyes, but when she did, they twinkled with unholy amusement.

"My lord, I can see how that might *seem* like an insult," she began, trying to think of a good explanation.

"It certainly does, Miss Fleming," Langley said. "I had hoped to rank above the fishmonger on your list of problems."

"Oh, you did," Amelia said truthfully.

"And I agree that there is no fault to be found with his appearance," mused her mother.

"Did you indeed write that, Miss Fleming?" Langley asked. "I'm flattered."

"It's a strange thing," said her mother. "His manners seem perfectly nice today. Eccentric, to be sure, but I don't think I would call him rude."

"I say," Adrian said again. "I think you're the one being rude. If you think it's acceptable to come to a man's house and call him rude and eccentric, you have some very strange notions of politeness."

"Come, Mama," said Amelia, taking her mother's arm and leading her away from the others. "Let me show you the gardens."

"I suppose I should congratulate you, Mama," said Amelia, when they were out of earshot of the others.

"Thank you," said her mother distractedly. She gazed critically at Amelia's face. "You're looking well, but I believe you have twice as many freckles as you did when I saw you last. The sun is truly horrid for a complexion like yours. What do you use on your face?"

"I wash it with soap, Mama," said Amelia, already bored with the topic. Her mother recoiled in shock.

"Oh no, dear. Let me give you some of my Denmark Lotion."

"Mama, I don't have time for Denmark Lotion," said Amelia impatiently.

Her mother bristled. "Really, Amelia, I don't know how you expect to be married if you don't look after your complexion."

"I don't expect to be married," said Amelia tartly. "I've been jilted twice and I have no dowry."

"*Chérie*, there's no need to be pessimistic."

But for once, Amelia was inclined to be pessimistic. Her problems seemed to have grown to an unmanageable size.

"Mama, when Mr. Garland asked me to marry him, he agreed to pay William forty thousand pounds as a settlement."

Her mother looked surprised. "I can't believe he agreed to that," she said dismissively. "But it's no longer important, as you're no longer going to marry him."

"Yes," said Amelia. "But William was going to use that money to pay the debt to the earl."

Her mother shook her head. "All this talk about debts! You are obsessed, Amelia, and it's not healthy. The debt was your Papa's, so I don't know why you and William are so troubled by it."

"It's a matter of honour, Mama."

"But that's ridiculous!" said her mother. "The debt was incurred by your father, and as your father is dead, he is no longer concerned about whether he is honourable or dishonourable. If Lord Langley keeps raising the subject, I consider it very dishonourable of him! It's not polite to talk about such things in company, and it's clear he doesn't need the money."

"Yes, Mama," Amelia said, realizing there was nothing to be gained from further discussion of the debt they owed Langley. "There is also the question of investments in Cliveden Manor. The home farm could be far more profitable with an investment in better machinery, and–" She broke off when she realized that her mother was staring at her in confusion.

"But Cliveden Manor belongs to William," her mother said.

"Yes."

"So it has nothing to do with Mr. Garland," her mother said decisively. "Really, Amelia, the boy has to learn to make his own way in the world."

"I suppose," said Amelia. "But it seems like miserable luck, inheriting an entailed estate with a mountain of debt." Amelia knew her mother's spendthrift nature was largely to blame, as it was her debts that had motivated her father to gamble.

"Here's what I'll do," declared her mother. "Mr. Garland has agreed to give me a thousand pounds a year as pin money. Whatever I don't spend, I'll give to William. Isn't that a generous scheme?"

"Very generous, Mama," said Amelia with resignation, for she knew that no part of the pin money would go unspent. Her mother would be surprised when there was no money left at the end of each quarter, and would appease her conscience with the argument that she wanted to help her children but was simply unable to do so. Amelia was tempted to give the new Mrs. Garland her honest opinion of her performance as a mother, but experience had taught her that it would be futile.

Adrian had returned to the house, and Langley took the opportunity for a private talk with Garland. "I must say, Garland, it's a foul thing to do to a girl." Had Garland not been married he would have hesitated to criticize him, for fear that he would renew his pursuit of Amelia, but now that Garland was safely hitched, Langley felt he could speak his mind.

Garland looked surprised. "I think any man would have done the same under the circumstances."

Langley raised an eyebrow. "Offered marriage to a girl and then married her mother? You're the first man I know who has done so, but I admit we move in different circles."

Garland had the grace to blush. "No, I don't mean marrying her mother. But that was beyond my control, you know," he said matter-of-factly. "I mean, I just looked at her and—well." He gestured in the direction of his wife. "You can see for yourself."

Langley glanced at Mrs. Garland and saw a vain and

selfish woman clinging desperately to the vestiges of her youth. There was certainly nothing to explain why a man would jilt a beautiful young girl like Amelia.

"But the decision to end the engagement to Miss Fleming was unrelated to my wish to marry her mother," Garland continued.

Langley raised an eyebrow and stared at him skeptically.

"In fact," Garland continued nervously, "that's something I wanted to talk to you about."

Langley looked more skeptical still. "I can't imagine what you think I could have to say about your engagement," he said, conveniently forgetting that he had opened the subject.

"But you're the reason the engagement ended."

Langley stared at Garland in disbelief. "I beg your pardon?"

Garland was finding the earl's stare decidedly uncomfortable. "I thought you knew," he said defensively. "I explained it all to Miss Fleming in my letter. I had heard, you see, that there had been—er—improprieties here at Stonecroft."

"Improprieties?" asked Langley. At that moment, he looked more like an icicle than a man, with an expression so forbidding that Garland could not imagine him engaging in improprieties with anyone. Garland understood why people called him the Stoneheart.

"Between you and Miss Fleming," confirmed Garland, who was beginning to sweat.

Then Langley's expression changed, and he laughed. "But that's ridiculous," he said. "Miss Fleming is here as a companion to my sister, Mrs. Templeton." He neglected to mention that his sister had returned to London the previous day. "All the proprieties have been strictly observed. Who was spiteful enough to make such an absurd suggestion?"

"As Miss Fleming's step-papa, I am pleased to hear it," said Garland, ignoring the earl's request that he name the source of the rumour. Langley cringed at the reminder that Garland was, indeed, Amelia's step-papa, but consoled himself with the thought that this relationship was far preferable to that of Amelia's husband.

"I have an obligation to the girl, you know, and that was one of the reasons for our visit," Garland continued. "I wished to ensure she was being treated with the respect she deserves." He winked. "That's not to say that I wouldn't look the other way if you were having a little fun with the chit, but nothing that would compromise her chance of marriage." He looked at Amelia, who was talking to her mother in the garden. "She's looking very well. The country air must agree with her."

Langley gritted his teeth. Garland had no idea how close he came to being knocked out. Langley was confident he could take him in a fistfight, and only held back because he knew a brawl would distress Amelia.

"I'm still waiting for the name of the spiteful cat spreading lies about Amelia," said Langley. He would put money on it being a woman, for gossip was a woman's weapon. As the gossip had brought an end to Amelia's engagement, Langley couldn't decide whether he wished to thank the person or flatten her.

"You know, that's the funny thing," said Garland. Langley fought to hold on to his temper, as he did not find it funny at all.

"I'm not sure I would have believed it had I heard it from any other source," Garland continued. "But I thought the lady who told me had reason to know, and certainly no reason to lie about it." He laughed nervously, for Langley's expression had turned fierce. "You know, I'm not sure I should tell you, as I would hate to cause a rift."

By now, Langley was fairly certain it was Mrs. Hunt, and had decided that regardless of the felicitous outcome, he would find a way to avenge Amelia. He gripped Garland's forearm, and Garland thought that for a man who had reportedly just recovered from a severe illness, the earl's grip was incredibly strong.

"Who was it, Garland?" Langley asked softly.

Garland's eyes widened as Langley increased the pressure on his arm.

"It was your mother."

It was the last answer that Langley had expected, and he released Garland's arm and stood gaping at him. Garland didn't know what to make of Langley's expression, but he was relieved to see Amelia and Adrian walking toward them. He had found his tête-à-tête with the earl unsettling.

"Ah, Miss Fleming," said Garland. "What have you done with my lovely bride?"

"She has gone inside to refresh herself," Amelia explained.

"I've always wanted to see Stonecroft," Garland said. "I came across an excellent book called *Noble Estates of the Nation*, and it listed Stonecroft as one of the eight finest estates in the country. Perhaps you've read it?"

"I'm not familiar with the work," said Langley, who

was acquainted with the owners of many of the country's noble estates.

"Although I admit I was surprised to read Amelia's description of Stonecroft," Garland continued.

"Indeed," Langley said, with a raised eyebrow. Amelia gave him a pleading look.

"Yes. It's certainly not as grand as Garland Castle will be, but that's not to be expected," Garland said, staring critically at Langley's mansion. "I don't think I would call it a rustic cottage."

Langley dropped his voice, as though sharing a confidence. "You know, Garland, among the nobility, it's common practice to underrate the home of an acquaintance. It emphasizes the gulf between his noble character and his physical dwelling, no matter how grand it might be. I'm sure Miss Fleming was paying me a compliment."

"I see," said Garland, with a look of dawning comprehension.

Adrian laughed. "Really, Robert, it's not right to–"

"It's time he was told," cut in Langley, with a reproachful look at his brother. "He married the widow of a viscount and the daughter of a duke–"

"And the sister of a duke," Garland put in.

"And the sister of a duke," Langley continued smoothly. "It's time we let him in on the secrets."

Garland looked at Langley with approval. "You put it very well, my lord. And after your kind explanation, I fully understand the custom."

"I think Garland Castle sounds too grand," Langley mused. "You could call it Garland Grange."

Garland looked thoughtful. "I like that. Thank you,

my lord. I should go find my wife, I daresay she'll be wanting her dinner," he hinted.

Amelia's cheeks burned, and she desperately hoped that Langley would not invite the newlyweds to stay. She hated to think about what they would find to discuss at the dinner table.

"We would be delighted to have you join us for dinner," Langley said smoothly. "It may be simple fare, I'm afraid. We have had some trouble in the kitchen over the past few days, but my housekeeper assures me we do not have mice."

"Robert, we've never had mice in the Stonecroft kitchens," Adrian protested.

Langley nodded. "Yes, Adrian, that's what I said."

Garland's brows knit together. "On second thought, my lord, perhaps we would do better to make a push for the coast."

"Most understandable," said Langley.

"Goodbye kiss for your stepfather, Amy?" Garland asked, taking a step towards her.

In an instant, Langley was between them. "You'd best get going, Garland," he said politely. "I expect you'll want to change horses at The Swan, and they have a shortage of good horses. It would be a shame to have such a fine carriage pulled by a team of hacks."

Adrian snorted at his brother's description of the carriage, but fortunately Garland didn't hear him. Despite the unpleasantness of their earlier conversation, Mr. Garland was starting to think that the Earl of Langley was quite a good fellow.

That night, Langley was filled with a joy that made it nearly impossible to sleep. Amelia was free, and there was no longer an obstacle to their happiness. Given the result, he couldn't even resent his mother's interference in his love affair. Garland had assured him he had kept his mouth shut, so there was no reason to fear the story had spread.

In a short time, it wouldn't matter; Langley had every intention of marrying Amelia, and he was tempted to seek her out and declare himself that very night. He thought of her in her bedchamber, no doubt asleep, and he remembered how weary she had looked after her mother and Garland had left. When he proposed, Langley wanted there to be no question of whether he was motivated by gossip, or honour, or even by lust. He would wait until tomorrow, when Amelia would be rested and there would be no distractions. The thought that she was sleeping down the hall from him, and no longer promised to another man, brought a smile to his lips.

But Amelia was too distraught to sleep. Now that her mother had married her former fiancé, she would not only be ruined, she would be a laughingstock. Amelia thought it was hideously unjust that she had experienced all the consequences of ruination but none of the enjoyment of it. She wasn't entirely sure what it meant to be ruined, but she suspected that given the immense social consequences, no lady would succumb to temptation unless the process was enjoyable. An inner devil argued she had nothing further to lose, and there was no reason not to walk down the hall and ask Lord Langley to educate her on the meaning of ruination. The only thing holding her back was the fear that Langley would think she was trying to trap him into offering her marriage.

Twenty-Six

"I'd like a word with you, Adrian," Langley said to his brother after breakfast the next morning. "Can you join me in my study?"

Adrian swallowed nervously. "Now, Robert?"

"If it's convenient."

"Of course," said Adrian, trying to think of what he had done to earn himself a private interview with his brother. Langley didn't look angry, but Adrian knew better than to think he had been summoned to his study for a social chat.

"If this is about the account at The Bull, Robert, I've been meaning to talk to you about that," Adrian said, once the door had closed behind them.

Langley raised an eyebrow. "Oh?"

"I know it might seem extravagant, but I stopped for lunch on my way down to Stonecroft, and stood a round for some fellows I met in the taproom. Then I realized I was short of ready money, so I had them put it on your account. I would be happy to reimburse you." He flushed as he remembered his pockets were still to let. "That is, if you'll give me an advance on the next quarter's allowance."

Langley smiled. "Nonsense, Adrian, I'm happy to stand the cost of refreshments for you and your–er–chance acquaintances."

Adrian sighed with relief. "Thank you, Robert. I don't suppose you'd like to give me an advance on the allowance anyway?"

Langley pulled a roll of banknotes from the drawer of his desk. "Here's fifty pounds," he said, handing the notes to his brother. "In exchange, I'd like a favour from you. I need an important letter delivered to Mr. Kincaid in London, and you're the only person I trust to do it."

As Langley had hoped, Adrian was flattered.

"Really Robert? You trust me with it?"

Langley nodded. "Yes, but you'll need to leave today. You don't mind, do you? You can spend a few days in London. Dine with Corky, see a play. The townhouse is at your disposal."

Adrian didn't really want to return to town, but he could hardly say no after his brother had been so understanding about the taproom bill.

"All right," Adrian agreed.

Langley almost sighed with relief. He wanted time alone with Amelia and was running out of excuses to send his brother away. "Excellent. I'll order the coach. Unless you'd prefer to drive yourself?"

"I'd rather go in the curricle. Can I take the chestnuts again, Robert?" he asked hopefully. Langley had always been particular about his chestnuts, but he seemed to be in a particularly agreeable mood.

"If you wish. Can you be ready in an hour?"

"I don't know, Robert, I'll have to pack, and–"

"Timms will help you pack," Langley said. "You won't want to be on the road after dark."

"All right. Where is the letter?"

Langley picked up a sheet of paper from a stack on his desk, scribbled a couple of lines, then folded it, sealed it, and wrote Mr. Kincaid's name on the top. "There," he said, handing it to Adrian.

"That's it?" asked Adrian, surprised by the brevity of the note. "I mean, I thought—when you said—it's an important communication, so I would have expected—at least, you know–"

"Quite," agreed Langley. "Fortunately, I can convey a coherent message with very few words."

∽

Less than an hour later, Adrian set off down the winding drive that led to the main road. He checked his horses when he saw Amelia, who was returning to the house after a walk on the grounds.

"Good day, Miss Fleming," he said. "I'm heading back to London, so I'll take my leave of you."

Amelia saw a solution to the problem of how to remove herself from the estate of a man who did not want her there.

"Take me with you," she said impulsively.

Adrian stared at her. "I beg your pardon?"

"I need to go to London. Please let me go with you."

"But Miss Fleming, surely you would be more comfortable in the travelling coach? And you haven't your luggage," Adrian protested.

"I don't need luggage," she said resolutely. "We'll reach London by evening, and I have clothes at home." This was something of an exaggeration, as the few presentable dresses she owned were at Stonecroft, but in a pinch she could borrow from Isabelle. "If you can give me ten minutes to change, I'll be ready to go."

Adrian shrugged, reflecting that it would be nice to have company on the journey. "All right."

Amelia rushed back to the house and slipped up to her room. After dashing off a note to Langley to explain her departure, she took a quick survey of her possessions and realized she owned almost nothing of value. She had left London with no jewellery and no money, and the trunk that Isabelle had packed for her contained only worn and outdated gowns. She shrugged into the green silk pelisse that Langley had given her and left everything else in the room.

Adrian was impressed when she rejoined him in less than the promised ten minutes, but looked askance at her pelisse, which looked far too fine for travel in an open carriage. "I mean to set a good pace and we won't be stopping long at inns, but if you don't mind that–"

"It sounds perfect," said Amelia, thinking that a fast drive away from Stonecroft was exactly what she needed.

An hour later, Amelia was wishing that Adrian would slow down. Although he wasn't ham-handed like Mr. Garland, he was reckless, and he drove as though his curricle was the only vehicle on the road. He raced around blind corners at full speed, causing Amelia to close her eyes and pray they wouldn't collide with an oncoming vehicle.

"Excited to get back to London?" Adrian asked conversationally. He turned to look at Amelia and pulled carelessly on the reins, causing the horses to veer to the side of the road.

"Yes," admitted Amelia, once he had corrected their course. "Would you like me to drive?" She thought the horses seemed anxious under his command.

"What?" asked Adrian, surprised. "Oh, no thank you, Miss Fleming. Robert's horses are all quite spirited, and they need a firm hand."

"I can see that," she said tartly.

"You must be distressed about that business with Mr. Garland," Adrian said, with his characteristic lack of tact.

"Yes," admitted Amelia. "And the most infuriating part of it is that after claiming to be put off by my scandalous behaviour, he went and married my mother!"

"What scandalous behaviour?" asked Adrian, whose ears had perked up at the mention of a scandal.

Amelia flushed. "Oh. Well, according to Mr. Garland, people are saying that your brother and I were engaged in an improper relationship."

Adrian nodded, as though this didn't surprise him. "Were you?"

"No!" she said vehemently. "There was nothing like that at all. And until two days ago, your sister was there."

Adrian appeared to be thinking hard. "I wondered," he said, and despite her denial, he suspected that there was more to Miss Fleming's relationship with his brother than she was willing to admit. "But I couldn't get past the fact that you're a redhead. Everyone knows Robert doesn't like redheads. I don't think he's ever looked at a redheaded girl in his life."

"Oh," said Amelia, irrationally hurt.

After three hours on the road, Adrian realized he had made a wrong turn, and effectively taken them in a circle. An hour after that, they reached an inn, and Adrian was able to reassure Amelia that they were now headed in the correct direction. They stopped to rest the horses and refresh themselves, but Amelia itched to get back on the road, as she feared they wouldn't make London by nightfall.

*

"Mr. Adrian seemed to be in a rush to get to London," Timms said to Langley as he helped him dress for dinner.

"What?" asked Langley distractedly. "Oh. Yes."

"It will be nice to have Stonecroft to ourselves again," Timms remarked. "I suppose Miss Fleming is the only guest remaining."

"I suppose she is," Langley agreed with a smile. He ran a hand across his chin. "Do you think I should shave again before dinner?"

"But we've already arranged your cravat, and I shaved you this morning," said Timms, confused.

"Right. Take off the cravat and let's do it again."

A footman interrupted with a letter for Langley. "One of the maids found this in Miss Fleming's room," he explained. "It has your name on it."

Langley jumped from his chair and grabbed the letter from the startled footman.

"That will be all, Timms," he said dismissively.

"Did you still want to be shaved, my lord?" he asked nervously.

But Langley didn't answer, for he was too distracted by the contents of Amelia's letter:

My lord,

I have trespassed upon your kindness for far too long, and I've decided it's time I left. So I have gone with Adrian.

I want to thank you for your hospitality. Despite the circumstances, I can honestly say that the weeks I spent at Stonecroft have been some of the happiest of my life.

As you have probably guessed, the end of my engagement to Mr. Garland means that my family won't be able to pay our debt to you for some time. We will strive to pay you in instalments, as previously discussed. I trust this will be acceptable.

Yours truly,
Amelia Fleming

Langley let out a loud string of curses, the likes of which his household had never heard before. The meaning of her note was not entirely clear, but his mind jumped quickly to the worst possible interpretation, which was that she had eloped with his brother. Had he been able to consider the matter rationally, he would have remembered that Amelia and Adrian hadn't demonstrated any particular interest in each other, but his love for Amelia made him irrational. He strode out of his room and down the stairs, yelling orders as he went. "Timms, bring me my riding boots. Matthews, send a message to the stables to have North Star saddled immediately."

"But sir, dinner is almost ready," Matthews said.

"If I wanted dinner, I would have asked for dinner," Langley roared. "Right now, I want a horse. I don't think I can state it more plainly. Timms, my riding boots."

"But you're in your dinner clothes, my lord," protested Timms. "If you wish to go riding, I can have your riding clothes ready in a trice, if you would only come upstairs."

"Hang my riding clothes," he barked. "Just find my boots, man." He rushed to his study to get some money.

His staff scurried around in confusion, shocked to see their usually cool-headed employer in such a temper. Within minutes he was off, galloping down the road in his dinner jacket, leaving his staff to speculate on the cause of his unusual behaviour.

∽

Adrian was telling Amelia the story of the monkey that had caused him to be sent down from Oxford when something spooked the horses and he lost control of the reins. The horses veered to the left, pulling the curricle into the ditch. Fortunately, the horses had the sense to stop, and the curricle came to rest with the left wheel in the ditch and the right wheel on the road.

"I'm terribly sorry, Miss Fleming," said Adrian sheepishly. "I'm afraid that was partly my fault."

"I think it was almost entirely your fault," said Amelia in frustration. Her criticism was not entirely reasonable, for only an exceptional driver could have kept the curricle on the road after the horses had been spooked like that, but Amelia had no doubt that Langley could have done it. She had been second-guessing her decision to leave with Adrian for several miles, and the fact that they were stuck in a ditch seemed to confirm that it had been a poor choice.

Adrian took stock of the situation. "I'm not sure we're going to get the carriage back on the road," he said pensively. "I suppose the best thing to do is to sit and wait until someone comes along to help."

"But that could take hours," Amelia protested. "I don't think we've passed anyone on this road since we left the inn. We could be here all night."

"I'm sorry, Miss Fleming, but I don't see an alternative," Adrian said apologetically.

"Do you know if we are close to a town, or an inn? We could lead the horses."

"I think the nearest inn is a few miles away," said Adrian. "We wouldn't get there before dark." Dusk had fallen, casting the surrounding fields in a beautiful purple haze.

"That seems like a better choice than sitting in here in the dark," said Amelia. She realized that when they made it to the inn, they would almost certainly be forced to stay the night, leaving what remained of her reputation in shreds.

Adrian frowned. "I'm not sure."

Amelia jumped down and inspected the carriage. "I

don't think anything is obviously broken." She went to the horses, who remained in harness and were anxiously pawing the ground. She spoke soothingly to them, and they seemed to settle.

"You know, Adrian, I think we could coax the horses to pull the curricle out of the ditch," she said.

But Adrian was no longer listening to Amelia, for he had heard hoofbeats. He turned to see Langley galloping toward them at a frantic pace.

∽

Langley hadn't thought that his heart could beat faster than it had when he learned of Amelia's flight, but the sight of the curricle in the ditch proved him wrong. He feared that she had been injured, and he pressed his tired horse to go faster.

When he found her standing at the horses' heads, apparently unharmed, he felt a rush of relief, which was quickly replaced by anger.

"Are you injured, Miss Fleming?" he asked curtly.

"No, my lord," she reassured him. "And I think your horses have escaped unharmed."

"I'm all right, too, Robert," Adrian said from his seat in the curricle.

Langley gave his brother an icy look. "I'll deal with you later," he said sharply.

"But Robert, I wanted to talk to you," said Adrian, hoping to distract his brother from the fact that he had driven his horses and his houseguest into the ditch.

"Later, Adrian," Langley repeated. He dismounted

from North Star and joined Miss Fleming. "By some miracle, it looks like the curricle may still be fit to drive. We need to get it out of the ditch so I can take Miss Fleming home."

"Actually, it was Miss Fleming that I wanted to talk to you about."

"I don't think that's a good idea, Adrian," said Langley, in a voice that could have cut diamonds.

His tone of voice would have quelled most men, but some inner demon drove Adrian on.

"I think it is. You know, Robert, I was thinking about her."

Langley's wrath was explosive. "No way in hell, Adrian," he said violently.

Adrian was confused by Langley's reaction. "Robert, think about it. She's from a noble family, although I know they've had difficulties recently. Her looks are tolerable, she seems reasonably well educated, and–"

"Her looks are *tolerable*?" asked Langley, who had long considered her the most beautiful woman he had ever met. "Adrian, are you blind?"

"It doesn't matter, my lord," cut in Amelia, hoping to put a stop to the critique of her looks and character.

"But Robert, I haven't explained the whole," persisted Adrian. "It seems there is gossip in town about her stay at Stonecroft, and people are saying you've compromised her. Her fiancé jilted her because of it, which puts her in a difficult situation. But I thought of a solution–"

"No, Adrian, you will not marry her," Langley said harshly.

Adrian stared at his brother in surprise. "Well, of course I'm not going to marry her, Robert. I don't know what's gone on between the two of you, but I wouldn't take what's yours. I thought that since you're no longer keeping Celestine, you might set Miss Fleming up in a house. Lord knows you have the money for it."

Amelia decided it was time to intervene. The brothers looked as though they were about to come to blows, and she was concerned Langley would reopen the wound in his shoulder.

"I'm afraid the horses are getting cold," she interjected. "Adrian, perhaps if you got out of the curricle, we could get it back on the road."

Adrian jumped down, and the three of them managed to get the curricle out of the ditch. Langley helped Amelia to climb into the vehicle, then climbed in beside her.

Adrian looked at them in confusion. "But where will I sit?"

"You won't," said Langley. "The curricle won't seat three."

"But it's my curricle," Adrian said indignantly.

"That's another thing I mean to discuss with you," said his brother. "How could you let Miss Fleming ride in this death trap?"

"You're proposing to let her ride in it," Adrian pointed out.

"Yes, but I know how to drive," Langley retorted.

"Really Robert, it's not like you to be so unreasonable," Adrian complained. "How am I to get to London?"

"Take North Star," said Langley, gesturing at the beautiful horse who was calmly grazing at the side of the road.

Adrian stared, open-mouthed. "You'll let me take North Star?" North Star was Langley's pride and joy, and despite frequent requests, he had never let Adrian ride him.

Langley nodded. "You need to get to London. Try not to ruin his mouth."

Adrian still looked uncertain. "I don't know, Robert. It's getting dark. Maybe I should come back to Stonecroft and set out for London first thing tomorrow."

Langley shook his head. "That letter needs to get to Mr. Kincaid without delay, so you'll have to go tonight. If you don't want to ride, you can hire a chaise at the Bull, and I'll send a groom for North Star tomorrow. Do you have enough money?"

"Just what you gave me this morning," Adrian admitted. Langley reached into the pocket of his waistcoat and handed his brother another roll of banknotes. "Here. If you're unable to hire a chaise, you can always stay at the Bull for the night."

"But I won't have any clothes," Adrian pointed out. "All my gear is in the curricle. Really, Robert, I think I should just come back to Stonecroft."

Langley let out a long-suffering sigh. "Adrian. You can't expect me to find solutions to every problem you face. You'll have to figure it out." With that, he set off, expertly turning the curricle and starting back toward Stonecroft.

Adrian mounted North Star and chased after them.

"Robert," he called. Langley cursed and checked his horses.

"Robert, I forgot the letter!" Adrian said. "It's still in my suitcase, in the curricle."

"It's no matter," said Langley. "I'll send a footman to

London with it tomorrow. He'll deliver it to you, and you can deliver it to Kincaid."

Something about that plan seemed off to Adrian, and he couldn't work out why his brother would trust a footman to take the letter to London, but not to Kincaid directly. He tried again. "Yes. But I don't understand–"

But Langley was already driving away.

Twenty-Seven

Darkness was falling and the horses were tired, and it took all of Langley's concentration to keep the curricle on the road. He and Amelia drove in silence, both recognizing that the road was not the place for the discussion they needed to have. They reached Stonecroft without mishap, and Langley lifted Amelia down from the curricle. Although his expression was inscrutable, the hands on her waist were gentle.

"I must see to the horses," he said shortly. "Tell Mrs. Prescott we'll want dinner in half an hour."

"Yes, my lord."

After delivering the message to Mrs. Prescott, Amelia went to change for dinner. After a month of good nutrition, she was no longer painfully skinny, and her dinner gown stretched tightly across her chest. It wasn't uncomfortable unless she breathed deeply, but the neckline was very low. She frowned at the mirror, but as she had no better options, she draped a shawl across her shoulders and decided it would do.

The cook had produced an excellent dinner, but neither Langley nor Amelia tasted the food. Tension was thick across the table, and Amelia talked of the weather with great determination, giving Langley no opportunity to discuss the issue closest to his heart.

At last, a footman came to clear the plates from a barely touched dessert course, and Amelia rose to escape to her bedroom.

"Miss Fleming, I wonder if you would indulge me in a game of chess?" Langley asked.

"Oh," said Amelia, trying desperately to think of an excuse. "I'm tired, and I don't think–"

"One game, Miss Fleming." She met his eyes, which were focused on her with such intensity that she found herself unable to say no.

"Yes, my lord."

They moved to the sitting room and faced each other across the chessboard. Amelia had trouble concentrating and moved her pieces without her usual deliberation. She was overwhelmed by the difficulties she faced, not least of which was her family's unpaid debt to the earl. She was hot, tired, and miserable, and her dress was too tight. For a moment she feared she would faint, and thought that fainting might not be such a bad thing, as Langley might carry her to safety as he had at Diana's ball. She then realized that since she was already sitting on the sofa, there would be no need for him to carry her anywhere, and the most likely result of a swoon would be a visit from the disagreeable Dr. Carter. She took off her shawl and draped it across the arm of the sofa.

The lightheadedness passed, and she decided to face the problem head-on.

"My lord?" she said, after moving a knight.

Langley moved a pawn and didn't answer. Amelia noticed his face was flushed and he had loosened his cravat.

"My lord?" she tried again.

"Yes?"

"I never intended to marry your brother, you know," Amelia said simply. For some reason, it seemed very important that he believed this. "I only wanted a ride to London."

"I never thought you did," Langley said lightly, although he was relieved to hear her say it.

"But I still think it's time for me to go home," she said firmly. "Your shoulder seems to be healing, and as I no longer have a chaperone it's not right for me to stay here with you. I wrote to William and asked him to come, but I don't expect him for several days still. I probably should have left with Diana and Templeton."

Langley raised an eyebrow. "You certainly shouldn't have done that." He moved a knight.

Amelia looked pensive. "You're right. But I could have joined my mother–"

"No," Langley cut her off with a pained expression. "You could not have joined your mother and Garland on their honeymoon."

"You're right," she agreed. "But I will have to go home."

"I think that problem can wait until tomorrow. If you're concerned about the lack of a chaperone, I can have Mrs. Prescott sleep in your dressing room."

She smiled ruefully. "Another night won't make a

difference to my reputation, and as to the other–" she paused and met his eye. "I trust you, my lord."

Langley's heart lifted. The chess game was forgotten, and he moved his chair around the table to be closer to Amelia.

"But I would like to talk about my family's debt," Amelia persisted. "With my reputation, I can no longer hope to gain a fortune through marriage, and I won't let Isabelle marry unless she falls in love. So it will be years before we can pay our debt to you, and I need to know what we're facing. What is the exact amount of the debt?"

"I have no idea," Langley said dismissively.

Amelia was nonplussed. "What do you mean?"

"I mean I don't know."

Amelia regained her wits. "But surely you have the IOUs, and–"

"I burned them," he said apologetically. "I've always hated clutter."

"What?" she asked incredulously.

"Threw them in the fire. They're gone."

"But surely you remember the amount?" she said in disbelief.

"My dear, I have a deplorably bad memory."

"But why?"

"I realized it would be awkward to collect a large sum of money from my brother-in-law."

Amelia's forehead wrinkled in confusion. "But I never planned to marry Adrian, and you seemed very upset by the idea of it." She stared at the floor. "I can't say I blame you. I understand your objection to an alliance with my family."

He looked her in the eye. "Amelia, you're right that I

don't want you to marry my brother, but you've misunderstood the reason. Although I think you are far too good for my family, I don't want you to marry Adrian because I want you to marry me."

"You can't marry me," Amelia protested in shock.

"Why not?" Langley asked reasonably. "And before you give me an answer, I want you to know that this has nothing to do with the debt. I have long regretted playing your father that night, and I never intended to collect money from your family. Your decision won't change that."

"But you don't even like me! You think I'm mischievous and meddlesome, and I've turned your household upside down."

Langley sighed. "You overheard me talking to Pettigrew."

Amelia nodded, unable to meet his eyes.

"Is that why you left with Adrian?"

Amelia nodded again. Langley was relieved to finally understand the reason behind her flight with his brother.

"How much of that conversation did you hear?" he asked.

"I left after you called me the most maddening girl you had ever met."

"Well, my darling, the lesson in this is that if you must eavesdrop, stay 'til the end," Langley said gently. "You missed hearing me tell Pettigrew that I didn't think I could live without you."

Amelia still wouldn't allow herself to believe it. "But Adrian told me you don't like redheads," she protested. "He said you had never looked at a redheaded girl in your life!"

Langley sighed. "I believe I will cut off his allowance," he muttered. "He's right that I had never been interested in a redheaded girl until recently. But since I've met you, I've had no interest in any other girl, of any hair colour."

Amelia frowned. "But Diana said you were interested in Miss Hunt."

"Miss Hunt?" Langley exclaimed in disbelief. "No. Diana would never have thought so. What exactly did she say?"

Amelia cast her mind back to her conversation with Diana in the garden. "Well, we agreed that Mrs. Hunt was an unpleasant person, so I asked Diana why you tolerated her visits," she explained. "Diana said you had a soft spot for her daughter."

Langley smiled. "Were you jealous, sweetheart?"

"Not at all," said Amelia, but the blush on her cheeks said otherwise.

"I think Diana meant that I pitied Miss Hunt, and I do," Langley explained. "Mrs. Hunt is a bully who makes her daughter's life miserable. But there was never anything more than that, and pity would never motivate me to make an offer of marriage."

Amelia's resolve was weakening, but she wasn't convinced. "I still think you're doing this out of a sense of obligation, and I won't let you. You feel responsible for my family's situation, and you're worried people will think that you compromised me, which is completely ridiculous!"

He raised an eyebrow at that, for it had taken an extraordinary amount of willpower to stay out of her bedroom. "Is it?"

"Yes!" she said emphatically. "And even if there is

gossip, I'll be all right. I'll have a home with William, and I can help him run the estate. And if he gets married, I'm sure I can find work as a governess."

"Would you teach your charges estate management?" Langley asked curiously.

"If they wish to learn it," Amelia said. "Or if I can't find a governess post, I could work as a housekeeper. Even a maid. I'm a hard worker, and I'm not proud. I would far rather work than let you marry me out of guilt."

"I don't feel guilty," he interrupted. "And I have it on good authority that I don't have a conscience."

Amelia flushed. "But you do! That Stoneheart business is all an act. I know you let William challenge you to that ridiculous duel to teach him a lesson. And it worked, much better than anything I could have said or done. For that alone, I must always stand in your debt."

"My darling, I wish you would stop talking about debts."

But Amelia was struck by another thought. "The hideous brass candlesticks!" she exclaimed. "That was you too! No one else knew about them."

"I hope you don't think I fit your sister's description of a funny little man," Langley said, looking pained. "That was Timms."

Amelia smiled. "Dear Timms," she said. "He's such a kind man."

"But I had the idea, and put up the funds," Langley said quickly.

"What will you do with them?"

"I've always had a fondness for hideous brass candlesticks," Langley said. "I think I will give them a prominent place in our townhouse. See if we can start a fashion for brass amongst the *ton*."

Amelia sobered at his implication that they had a shared future. "I won't let you marry me because of some spiteful gossip."

"It seems I should be worried about my own reputation," he teased. He moved next to her on the sofa and put his arm around her. "If word gets about that I'm soft-hearted, I'll be a target for everyone in the *ton*." He sighed. "The problem, my darling, isn't your reputation."

"It isn't?"

"No. The problem, Amelia, is that I love you. I think I've loved you since the first day you came to see me, wearing your brother's ridiculous clothes. Try as I might, I haven't been able to get you out of my head or my heart, and I don't think I can be happy without you. Will you marry me, Amelia?"

Amelia was so overcome by joy that she was temporarily bereft of speech. She had imagined such a moment many times, but it had always seemed like an impossible dream, and Langley's declaration of love was literally a dream come true.

Langley misread her silence as hesitation, and waited anxiously for her answer. For the first time in his life, he was having to fight for something he desperately wanted, and he wasn't sure of the outcome.

When Amelia finally turned to face him, the look in her eyes left him in no doubt of her feelings. Seconds later, she found herself locked in a ruthless embrace, as Langley took possession of her mouth. They tumbled sideways on the sofa.

"Your shoulder!" Amelia cried, jumping up. "I forgot."

She realized that with his injury, the ride to catch her and Adrian must have been harrowing. "You'd better let me look at your wound. I'm afraid this afternoon's ride may have reopened it." She reached for the buttons of his waistcoat.

Langley reached up and drew her back down to him.

"My shoulder's been healed for well over a week," he said roughly. "But you're welcome to undress me if you like."

She looked confused. "But the pain?"

"Has miraculously disappeared. You have a sort of drugging effect on me."

Amelia still looked cautious.

"If you must know, I've been exaggerating my symptoms to prolong the pleasure of your company," Langley confessed.

Understanding finally dawned on Amelia.

"And to think how I worried over how long it was taking to heal! What a despicable trick. You are entirely without a conscience!"

"So I've been told," he agreed. "I'm sure you'll think of an appropriate punishment. I know it was selfish, but I wasn't sure I could convince you to stay at Stonecroft otherwise."

"I would have stayed," Amelia said shyly. "If you said you wanted me here, it would have been reason enough. I love you, Robert. I'm not sure when it started, but by Diana's ball I was in the middle of it, and at the duel I was as terrified for you as I was for William. I tried to fight it, but I couldn't."

Langley answered by kissing her thoroughly.

Some time later, Amelia looked lazily at the chessboard, and realized that she was two moves away from putting the earl in checkmate.

"Care to finish the game, my lord?" she asked saucily.

Langley studied the board and reached the same conclusion that she had. He sighed and toppled his king. "I believe the outcome was inevitable."

"I can't believe I won so quickly," Amelia remarked. "That was less than ten moves." A suspicious look crossed her face. "You let me win, didn't you?"

"I would never. But you had an unfair advantage."

"I did not!" she protested indignantly. "I would never cheat!"

"I don't know if it was cheating exactly," he mused. "But you are wearing the most indecent dress. I was completely unable to focus."

She looked down and flushed. "I was worried it was too tight," she admitted with a rueful smile. "I won't be able to pass for William anymore."

Langley raised his eyes to the ceiling. "Thank God."

"But speaking of William," she continued.

"Must we?"

She looked at him seriously. "Yes Robert, we must."

He smiled at the sound of his name on her lips. "All right, my darling. What about William?"

Amelia took a deep breath. "I was hoping you would help him with Cliveden Manor. Not financially, of course," she said quickly. "You have already been incredibly generous in forgiving our father's debt. But after I marry you, I won't be able to help William as I did before."

The earl's lips twitched. "And by help William, you mean run the estate for him?"

She flushed. "It wasn't quite like that. But I think he would benefit from advice, and I think your estate is quite well managed."

"Thank you," said Langley with a smile.

"So I was hoping you could . . ." She trailed off, searching for the right phrase.

"Loan him Pettigrew? That's an excellent idea," said Langley, thinking that it would be fitting revenge on his land agent, who had just enjoyed over a week of Amelia's company.

"Oh no, Robert," said Amelia seriously. "I mean, Mr. Pettigrew is an excellent manager, but I'm not sure he's–" she paused. "I'm not sure how to explain it. He's just not *you*, Robert."

"You have explained it admirably, my darling. I would be pleased to advise your brother."

Amelia was struck by another thought. "And Robert?"

"Yes, Amelia?"

"You realize that if you marry me you will be related to Mr. Garland?"

He smiled. "It had crossed my mind. But it would take far more than Mr. Garland to scare me off." He played a fingertip under the tight neckline of her dress, causing Amelia to sigh.

"I will have to have this gown altered," she said.

"You will do no such thing," Langley said firmly.

Amelia looked up at him, confused. "But you said it was indecent," she protested.

"Oh, it is," Langley agreed. "When we're back in London we'll have new gowns made for you. I've wanted to buy you new gowns for some time, and I am pleased to finally have the right."

Amelia frowned. "You don't like my gowns?"

"On the contrary, I am inordinately fond of them. This one especially, and I hope you will wear it often around our house."

"I could do that." Amelia nestled into his side.

"But if you let me have input into your clothing choices, it's only fair that I let you have a say in mine," Langley mused. "I remember you once said I wasn't to wear anything but a dressing gown for a week. At the time I thought it was an outrageous suggestion, but now I think I could be convinced."

Amelia's brow furrowed in confusion. "But that was because of your shoulder, and you said it's healed."

"I meant I could be convinced to spend a week in my bedroom," he said, squeezing her closer. "If I had the right company."

Amelia blushed as she grasped his meaning. "Robert," she protested, suddenly shy. "I'm not sure–"

He kissed her to silence her protests.

"You're right," he said when they finally broke apart. "A week won't be nearly enough."

―

Two days later, a letter was hand-delivered to Mr. Lucas Kincaid in London by Mr. Adrian Stone. It was brief, but as Langley had promised, its message was perfectly clear to its reader, and it brought a smile to his face.

Lucas,
You were right. I'm going to marry her.
Robert

Epilogue

Nine Months Later
Notes from the diary of the Earl of Langley

January, 1817

I must admit that married life has much to recommend it. It helps that I am married to the most beautiful, intelligent, generous, witty, and desirable lady in the country.

In short, my wife is a paragon. My only complaint is that I think she reads my diary.

Langley assisted his wife into the phaeton and tucked a blanket around her legs. He was still getting used to having someone to look after, and he found he liked it very much. Langley had wanted to take the coach, but Amelia had recently found that travelling in closed carriages made her nauseated. They were going to visit Diana's newborn daughter.

"Robert," said Amelia shyly as they made their way through the streets, "I have been wanting to talk to you. I think perhaps I should see the doctor."

Langley smiled. He had wondered when his lovely wife was going to tell him she was expecting their first child.

"This is a surprise, my love," said the earl, feigning concern. "I didn't think you liked doctors. If I recall, you said they were ignorant bloodsuckers."

"Yes, I did say that," Amelia admitted.

"I'll turn around, sweetheart," he said solicitously. "If you're unwell, you'll be more comfortable at home, and I'll send for the doctor directly. We can see Diana's baby another time."

"No, I'm not unwell exactly," she began. "I think—that is, I've wondered if perhaps—but I'm not certain," she stammered, afraid to give voice to her hopes.

Langley, who had been fairly certain for over a month, was having trouble keeping a straight face. "If you're having difficulty finding words, we should definitely send for the doctor," he said. "This is unlike you, my love."

"It's just—oh, I very much wanted to talk to Diana," she said miserably.

"You can talk to her today," Langley pointed out.

"Yes, but I wanted to talk to her *privately*," explained Amelia. "And I imagine Templeton will be there, as Diana wrote that he's so besotted with little Cecily that he rarely leaves her side." She paused and turned to her husband. "Do you like babies, Robert?"

The earl took pity on his wife. He checked the horses and turned to face Amelia.

"Are you trying to tell me, my love, that you are expecting a baby?"

Amelia nodded shyly. "Are you pleased?"

Langley didn't answer in words, but kissed her instead. Curious passersby in Mayfair were treated to the sight of the Stoneheart passionately kissing his wife in an open carriage, with an expression of joy on his face.

Acknowledgments

Thank you to my mother, for being my first and most enthusiastic reader, and to Mary Matthews, for her valuable editorial suggestions.

Printed in Great Britain
by Amazon